Evil Above the Stars
Volume 1

Seventh Child

4

Evil Above the Stars
Volume 1

Seventh Child

Peter R. Ellis

Elsewhen Press

Seventh Child
First published in Great Britain by Elsewhen Press, 2015
An imprint of Alnpete Limited

Elsewhen Press, PO Box 757, Dartford, Kent DA2 7TQ
www.elsewhen.co.uk

British Library Cataloguing in Publication Data.
A catalogue record for this book is available from the British Library.

ISBN 978-1-908168-60-3 Print edition
ISBN 978-1-908168-70-2 eBook edition

Printed and bound by CPI Group (UK) Ltd, Croydon, CR0 4YY

This book is a work of fiction. All names, characters, places and events are either a
product of the author's fertile imagination or are used fictitiously. Any resemblance
to actual events, places or people (living or dead) is purely coincidental.

To Alison

Map of Gwlad

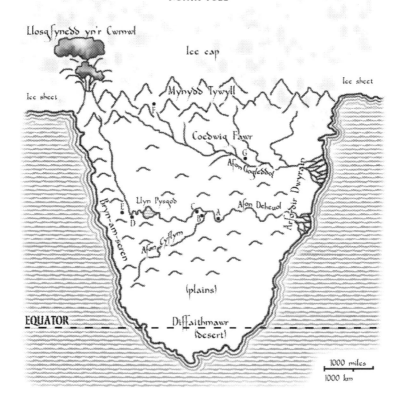

NORTH POLE

Llosgfynedd yn'r Cwmwl

Ice cap

Ice sheet

Ice sheet

Mynydd Tywyll

F

Coedwig Fawr

G

Afon Gogleddol

Brym-am-seren

Llyn Pysgod

E

C

Afon Deheuol

Arfordir Dwyrain

D

B

A

Afon Cyflym

(plains)

EQUATOR

Diffaithmawr
(desert)

1000 miles

1000 km

Towns and Villages:

A-Amaethaderyn

B-Abercyflym

C-Glanyrafon

D-Dwytrefrhaedr

E-Arsyllfa

F-Mwyngloddiau Dwfn

G-Trefyncoed

7

Pronunciation guide

The 'old tongue' used by the people of the Land is derived from Celtic languages such as Welsh. General guidelines on pronunciation are as follows.

'll' does not occur in English, in the glossary it is written as 'LL'. The sound is made by partly opening the mouth, pressing the tongue against the roof of the mouth and blowing gently.

'dd', written as 'TH' in the glossary, is the hard th sound in 'this' and 'that' but not as in 'path'.

'a' is always as in 'cat' and not as in 'ape'.

'e' is always as in 'pet'.

'f' is the v in 'van' while 'ff' is the f in 'fan'.

'c' is always the hard 'k' sound in 'kid'.

'ch' is similar to ck and pronounced as in the Scottish 'loch' and not the English 'church'.

'g' is always hard as in 'god' and not as in 'german'.

'o' is like in 'on' but not 'open'.

'i' and 'u' are pronounced 'ee'.

'r's should be rolled.

'si' is between the sh in 'shone' and the j of 'john'.

'w' is oo as in 'cool'.

'y' is sometimes the u sound in 'run', sometimes the i in 'bin' and occasionally the ee sound in 'been'.

'yw' is pronounced 'you'.

'ae', 'ai', 'au' and 'ei' are all pronounced 'eye'.

'eu' is the oy in 'boy'.

Glossary

Word	[Pronunciation] Meaning
Abercyflym	[a-ber-kuv-lim] village at the mouth of the river Cyflym onto the river Deheuol
Adarllwchgwin	[ad-ar-LL-ook-goo-in] giant eagle bearing red devil-like figures with tridents, air manifestations of the Malevolence
Adwyth	[ad-oo-eeth] The Malevolence, the evil from above the stars
Afon Deheuol	[a-von de-hoy-ol] Southern River, one of the great transport links of Gwlad
alcam	[al-kam] tin, a silver-grey malleable metal
Aldyth	[al-dith] a sword
Amaethaderyn	[am-eyeth-ad-er-in] Farm of birds, a village on the Afon Deheuol, the southern river
arian	[ar-ee-an] silver, a rare silver metal
arianbyw	[ar-ee-an-byou] mercury, dense silver liquid metal
Arsyllfa	[ar-siLL-va] The observatory-cum-fortress in the Bryn am seren in the west of Gwlad
Aur	[eye-er] gold. A rare, maleable, yellow metal
Bryn-am-seren	[brin-am-ser-en] Hills of Stars, a range of low mountains in the west of Gwlad
carregmam	[kar-reg-mam] mother stone
Ceffyl dwr	[kef-ill doo-er] Water horse, a giant aggressive winged horse, a water manifestation of the Malevolence
Cemegwr	[kem-egg-oo-er] Creators, chemists, the Makers of everything
Clogwyn Llwyd Uchel	[klog-oo-in LL-oo-id ee-kel] high cliffs at the western side of Llyn Pysgod
Cludydd	[klee-deeTH] bearer or wielder
Coedwig Fawr	[koy-doo-ig vow-er] The Great Forest, region of the Land between the northern river and mountains

Word	[Pronunciation] Meaning
Cyrhyraeth	[kir-hir-eyeth] a moaning, disease-bearing wind, an air-manifestation of the Malevolence
Cysegr	[ku-seg-er] Refuge or shrine near Amaethaderyn
Daear	[die-ar] Earth, the planet at the centre of the universe
Draig tân	[dry-g tarn] Fiery dragon, comet. A fire manifestation of the Malevolence
Dwytrefrhaedr	[doo-ee-trev-rheye-der] The two towns by the waterfall, on the River Deheuol
Dyfrgi	[du-ver-g-ee] The Otter, one of the trading barges on the river Deheuol
efyddyn	[e-vu-TH-in] copper, a malleable red metal
Glanyrafon	[glan-ur-avon] Village on the bank of the river Deheuol
Gleisiad	[gl-eye-see-ad] The Salmon, one of the trading barges on the river Deheuol
Gwener	[goo-en-er] Venus, the 3rd planet from the Earth in the geo-centric system
Gwlad	[goo-lard] The Land – the occupied continent on Daear
Gwyllian	[goo-iLL-ee-an] old women, earth manifestations of the Malevolence
haearn	[heye-arn] iron, a hard grey metal
Hafn	[hav-en] cleft or gorge
Haul	[h-eye-el] Sun, the 4th planet from the Earth in the geo-centric system
Iau	[ee-aye] Jupiter, the 6th planet from the Earth in the geo-centric system
Lleuad	[LL-eye-ad] Moon, the 1st 'planet' from the Earth in the geo-centric system
Llyn Pysgod	[LL-in piss-god] The Lake of Fish, the great lake on the river Deheuol
maengolauseren	[mine-gol-eye-ser-en] stone of starlight or starstone, the stone of power held by September
Malevolence	[mal-ev-o-lens] the power of evil from above the stars

Word	[Pronunciation] Meaning
Mawrth	[ma-oorth] Mars, the 5th planet from the Earth in the geocentric system
Mercher	[mer-ker] Mercury, the 2nd planet from the Earth in the geo-centric system
Mordeyrn	[mor-day-ern] Leader
Mynydd Tywyll	[mun-iTH tu-oo-iLL] the dark mountains in the north of Gwlad
o	[o] of
plwm	[ploom] lead, a dense, soft grey metal
prif-	[preev] chief, head
Pwca	[Poo-ka] a shape-changer, an air manifestation of the Malevolence
Sadwrn	[sad-oo-ern] Saturn, the 7th planet from the Earth in the geo-centric system
Seren Gogledd	[ser-en gog-le-TH] north star, the Pole star
trawsffurfio	[trows-feer-vee-o] to transform, the talent of a cludydd o arianbyw
Ymadaelwch	[um-a-dial-oo-k] "Be gone!"

Dramatis Personae

Alawn	[ala-oon] young guide to Bryn-am-seren
April	30 years old, oldest sister of September
Arianwen	[a-ree-an-oo-en] The cludydd o arian, silver-bearer, of Amaethaderyn
Augustus	18 year old brother of September, also called 'Gus'
Aurddolen	[eye-er-TH-olen] chief bearer of gold and leader of the Land
Berddig	[bear-TH-ig] The cludydd o alcam, tin-bearer, of Amaethaderyn
Breuddwyd	[broy-TH-oo-id] September's mother
Catrin	[kat-rin] The cludydd o efyddyn, copper-bearer, of Amaethaderyn

Collen	[ko-LL-en] elderly guide to Bryn-am-seren and cook
Cynddylig	[kin-THil-ig] older man, boatman and river guide
Eluned	[e-lee-ned] The cludydd o arianbyw, mercury bearer, of Amaethaderyn
Elystan	[el-is-tan] young guide to Bryn-am-seren
Emma	schoolfriend of September
Gwrion	[goo-ree-on] mature guide to Bryn-am-seren
Heulwen	[hoyl-oo-en] daughter of Aurddolen
Heulyn	[hoyl-in] chief bearer of gold and leader of the land at the last conjunction
Iddig	[i-TH-ig] bearer of iron in Dwytrefrhaedr
Iorwerth	[ee-or-oo-er-th] The cludydd o haearn, iron-bearer of Amaethaderyn
Julie	21 year old sister of September
June	24 year old sister of September
Malice	servant of the Malevolence, twin sister of September
May	27 year old sister of September
Merryl	[mer-ril] woman of Dwytrefrhaedr, housekeeper for the Mordeyrn Aurddolen
Meurin	[moy-rin] young man of Amaethaderyn
Mr Bloomsbury	Chemistry teacher
Mr Jones	Physics teacher
Mrs Roberts	English teacher
Nisien	[nis-ee-en] mature guide to Bryn-am-seren
Padarn	[pad-arn] The cludydd o plwm, lead-bearer, of Amaethaderyn
Poppy	schoolfriend of September
September	16 year old girl, surname Weekes, also called 'Ember' and 'Em'
Sieffre	[jef-re] young man, lead guide to the Bryn-am-seren
Tudfwlch	[teed-voolk] young warrior and ironsmith, apprentice to Iorwerth

Part 1

~

Arrival

1

The dark embraced her. It had always been dark, not that she had any understanding of 'always'. That implied a memory of before. She had no memory. Memories are born with the passage of time and in the dark there was no time. Nevertheless she was unique, an anomaly, the one amongst thousands, millions, billions, who was aware. Around her, filling the dimensionless space without time, were the other souls who had never experienced life. They had no awareness, no sense of self, just one emotion – hate. She felt it too, along with anger, spite and malice – anger that she had been denied existence; spiteful resentment of those, unknown to her, who had life; malicious intent to harm them all. The urge to wreak vengeance, to destroy, sustained her through the endless timelessness.

Something changed. Time began. No longer was the dark complete nor her existence formless. There was light and she had eyes to see. The light was only a speck, a pin-point of brightness. Slowly it grew. Was the light itself growing, was it moving towards her or was she drawn towards it? She didn't know or care. It didn't matter but the light held her attention, became the focus of her malice. This was the source of her injustice, the denial of her life.

Around her she could feel the power of all those nameless souls growing. A dark energy of malevolence directed, like her own feelings, at the growing orb of light. It was an old emotion that waxed and waned but now was building to a new peak. And she was at the heart of it, aware and eager, hungry for revenge.

2

September held the object in her hand. It looked like a pebble but she was sure it was not simply a piece of rock, more like a chunk of smoky glass. It was oval, about four centimetres long, a centimetre less in width and its thickness varying like a lens. It could have been a pendant, she thought, but there were no marks of a clasp. She put it down on her dressing table-cum-desk and finished getting ready for bed. Standing in her sleep-shirt and knickers she picked the object up again. It felt smooth and cool, like glass, except that it was opaque. Well, that was the odd thing. The surface seemed clear but the interior was cloudy. She thought it was quite pretty.

She looked out of the window in front of her. The sky was black and there were no clouds to reflect the city lights. The Moon had risen above the rooftops, casting its silver-blue radiance over the gardens below. A few stars out-shone the streetlights. September lifted the glass pebble and stared into it. It caught the moon beams and seemed to sparkle for a moment. The cloudiness seemed to move like mists swirling away on a cold morning.

"Are you ready for bed, Ember?" The call came up the stairs and September immediately felt her hairs rise on her neck and her cheeks flush. Why did Mother still treat her like a child, checking that she was settling down? In another two weeks she would be sixteen. Surely she could decide when it was time to go to bed. The feeling quickly passed. She'd grown up with Mother's attention. She seemed to fuss over September more than over her sisters and brother, but perhaps that was just because she was the youngest. The bedtime call was one of Mother's little rituals. Mother liked ritual and orderliness; that was why she still went to chapel every week. The rest of the family copied Dad's atheistic laziness on Sundays.

"Yes, Mum," she replied.

She dropped the pebble into her pencil case and climbed

onto the top bunk. During term time she had the choice of beds but in college vacations, Julie exerted her rightful choice as the next older sister. School had only just begun again after the summer holiday but Julie was away with her friends. September pulled the duvet up round her neck and waited for the inevitable tap on the door. It came moments later, followed by the door opening and a head appearing in the gap. None of her teachers or friends ever failed to recognise September's mother. Both of them had white hair that looked almost blue in some lights. September now had hers cut short but Mother's flowed in waves to her shoulders. Their faces too were similarly round, with pink cheeks, short up-turned nose and wide pale blue eyes, and both had the same build, short with broad hips and a tendency to plumpness.

Mother smiled at her.

"Everything done, love?"

September sighed; another of Mother's rituals. Homework and getting qualifications was a top priority.

"Yes, Mum."

"No problems today?" She didn't say more, didn't need to. They both knew that hardly a day went by without a bit of name-calling or worse. There was always a knot of fear in September's chest when she was out of the house, a nervous apprehension of what other girls and boys may do or say when they saw her. Snowy! Fatty! Or they ridiculed her stupid name. Teachers were hardly better, always assuming she was an idiot as she blushed and stumbled over answers. But today had been bearable and she was trying to be grown up and not run to Mother every time something went wrong.

"No, it was alright."

"Well, sleep well darling," Mother paused looking out of the window, "Do you want the curtains drawn?"

"No thanks. It's a full Moon and I love the moonlight in my room."

"Ah, yes, the Moon." Mother seemed wistful for a moment but then recovered, "Shall I turn your light off, love?" There was a lamp on the desk beside the bed but the switch for the main light was by the door.

"Yes, please."

"'Night, love. God bless." The head withdrew and the light went off as the door was pulled closed.

"Night, Mum." September rested her head on her pillow, and lay in the dark absentmindedly rubbing the slightly raised birth mark on her right hip while listening as the steps padded along the landing. There was the muffled sound of another exchange at Gus' door but Mother had been persuaded not to burst in on her son as he prepared for bed. Heaven knows what went on in a teenage boy's bedroom. He might have been two years older than September but maturity didn't correlate with years. Then there was the sound of Mum and Dad's bedroom door closing. Her other three sisters lived in their own homes.

September slipped from under the duvet and gently lowered herself from the bunk. She picked the pebble from her pencil case and caressed it in her hand. She had found it while rummaging for a paper clip in a drawer in the living room. It seemed more like the stone had found her because she had never seen it before and she must have looked in that same drawer hundreds of times. It was so distinctive it would have caught her attention if it had been anywhere in the house. Resting on her hand, just visible in the pale moonlight, it still looked dull and opaque.

She glanced out of the window. The Moon looked so big against the roofs, much bigger than it usually looked when it was higher in the sky. The stars around it had been rendered invisible by the greater light, but now the whole sky elsewhere was filled with starlight. She lifted the pebble up and lined it up with her eye and the Moon. The cloud seemed to swirl as before but this time the mists started to clear. They formed a whirlpool that spun and faded as if falling down a plughole. September stared in wonder. What strange trick of the light was this? The glass cleared and just for a moment she saw an image of the Moon surrounded by brilliant stars clearer than seen through the window.

The light came like a breaking wave, silver-blue like the moon and starlight but much brighter. It burst through the stone like a tsunami through a port-hole, forcing September to turn her head, squint and hold her hand up to shield her eyes. The surf of light broke over her; a deluge of blue-white luminosity engulfed her and she was immersed in dancing beams and droplets of light. The room disappeared in the dazzling illumination. September staggered; her sense of balance shaken. Up and down lost meaning. Her head spun. She reached out to steady herself on the desk but her hand found nothing. She fell to her knees.

3

Her hand touched damp grass. She flinched and drew it back but then was toppling forward. She reached out to break her fall and rested her hand on the turf. She was crouching. Her eyelids were squeezed shut waiting for the jumping spots of light in her eyes to fade. Dizziness filled her head. It took a few moments before she felt confident about opening her eyes again. When she did, when the orange flashes on her eyelids had faded, she found it was dark again, but she was not in her bedroom. Her bare feet and hands rested on cool, damp grass. Her heart hammered in her chest. What had happened to her? Was she dreaming or was this some sort of mental attack?

Slowly she straightened her legs and stood up, gazing around in wonder. Although it was night the full Moon provided ample light for her to examine her surroundings. She was standing on a low ridge. In front of her, a meadow sloped gently down to a broad, tree-lined river that gleamed like mercury in the light of the Moon. Beyond the river there seemed to be cultivated fields among woodland and a dark shadow speckled by starlight, a lake. Turning her head she saw behind her that the grassy hillside fell away steeply to the edge of another wood which receded into darkness. September looked to her right. The ridge reached up to the brow of the hill where there was a small stand of tall, broadleaved trees.

She knew this place. It appeared in her dreams; dreams which had been recurring frequently of late. But now September was sure she was not dreaming. In her dreams there had been a hazy quality to the view. Now it was crystal clear. Previously she had been unaware of her other senses but now she felt the ground beneath her feet, the smell of grass filled her nose and the light, warm breeze ruffled her gown and hair. Her gown and hair? She looked down and saw that the long T-shirt she wore to bed no longer covered her, but instead she was clothed in an ankle length white linen robe with long loose sleeves. Her hair had changed too. Long waves, rippling over her shoulders like Mother's, had replaced her short bob. Now that she examined herself she felt different. She had been aware of the changes in her body since her periods had started, had despaired of getting rid of what Father called her puppy-fat, but now her body seemed harder, tuned, more mature; even her breasts felt larger – what did it mean? She barely had folds of flab but these were really rounded and firm. She must be dreaming to have acquired the body she desired.

The glass pebble was still gripped in her left hand. She looked at it. It too had changed. It was no longer dull and opaque but clear and it sparkled with its own internal lights like tiny stars. It was warm too, a warmth that seemed to come from within it.

What has happened to me? Am I really here, wherever here is? September had no answer to her questions but she knew where she had to go. She turned to face right and began walking up the ridge towards the copse at the top of the hill. In her dreams, that was where 'they' had been, although she had no idea who 'they' were or whether they could help her.

She was not used to walking outdoors in bare feet but her feet seemed accustomed to it. The moon provided sufficient light for her to feel confident of finding her steps. It was quite a walk to the brow of the hill. She knew that she would soon be puffing and sweating if she had done this walk normally even on a typical early Autumn night. Here the air was comfortably cool and although she felt the climb in her leg muscles her lungs barely felt the strain. She felt fit, not a feeling she was accustomed to. Was that a sign that this was still a dream?

As she neared the stand of trees at the summit she caught glimpses of movement between the trunks, flickers of white-garbed figures processing. As she approached she noticed that the trees were not arranged randomly as in a wild wood but in concentric circles as close together as their outstretched branches would allow. When she reached the outer ring she saw that there was an avenue leading to the centre of the copse. Not far away she could see light, a fire burning and flashes of white robes and shadows as the figures circled the flames. September ventured towards the light. As the canopy of leaves closed over her she felt vaguely scared at losing the moonlight. Within the circle of trees there was no light except that which beckoned her forward.

The sound of soft tuneful humming broke the night-time silence. The figures hummed in unison as they walked. September reached the inner ring of trees and paused. The sight before her almost made her giggle it seemed so corny: a bunch of druids carrying out some arcane ritual, or a coven of witches and wizards rehearsing their magic spells. A huge, circular stone altar with a fire burning in the middle of it formed the centre of the circle. The humming figures, each dressed in a white robe like hers with hoods pulled over their heads, shuffled slowly around it. Facing her, standing beside the altar, his hands raised to the sky, was a man, dressed the same except that his head was uncovered. He was tall and his hair and his short, neat beard shone gold in the yellow firelight. He saw her standing there and immediately he lowered his arms and beckoned to her. The congregation stopped moving and ceased their chant. Each turned their hooded heads to gaze at September.

"Come, join us, do not be afraid," the chief druid, as September thought of him, said in a warm, kindly voice. She stood still, nervous of making a move. She had glimpsed this scene in her dreams but never been part of it. "We have been awaiting you and praying for your safe arrival." Waiting for her? Praying? What did they mean? Why was she special? The man's voice was, however, welcoming and kindly. September took one step forward, and another.

The circle of druids parted to allow September to approach the altar. The man took her right hand and guided her to his side.

"You were expecting me tonight?" September asked.

"Last night, tomorrow night. We knew you would respond to our summons at some time."

"Why?"

"Because you are the Cludydd o Maengolauseren."

"The what?"

"Ah, you do not yet understand the old tongue. You are the bearer of the starstone."

September held up the glass jewel which glistened and sparkled in the flames of the fire. The people gasped.

"You mean this?"

The man stared at the pebble and nodded.

"But it's just a piece of glass," September said, knowing as she spoke that it was not true.

"I do not know of a material that you call 'glass'," the man said gently, "it is a piece of the hardest substance known in the world, retrieved from the deepest mine at the dawn of history and fashioned by the power of light to give the Cludydd great power."

"The hardest substance?" September recalled that phrase. Chemistry wasn't her best subject, she wasn't sure what was, but that phrase brought forth a memory of something she had heard in lessons, "You mean, it's a diamond. It must have been shaped by a laser to make it this smooth. Is that what you mean by the power of light?"

The man looked confused.

"I do not understand the terms of which you speak. No stones like yours are found today, just tiny grains, and none have the fabled power of the stone that you bear. You hold the Carregmam, the mother stone, the oldest and largest and most powerful. For centuries it has been hidden within but beyond this world, but now that we have need of its power it has been recalled and its bearer with it."

"Me?" September felt weak. The man nodded. "Why is it needed? And who are you?" She was filled with questions which overwhelmed the nervousness that she had felt.

The man smiled at her.

"There are a lot of things to tell you, but I apologise. You have come from afar and we have not welcomed you as we should. Come and sit. Eat and drink and I will begin to tell you what you should know."

The congregation, which had been watching and listening, now broke up. They threw back their hoods revealing themselves as men and women, young and old, fair and dark. They dispersed as if each knew what they had to do. Some ran to the edge of the clearing where smaller fires burned and returned with bowls and cups filled with steaming liquid. Others ran to bring cushions to lay at the foot of the altar for everyone to sit on. September sank gratefully onto the cushion offered to her, feeling very tired. A cup was placed in her hand. She took a sip and found it to be cool, clear water. Suddenly she was thirsty and she drained the cup. A bowl was offered to her. For a moment she hesitated, wondering what to do with the starstone still gripped in her hand but decided to just drop it into her lap. The young woman proffering the bowl gazed at the stone with something like awe on her face. September took the spoon and bowl which contained some sort of soup. She thanked the woman who nodded her head and backed away still looking at the stone.

September scooped up the thick liquid and touched it to her lips. She wasn't used to eating in the middle of the night but the aroma of the soup made her feel hungry. It tasted wonderfully of cheese and a variety of vegetables which she couldn't quite identify. The man wrapped his robe around himself and sat down cross-legged next to her. He smiled at her as she ate and began to speak.

"I am the Mordeyrn. It is my honour and duty to guide these people, to help them live in peace and to sustain them." His modesty impressed September. It was strange having an older man give her this sort of attention but she felt comfortable sitting alongside him amongst the crowd and was surprised that she felt at ease. What is happening to me? she thought. Have I gone barmy, thinking that my dreams have become real? But the warmth and the flavour of the soup certainly seemed real as did the hardness of the stone behind her back. Surely I can't be imagining all these people slurping from their spoons?

"I'm September," she said.

"Ah, yes," the Mordeyrn nodded.

"Who are these men and women and where are we?" September inquired between mouthfuls of soup.

"We are the People and we live in Gwlad, which in the old speech means our Land,"

"Doesn't it have a name?"

"Why should it? There is nowhere else which we inhabit."

"But what about this place? It seems pretty special with its rings of trees and this stone altar thing. Do you live here?"

"No, we live in the valley at Amaethaderyn. This is our Cysegr. How should I say it? Our refuge, our shrine."

"Refuge? Are you being attacked?"

The Mordeyrn frowned. September sensed a great sadness in him.

"Not seriously, but the forces of darkness are growing in strength and soon they will threaten us." September giggled a little. Mother, in her religious moods, talked of hell and the forces of evil and September knew about the plots of fantasy stories from the way that Gus went on about them. She must be dreaming and drawing together the images she had seen in Gus' books and magazines and the films he watched on their one TV.

"I suppose there is a Dark Lord out to enslave you," September said cynically. The Mordeyrn looked confused again.

"There is no Dark Lord. Evil has no leader, no organisation. It is Chaos, Disintegration, the breakdown of order. Nevertheless the Adwyth would destroy us all."

"The ad-oo-eeth?" September struggled with the word.

"The evil that threatens us or the Malevolence as it is commonly called."

"Oh," September felt as though she had been silly, "What can you do to stop it then?"

"We are not without power," the Mordeyrn said rising to his feet. He clapped his hands. All the people got up and began to organise themselves. Some collected the cushions, dishes and cups. Others went to the edge of the clearing while the remainder arranged themselves into curved rows facing the altar. September rose to her feet too, grasping the starstone in her right hand.

The Mordeyrn spoke directly to September but in a voice that all could hear.

"We have the Maengolauseren, the starstone, which is the most powerful guardian of the Land and its people, but we have other gifts won from the rock beneath the Mynydd Tywyll, the dark mountains. Look." He pointed to a procession of people who approached the altar. Each was carrying an object. The first was a young woman with large eyes and shiny black hair, who walked up to the Mordeyrn and handed him a wooden cup with a small dip of her head as a sign of ritual. The Mordeyrn turned to place the cup on the altar in front of September. The polished cup was filled with a silvery liquid which moved languorously and didn't wet the sides.

"It looks like a metal but it's liquid," September said, struggling to make her brain work, "What is it called?" it was there in her memory she was sure. Suddenly, the answer was there, " I know, it's mercury,"

"That is one name for it; Arianbyw has been its name since the dawn of time; quicksilver is another. It has no shape of its own but has the power to shape others, even things made from other metals that are themselves hard and rigid. Those that are expert in its properties can use it to change their form or the form of other things or beings."

The Mordeyrn's words meant little to September. She was confused. Was he describing the properties of the liquid metal or the young woman that carried it to the altar? There wasn't time to say anything because the girl bowed again and moved away. Her place was taken by a grey haired man who carried a dull grey slab the size of a tile. He too nodded and lifted the object up for the Mordeyrn to take. It was obviously heavy because the Mordeyrn's hands sank as he took it with an answering nod. He placed it on the altar.

"Plwm," he said, "soft and malleable but so dense that it can absorb energies that attack it. The bearer can shape it to defend himself and his companions from danger."

"Um, lead, I think," September recalled seeing the metal in a school lesson but again the description of its properties was beyond her.

A third person, a young man with a jolly smile on his round face arrived carrying a roll of silver coloured foil. Once again the Mordeyrn took it solemnly and placed it on view.

"Alcam," he said.

"It's the foil we use in the kitchen, uh, aluminium," September said, pleased that she had recognised something. She reached out to lift the lump of metal but found it heavier than she expected. Her confidence was dashed, "No, it can't be, it's too heavy. I don't know what it can be." She found herself struggling to remember all the metals that she had learned about at school.

"Tin," the Mordeyrn announced, "the great mixer. It hardens and protects other metals. In the hands of a bearer it reinforces and reinvigorates, building confidence and companionship." September had an image of tins of beans on a supermarket shelf; tin as a metal meant little to her.

A striking blonde woman stepped up to the altar carrying a bell made of a shiny orange metal.

"I know that one," September said eagerly, "it's copper, a good conductor." She was proud of herself; she had remembered something.

The Mordeyrn nodded as he placed the gently tinkling bell on the altar, "Copper yes, Efyddyn. Fashioned into sheets or rods or bells it reflects light, and carries heat and sound. Those who understand its powers use it to communicate across great distances and exchange energy." Once again September felt flummoxed by the Mordeyrn's description of properties that sounded like nonsense.

The woman bowed and stepped aside to allow a burly young man to approach. He carried a broadsword. The Mordeyrn took it from him and lifted it with some difficulty on to the altar. The blade was over a metre long and was polished to a silvery-grey lustre. The hilt and handle were a darker dull grey, engraved with spirals and curlicues. The pommel was a polished sphere.

"A sword, that must be made of iron," September guessed.

"Haearn," the Mordeyrn nodded emphasising the 'h' at the beginning of the word, "strong and hard. In weapons like this great old sword, Aldyth, it gives the Cludydd the strength and skill to fight beasts and warriors more powerful than themselves. In other forms it can move great loads." September wondered whether he was referring to trucks and ships. They were made from iron weren't they? The swordsman, for surely the young man was such, withdrew with a deep bow and his place was taken by a noble looking older woman. She bowed and handed a wide silver amulet to the Mordeyrn. He held up the piece of jewellery.

"Arian, the queen of metals," he proclaimed, "Silver draws its power from Lleuad, the Moon, the nearest of the other worlds. It is the healer and protector of life. The bearers are always women who are held in great esteem amongst the people."

September looked from the Mordeyrn and the woman to the array of objects on the altar. Six different metals, each according to the tall druid something special, although she had not taken in the various powers that the bearers were said to have. She had noticed something that the Mordeyrn has said about the last metal.

"If silver is linked to the Moon, what about the other metals?"

"A good question, Cludydd," the Mordeyrn nodded, "Each of the metals draws its power from one of the heavenly bodies. Plwm takes its energy from Sadwrn."

"Saturn?"

"Yes, Alcam from Iau, Haearn from Mawrth,"

"Hold it," September held up her hands. Her head was spinning. The Mordeyrn had mentioned the Moon and Saturn but what were these other places? The language meant nothing to her but perhaps he was referring to the other planets. She struggled to recall what they were.

"Um. What's next to Saturn? That's Jupiter, I think. Do you mean Iau is Jupiter?" The Mordeyrn nodded. September was excited, she'd remembered the next.

"And Mawrth is Mars."

The Mordeyrn smiled and continued, "That's correct and Efyddyn is connected to Gwener and Arianbyw to Mercher."

"Oh, I don't know. What are the other planets called?" September appealed for help.

"Venus and Mercury in the common tongue," the Mordeyrn answered.

"Oh, yes, of course," September felt silly. The Mordeyrn ignored her grimace of embarrassment and went on.

"Which just leaves the champion of metals and one heavenly body." Two children approached the altar struggling to carry a plate. It was half a metre in diameter and although thin, was obviously a great weight. In the light of the fires it shone with a bright yellow lustre.

"It's gold," September said in amazement. The Mordeyrn took the plate from the two children and raised it above his head to show the congregation before turning to lay it with the other metals on the altar.

"Aur," he said, "the metal of Haul." September looked at the gold plate. She had never seen such a large piece of the precious metal. It was embossed with pictures and patterns that she could not take in at a glance. "Incorruptible and unchanging," the Mordeyrn continued, "the Cludydd o Aur can withstand evil and brings goodness and hope."

September felt quite overwhelmed with all that she had learned but was bothered. She couldn't remember a lot of her chemistry but she was sure there were more.

"Just seven metals? What about aluminium, sodium and all the others?"

It was the Mordeyrn's turn to look confused.

"I do not understand," he said.

"There are lots of other metals so my teachers tell me, and what about the other planets, um, what are they called? Uranus, Neptune."

The Mordeyrn shook his head, "These names are unknown to me. The seven astronomical bodies circle Daear in their orbits and share their powers with the metals that we win from the rocks.

"Daear?"

"Here, this world."

"You mean Earth."

"So it is also named."

"They all orbit the Earth, the Sun included?"

"That is correct."

September was quite sure that idea had gone a few hundred years ago. Wasn't there a guy called Galileo who said it was different. "Are you sure?"

The Mordeyrn smiled, "It is well known. When the Cemegwr made the world they fixed Daear at the centre and all else revolves around us. The evil of which I have spoken comes to us from beyond the sphere of stars."

September frowned, "Who are these Cemegwr?"

"The Makers of everything, the Creators of all that there is.

"You mean God?"

"What is god? At the beginning of time the Cemegwr fashioned Daear and the seven planets; they are the Providers of the seven metals that we find in the rocks of the Mynydd Tywyll."

"Seven metals and seven things in space. Seven days in a week. Seven keeps on cropping up."

"That is true. The number seven carries great importance in our world. That is why the Cludydd o Maengolauseren is always the seventh child."

"Hold on. The Clud... whatever, is what you called me."

"Yes, my child."

"But I'm only the sixth child. My mother had my sisters, April first, then May, June, and Julie, then Gus, and finally me. That's six of us."

The Mordeyrn shrugged, "The Maengolauseren always finds the seventh child. You must have six siblings, not five. But the night draws on and soon we will lose the light of the Moon. It is time the people returned to their homes, and you too. The time when the power of the Maengolauseren will be needed is not yet come, although I fear it will not be long. The connection has been made so you should return to your home until the starstone carries you here again."

September looked around. The congregation was starting to disperse, collecting together cushions and cups and the other things. September's head was in a whirl. She had barely followed all that she had seen and heard. What did he mean by saying she must be the seventh not sixth child? She recalled something about evil from beyond the stars, and a task for her and the stone that she still held in her hand, but the man, the leader of these people was saying she could go home. How? Where was home? How did they expect her to help them? Her! Silly, fat September. Except she wasn't fat – not here. She felt fit and full of energy. She wanted this dream to go on.

The six bearers approached the altar to reclaim their objects. The older woman who collected the silver amulet slipped it on to her arm and came to stand at the Mordeyrn's side. September noticed she was carrying something, another silver object. She held it out to September.

"You will find this useful," she said. September saw that it was a locket on a chain. The locket was about the size of her starstone. The woman pressed on the edge of the locket. The front and back covers sprang back and the top of the case hinged open.

"Place the stone inside," the Mordeyrn said as the woman presented the locket to her. September carefully inserted the starstone within the silver frame. The woman closed the case up without touching the stone and handed it to her.

"There, now you can keep it with you. The silver will protect you from all ills."

September placed the chain around her neck. The locket hung between her breasts. She was not used to wearing such a heavy pendant; its weight tugged on her.

"This is for me to keep?"

"It is yours as much as you belong to the starstone. Your futures are as one and when you return to us you will soon learn to control the powers of the stone."

"So I will see you again, Mordeyrn?"

"I hope so, my dear. Your presence will be of great assistance to us in our time of trial and the starstone will certainly draw you to us."

There was a great shouting from the edge of the throng that travelled with increasing volume towards them.

"Draig tân!"

"A comet comes!"

"The fiery dragon!"

The people huddled together, retreating from the circle of trees until they were pressed against the altar, but they took care to leave space around September and the Mordeyrn. The Mordeyrn lifted the gold plate and stepped away from the altar. He strode through the people and between the avenue of trees.

"Wait, Mordeyrn!" September called, trying to run after him but finding the long gown tripping her. She caught him as he reached the outer ring of trees. A wind had blown up and the branches of the trees creaked and leaves rustled. Her hair was blown back and the cloth of her robe pressed to her body.

"Comets don't hurt people," she said.

"In your world, perhaps," he pointed to the northern sky.

September looked along his outstretched finger. Sure enough there was a comet clearly visible in the night sky, a bright spot and a white curved tail.

September stared – the comet was moving. "Comets don't move that fast do they. Don't they go round the Sun?"

"No, they are born of the evil beyond the sphere of stars and come into existence beneath the orbit of the Moon."

September was even more confused. This sounded like the ravings of a madman. But her eyes did not deceive her. She was seeing a comet approach.

"But surely it can't harm us?"

"Comets bring fire, famine and pestilence. They are a manifestation of evil. I must protect my people." The Mordeyrn stepped forward holding the golden plate aloft facing towards the comet. His arms shook with the weight of the gold. He began mumbling words that September could not understand. Still the comet approached, its tail now spread across half the northern sky and its head growing to become a ball of fire. She was mystified. What she was seeing was like nothing she had heard about, but then she had another surprise.

The golden plate began to glow in the Mordeyrn's up-stretched arms. A beam of yellow light groped out from the plate in the direction of the comet, but faded quickly in the distance. September could see that the Mordeyrn was straining with all his might to hold the plate up and give it power. Veins stood out on his forehead and sweat ran down his cheeks but it was to no avail. The glow from the plate slowly faded. The comet was closer now and obviously coming straight towards them. The head of the comet was as big as the Sun appeared to be, growing still, and its tail obscured the distant hills and forests.

"It's no good," the Mordeyrn sighed, lowering his arms, "without the Sun in the sky I do not have sufficient power." He took a few deep breaths. "Unless, you September, the Cludydd, you could help."

"What can I do?" September asked.

"The starstone. It gathers power from the stars and all the heavenly bodies. Direct the moonlight on to the plate of gold. It will boost my power. Hold the stone aloft. Open the locket." Once again he held the plate over his head directed at the growing threat of the comet.

September had no idea what he was expecting of her but she lifted the silver locket from her breast and opened the front and back cover. She looked at the stone. It was dark and clear. She looked to her left; the full Moon was sinking towards the horizon where the river flowed through the woods. September held the stone between her finger and thumb and tried to line it up between the Moon and the gold plate. The wind was a gale now and the approaching comet had grown huge. She was scared. Fear made her sweat and tremble and her hand holding the stone shook. The birthmark on her hip itched and she wanted to rub it but she had to concentrate on her task. It was difficult to judge the correct position but she must have succeeded because a shaft of blue light burst from the stone and onto the gold plate. She flinched and moved the stone. The beam of light faded.

"That's it," the Mordeyrn cried out, "Again! Hold it steady!" The comet was even larger, flames flickering around its circumference.

September wanted to do what she was told. She raised her hand again, struggling to find the right angle. A beam of blue-white light shone from the stone to the golden plate. At once the plate glowed with an intense yellow light which sprang out towards the head of the comet. September felt a tingle, like an electric current, in her hand holding the starstone. The tingle passed up her arm and into her body. It grew in intensity like a cramp locking her muscles. The birthmark burned. She held firm and the beam of light from the plate groped further towards the comet which now seemed very close and immense. Now it did seem like a great roaring dragon spewing fire with its glowing tail spread across the sky. September felt afraid. What might happen when the comet, or dragon, reached them? It was coming straight at them and already she could feel the heat of its breath. What if it fell on their heads? It grew till it seemed to September to be covering half the sky. She was locked in position, too scared to attempt to move, her hip a fiery agony, but the blue light from her stone grew in intensity.

The Mordeyrn roared out, "Ymadaelwch!"

The golden beam reached the comet. A black spot appeared where the beam touched it. The spot grew then there was a huge explosion of light and a roar like thunder tore the sky. The head of the comet broke into gobbets of fire that scattered in all directions. September thought that they were going to fall all around them. Then all the flames were gone. The Mordeyrn's plate ceased its glow and the gleam disappeared from September's stone. The sky was dark again except for the twinkling light of the stars and the Moon sinking towards the horizon.

The Mordeyrn lowered his arms with a relieved groan and sank to the ground cradling the plate. September found she could move again but her whole body ached as if she had been on a long run. The pain in her hip receded to a dull throb. She shivered as if she was icy cold although the air was warm. She fumbled with the locket enclosing the starstone and let it drop to her chest, taking a deep breath as if she hadn't been breathing at all.

The people came out of the copse, cheering and whooping with joy. They gathered around her and the Mordeyrn expressing their thanks.

The Mordeyrn struggled to his feet and faced her.

"Surely you are a worthy Cludydd o Maengolauseren. No one else could have given me the power to destroy that evil."

September wrapped her arms around herself still trembling and bemused. What had she seen? Surely that was not a real comet or even a meteor. What had she done?

"Where did it go?" she asked, "What happened?"

"That was surely a most powerful Draig tân but with the help of the power of the Moon and stars, my energy as Cludydd o Aur was sufficient to dissipate the evil and save us from its malevolent influence. But I could not have done it without you even though you are untrained in the handling of the Maengolauseren. I am sure you will prove to be a most powerful bearer." He glanced to the west. The Moon was touching the horizon. "But now my child, you must go."

"But if you are already being attacked, surely I must stay." September was not sure that she wanted to stay, she felt drained of energy and scared and didn't know what was expected of her but it seemed she was needed. That was an unusual feeling. It felt strange having the people cheering her and while she understood few of the Mordeyrn's words he was thanking her. She did not want to leave now; she wanted to relish this feeling of success for a bit longer.

"Comets are not unknown even when the Adwyth is not growing, but that was a most powerful example. Your arrival may have triggered a response from the Evil."

"So my coming brings evil with it." September was despondent. There had to be a downside.

"All actions have a reaction, my child. Some say the destructive evil of the Malevolence is just a response to the creativity of the Cemegwr. I do not know, but the Draig tân are just one of the horrors that await us. Your time has not yet come. You must continue your growth and when the starstone is ready you will return. The good you will bring will outweigh any response from the Adwyth. Now go to your own world with all our love and thanks."

"How? How do I get home?"

"The same way in which you came."

September tried to remember what she had done before she had found herself in this place.

"I just looked at the Moon and stars through the stone."

"That is it then. Do it."

Again, September took the locket in her hand, undid the clasp holding the covers and held the stone up to her eyes. The people standing amongst the trees behind began a chant that warmed and encouraged her. She looked at the people, men, women, young and old, children, all looking at her with faces that showed love, admiration, hope. She turned away, held the stone up and looked through it. She scanned the western sky for the Moon. The silver orb moved into view through the stone. For a moment she saw it clear and bright sitting on the horizon with a semi-circle of brilliant stars around it.

Blue-white light bathed her, dazzling her. She closed her eyes as the wave of light rolled over her, her ears catching cries of "Farewell Cludydd!" and "Praise to the Cemegwr!".

She knew she was back home by the feel of the carpet on her bare feet. September opened her eyes and found that she was standing once again at her desk facing her dark window.

The Moon was as it had been, just above the rooftops. She felt dizzy for a moment and rested both hands on the desk. Her eyes fell on her alarm clock. Apparently no more than a few moments had passed since Mother had called to say good night. Perhaps I've been dreaming, and sleepwalking, she thought. She stood up straight and felt a weight press between her breasts. She reached for it. In the moonlight she could see it was the silver locket. She gasped; it was true, it had happened. She undid the case and looked at the stone. It was dull and cloudy; no more than a piece of old glass. And yet the locket proved it to be more.

September closed the locket up and took the chain from around her neck. She placed the stone in the bottom drawer of her desk under some papers. As she straightened up she felt her body. She was back to as she had always been. The delightful tautness of her body in the Land was replaced by the soft roll of fat around her middle and the weak, flabby muscles in her arms and legs. A sigh escaped her and she climbed onto the bunk and beneath the duvet. She laid her head on the pillow feeling exhausted, hoping sleep would come, but instead her head was filled with many mysterious images.

4

"Are you up, September?"

Mother's shrill call woke September from a deep, disturbed sleep. She peered through half open eyelids at her alarm clock and was astounded to find she had overslept. It felt as though she had been awake all night, tossing and fidgeting in bed. Her mind could not reconcile her visit to the Land and the defeat of the comet with normal life. Surely it must have been a dream, and yet it felt so real. She recalled the fire dragon bearing down on the wooded shrine, the Mordeyrn fighting it off with his gold plate and her part in the victory. She could smell the grass and the trees and smoke from the bonfires; she could still taste the delicious soup and the last chant and farewells of the people rang in her ears.

"September!"

"Yes, Mum, I'm coming." Her reply came out weak and strained.

"Are you ill?" Was Mother coming upstairs? September swallowed, coughed and forced her voice to sound stronger.

"No, I'm fine. I'm coming." She rolled off the bunk onto the floor and pulled open the drawer of her desk. She fumbled under the papers until she retrieved the pendant. There it was, the silver locket and chain. She clicked it open and gazed at the milky stone inside. It was true. She had visited the Land and seen all those things. She stared at the stone for a moment longer before closing it up and hiding it back amongst her things. She had to hurry or she would be late for school.

In less than ten minutes she was washed, dressed and entering the kitchen. Gus looked up at her with a thick slice of toast halfway to his mouth.

"Gosh, Sis, you look dreadful."

September glowered at him. Mother, busy at the sink, turned to examine her.

"Are you sure you feel all right, Ember," she asked gently. September ran her hands through her hair.

"Yeah, didn't sleep very well. Feel a bit tired but I'll be fine."

"Did you have nightmares then?" Gus mocked. September ignored him and put some jam on a slice of bread. She hurried out into the hallway to put her blazer on with the bread flopping in her hand, trying to be lively and ready for the day but in truth feeling exhausted.

It wasn't a good day at school. She couldn't concentrate. Every few minutes something from her visit would come back to her; a face, the metal objects, something the Mordeyrn had said, the enlarging ball of fire coming straight towards her. Mrs Roberts, the English teacher, asked if she was unwell, while Mr Jones in Physics had snapped at her to wake up and pay attention. Her friends, her only friends, Poppy and Emma, mothered her and fussed during the lunch break but they could see that she was preoccupied. They thought there had been an incident: one of the other girls calling out names at her, the boys blocking her way along the corridor, a teacher getting at her. She shook her head denying that it was any of the usual problems that made life at school a misery.

Last lesson of the afternoon was Chemistry. September wasn't one of Mr Bloomsbury's star pupils but he was quite nice. When the bell went she hung around as everyone else fled.

"Oh, hi, September. Do you want something?" he asked when he noticed that she wasn't rushing to leave the laboratory as she usually did.

"Um, yes. I was wondering. Was there a time when we only knew about seven metals?"

Mr Bloomsbury looked surprised. September guessed he had been expecting her to ask for some trivial help with the homework he'd set or a question about the GCSE examinations.

"Well, yes, I suppose there was. Most of the metals in the Periodic Table have been discovered in the last two hundred years, so, uh, yes, earlier than that there would have been about seven. Why?"

"Oh, it's just something I read somewhere," September realised that she was flustered and hadn't worked out a story, "and were they linked to the planets?"

"Ooh, now you've got me. I think that was an idea that the alchemists had."

"Alchemists?"

"Yes, you know. The guys who tried to turn lead and stuff into gold. I don't know much about it but they were the people who sort of did chemistry before it became a real science. I think a lot of their ideas came from the Arabs."

"When was that?"

"Oh, gosh, I'm not sure. I suppose alchemy started to fall out of fashion in the seventeenth century, although I've heard that Isaac Newton was a keen alchemist."

"Newton? The physics guy who discovered gravity?"

"Well, he discovered the laws of gravitation that explained the motion of the planets around the Sun."

"Didn't Galileo have something to do with that?" There was another look of surprise on Mr Bloomsbury's face.

"Yes. Galileo was just before Newton."

"So all this alchemy stuff was at the same time as people thought the Sun and everything went around the Earth?"

"Yes. What's got you into all this, September?"

September blustered, what could she say?

"Oh, it was just something I read." Mr Bloomsbury's expression showed September that was another surprise.

"Right, well, good. Look I don't know a lot about the history of science but I'm sure there are some good books around, or you can find lots of stuff on the internet." The teacher looked as though he was keen to get away.

"Thanks. Actually you've helped me get things a bit clearer."

"I'm pleased. Goodbye September." He turned away from September and started to pile pupils' books and papers together. September left. She didn't meet up with her chums for the usual post-lessons natter, but hurried home. Gus wasn't back from college yet, Dad was at work of course, and Mother was too.

September hung up her blazer and went upstairs to her

Peter R. Ellis

room. She sat at her desk and switched her old, clunky
computer on. While it was taking its usual long time booting
up she reached into the drawer and pulled out the starstone.
She needed to see it and feel it to reassure herself that she
wasn't going daft and pursuing silly dreams. Something real
had happened last night, and if that was true then some time
she would be going back and she was expected to be
someone special – what had the Mordeyrn called her? The
Cludith o Mine-golly-seren or something? The bearer of the
Starstone, slim and strong and fit. She recalled the cramp and
stiffness in her arm as the shaft of blue light had leapt
between the stone and the gold plate, and the waterfall of
light that had engulfed her when she had travelled to and
from the Land. She remembered the adulation of the crowd
as the comet was destroyed. She half dreaded and half looked
forward to it happening again. Now though the stone looked
dull and dead in its casing.

The computer was awake. It didn't require much skill or
knowledge to google alchemy and metals, confirming what
Mr Bloomsbury had said and what the Mordeyrn had told her
of the connections between the metals and astronomical
bodies. But there was nothing about the magical properties of
the metals or such things as starstones. That belief seemed
peculiar to the people of the Land. Indeed while she found
hints of ideas that she had heard from the Mordeyrn, such as
that comets were once thought to be below the Moon, the
Land seemed strange and different and its creators, the
Cemegwr were not mentioned anywhere.

She heard Gus come in and tramp up the stairs to his room
followed soon by the thudding bass of the heavy metal music
he seemed to be unable to live without. Shortly after there
was a clatter of pans from the kitchen; Mother had returned.
September went downstairs to see her.

"Oh hello, love. I didn't know you were in. School alright
today?"

"Yeh, it was OK."

"You didn't stay to chat to your friends?"

"No, I came straight home to get on with some work."

"Are you feeling better? You did look poorly this
morning."

"I'm fine, just tired. I'll have an early night and hope I can get to sleep."

"Well, we'll have supper soon and then you'll have time to let it go down before you settle. Got much homework?"

"A bit."

Mother busied herself collecting items for the meal. September sat at the kitchen table idly watching her. A thought occurred to her.

"Mum?"

"Yes, Em."

"You had six children, didn't you?"

Mother stopped in the middle of chopping an onion and turned to face her. There was an expression of surprise in her face.

"Yes, love. You're my sixth. You know that."

"There wasn't a seventh?"

There was silence for a few heartbeats. September noticed her mother's pale face turning pink.

"I had six lovely children," Mother said slowly and deliberately, "Now don't you think you should get changed out of your school clothes?"

September took the hint and returned to her room. There was something mysterious in Mother's response. Previously September had never suspected that there may have been a seventh offspring. She could not recall any mutterings or passing remarks at any time in her life, but Mother's guarded reply suggested something had happened. If she was the seventh child and not the sixth as she thought then another of the Mordeyrn's statements would prove to have some truth. She changed into leggings and a loose tunic that slightly disguised her round tummy, and settled down to start some homework.

Later, when Father had arrived home, September joined Gus and her parents around the kitchen table. Usually conversation was lively but this evening Mother remained silent and pensive. Was it because of her question, September wondered? The two men didn't seem to notice and munched their suppers with a bit of chat about football. Once the table had been cleared, Gus headed back upstairs. September followed him. As he was about to disappear into his den of a room, September called to him.

"Gus." He paused and turned, surprised to find September right behind him.

"What is it Em?"

"Do you know anything about Mother having another child?"

"What? She's a bit ancient to have another baby isn't she?"

"No, not now, silly. I mean in the past, before I was born."

"What are you talking about? There's April, May, June, Julie, me and you. Six of us. That's enough isn't it? Perhaps you don't remember how crowded this house was, full of women – before April, May and June left."

"So, no mention of another boy or girl?"

"What are you on? Didn't you hear me? There are six of us – that's enough for me." He went into the room and slammed the door on her.

September returned to her room and got on with a bit more work. It was Maths. She always got stuck with Maths homework and this evening her thoughts kept wandering. She gave up and went back to her internet search for information on alchemy and pre-Galilean science but couldn't find anything to match what she had seen the previous night.

About nine she went downstairs to collect a glass of orange juice and said she was going to bed. She undressed and stood in her T-shirt looking out of her bedroom window. She held the starstone in one hand and absentmindedly rubbed the strawberry mark on her right hip with the other. It was dark outside but unlike the previous evening the Moon and stars were hidden by cloud. The stone remained dull and lifeless. September returned it to its hiding place and jumped into bed. She really did feel exhausted, as if she had been awake for two whole days. Sleep came quickly and with it dreams. Dim, clouded, confused dreams of the circle of trees on the hill, the stone altar, people processing and chanting and the comet bearing down on them.

5

Despite sleeping all night she still felt tired and disturbed by the dreams. Were they memories of what she had seen or was she an observer of things that had happened since she had returned? An observer looking through frosted glass at moving shadows and deaf to any sound or conversation? The alarm going off was a relief and she got up quicker than usual for a school day. There was the usual breakfast routine, trying to ignore Gus' inane comments and Mother's concerned questioning.

She got to school a few minutes earlier than usual. Poppy and Emma weren't there but there were a few boys from her year clustered round the entrance, trying to look cool despite their uniforms, with their collars up and trousers tugged down on their hips.

"Oh, look it's the fat snowball with the daft name," one of them said. She didn't see which as she was trying to ignore them by looking away.

"Hey, blubber-girl, couldn't your parents think of a name?"

"Perhaps they couldn't be bothered."

She hurried past them, avoiding their attempts to jostle her. Tears filled her eyes and her foot caught the top step. She staggered and the boys laughed. She hurried to the cloakroom trying to find a place to hide so no-one would see the tears in her eyes. She should be used to it by now, the teasing about her weight, her flab, her white hair and pale skin and her silly name. Most of the time she was proud of her name, no-one else was called September, but at times like this she wished Mother and Father hadn't got stuck on naming their children after months as a way of getting round the bible names or family names argument. It was OK for April, May, June and Julie; their names were normal. Even Gus didn't mind so long as he wasn't called Augustus out loud, but September, well! She liked being called Ember, it seemed lively, but only

Mother and Father and her best friends seemed to remember to call her that.

Sitting there on the floor amongst the lockers and coat hooks, she recalled the image of the crowd of gown-wearing people standing at the edge of their copse of trees that they called their Refuge, cheering her after she had helped destroy the comet; the 'Draig tân' they called it. She remembered the feeling of a mature body, lithe and fit. Had she imagined it? She had felt so alive and full of energy. Wielding the power of the starstone, whatever it may be, seemed real then. Here she was plump, unfit, thick. The boys were right to call her fat – what guy would think of asking her out even though she was sixteen in a couple of weeks' time?

It wasn't a good morning. She was pre-occupied with her internal debate all day. She drifted through lessons, ignoring the teachers who urged her to get down to work. They just shrugged when she failed to respond. After all they didn't expect much from September Weekes. She didn't have a lot to say to Poppy and Emma either. At lunchtime she opened her packed lunch and saw her usual crisps, biscuits, Nutella sandwich. It was what she always insisted on. Mother had given up trying to get her to bring a more 'healthy' meal. Now for the first time she saw the whole lot as fat, fat, fat. She tipped it into the waste bin. She was going to change. She wasn't going to be a sixteen year-old fatty. She was going to turn over a new leaf and become the figure of her dreams.

The afternoon wasn't much better. Her stomach rumbled and she couldn't concentrate. She hurried home at the end of school not waiting to chat with her friends. In the kitchen the biscuit tin caught her eye. It would be so natural to open it, take out a handful of biscuits and chomp them down. No, she told herself, she was hungry but she mustn't eat the fattening stuff. She found an apple and ate that instead. She drank a glass of water instead of her usual cola. Feeling less starved and quite virtuous she went to her room, and took off her uniform. Standing in front of her long mirror in her knickers and bra she took a good look at herself. It wasn't something she normally did; she didn't like what she saw. She tried to see the woman she felt herself to be holding the starstone above her head. It seemed like a dream but the pendant was there at the bottom of her drawer. She got it out, unclipped the casing and looked at the dull milky white stone. She stood in front of the mirror again holding the stone above her head. It was disappointing. Her image didn't resemble her memory of herself as a strong, fit woman wielding the magic stone but, she remembered, she would be going back to the Land. They had told her so. That body would be hers again and there was no reason why she couldn't have it here as well. She was resolved. She would diet, she would exercise and she would show that she wasn't a dumb idiot. She was the Bearer of the Starstone, the Mine-golly-thingy and the people loved her.

She found a pair of jogging bottoms at the bottom of her wardrobe, hardly worn. She put them on with a T-shirt and a pair of trainers. Then she hit the road. In twenty metres she was puffing, after fifty she was reduced to a trot. Once round the block and she was sweating and panting. She got back to the front gate just as Gus got home.

"What on earth are you doing, sis?" he said.

"Exercising," she said between breaths.

"Why? You never exercise."

"I've decided. I'm fed up with people saying I'm fat."

"But you are."

"Well, it's going to change. It's my birthday in a fortnight. There's going to be a new me. I'm going to diet and exercise."

"Huh. I give it two days max before you're back on the crisps and slouched in front of the TV." He went indoors, leaving September at the gate.

"No, I mean it. I'll show you," she said to herself.

It was a struggle. She was hungry, tired, irritable, despondent. School was difficult as teachers fretted about the exams that would be looming like a great high wall at the end of the year that she would have to clamber over. September gave in to temptation once, twice, three times as a packet of chocolate biscuits disappeared almost before she realised she was eating them. But Gus' repeated taunts, the remembered insults of the boys and girls at school and the memory of the image of herself wielding the starstone kept her vow firmly in her mind.

In some ways her focus on dieting and fitness made her memory of her experiences that night become less vivid and she sometimes wondered whether they had really happened. She even found herself questioning her 'proof' – the pendant. Perhaps it had the silver clasp and chain all along and she had just forgotten. Each evening and morning she looked out of her window for the stars and Moon. When the sky was clear she held up the starstone and peered into its cloudiness, but nothing happened. She watched the Moon pass the third quarter as it became old and saw the changing shape for the first time.

She wanted to question Mother more about the seventh child but she felt that Mother wouldn't welcome the subject coming up and an opportunity didn't arise. Mother did of course notice the change in her. She responded cheerfully to September's sudden desire for healthy food, and she encouraged her on her jogs around the housing estate. September was grateful that she didn't question too much the reasons for the sudden change in her habits but seemed to accept September's explanation that turning sixteen was the incentive. Despite mother's quiet assistance September still found it difficult to maintain her programme. She felt starved most of the time and she feared being seen and ridiculed on her runs, well trots, around the houses. The most depressing thing was that despite all the effort there didn't seem much change. She had barely lost any weight, she couldn't see much difference in herself in the mirror and concentrating on her work seemed more difficult than ever.

A weekend came and passed. Gus remained in his room, with a mate or two, making loud crashing noises which he called music. September met up with Poppy and Emma for a visit to the shops but she found her heart wasn't in shopping even though her birthday was just a few days away. There was homework too of course. Although it was months till exams teachers were piling on the homework as preparation and nothing came easily to her.

The Moon became a crescent getting slimmer and slimmer. She wished her diet was having a similar effect on her but any changes were impossible to detect after just a couple of weeks. Now the Moon was a thin sliver, her birthday was just a day away. She had checked up on the internet and confirmed that her birthday would be on the new Moon. Perhaps because that was on her mind the dreams were troubling her more. It seemed each night she witnessed vague disturbing events in the Land. Comets and strange winged creatures filled the sky and there was fire all around. Each morning she awoke sweating and trembling. What did these foggy and indistinct images mean? She was torn between wanting to discover what was happening and dreading what was expected of her. The memories of her visit seemed distant and unreal now but the dreams kept her unsettled and wondering what would happen.

The Saturday of her birthday dawned at last. September stayed in bed, reluctant to meet the rest of the family and tired after another night of broken sleep. Eventually Mother came up to her. At least this morning she knocked on the door before opening it.

"Happy Birthday, love," she looked at September with a worried frown on her face, "are you all right, Em? Your eyes look tired."

"I'm fine Mother," September said, a little annoyed with herself that it came out rather more petulantly than she intended.

"Are you sure? You've been looking a bit run down for days. You're not overdoing it with your exercise?"

"No, Mother."

"You're not worried about your school work are you?"

"No. Well not much. I'm trying to learn it, I really am."

"We know you are, love," Mother said softly, "Your father and I have been really impressed with how you've been looking after yourself these last couple of weeks and how you've been working since the new term started. We know the exams will be difficult for you, but we're proud of you." She gave September a broad smile, "Anyway, give it a break today. It's your sixteenth birthday. Come and open your cards."

Mother left and September hauled herself out of bed.

Soon she was immersed in the celebrations. The house filled up with her other sisters. Even April and her boyfriend arrived. Well, sixteen was quite special, September thought. Gus kidded her about all the things that she could now do legally. She ignored him.

September tried to look pleased at seeing everyone and oohed and aahed over her presents but drifted through the day as if it was someone else having the birthday and she was just a watcher. By the evening the kitchen and living room were full of sisters and boyfriends and aunts and uncles. Mother was careering around trying to keep everyone happy and produce food for all. September slipped outside into the garden. It was still daylight but cooling quickly after a sunny day – it was September after all. She looked up into the sky. No moon this evening of course. She shivered, not just from the cool air, but with apprehension. Was a new Moon significant? A new beginning. Was this was the night she would be called back to the Land? What would she find there? What was expected of her?

She realised that April was standing next to her, puffing on a cigarette. April had dark hair like her father and there was little resemblance to September or Mother, or her father for that matter. April had always tried to be different so had her hair spiked, wore heavy make-up and there were various rings and studs piercing her face and ears. Gosh, she's thirty now and still acting the rebellious teenager, September thought; the product of Mother's youth and inexperience, the daughter who, as the oldest, always had to look after herself.

"Finding it too crowded, then?" April said, puffing on her fag then offering it to September. She shook her head.

"A bit," she replied.

"You seem a bit, sort of subdued; not the September I remember always bouncing around with a smile and a laugh. You look different, too. Mother says you've been on a slimming thing."

September shrugged but was secretly pleased that April could see a change in her.

"Got a problem? Try it out on big sis April."

"No, it's nothing..." September was going to deny everything, and then a thought came to her, "Well there was something."

"What is it? A boy?"

"No, don't be silly. Would a boy look at me?"

"'Course he would, now you're losing that flab, and especially if he thought he was going to have it off with you."

"Thanks."

"My pleasure. So what is it?"

September paused, wondering if she should ask the question, then decided that this was her chance to find out.

"Did Mum have another child before me?"

April stared at her through her black shadowed eyes.

"You mean between Augustus and you."

"Yes, I suppose so."

"No-one's told you?"

"Told me what?"

"Well..."

"Look, come on April, if you know something, tell me." The normally sullen and impassive April suddenly looked on edge.

"If Mother doesn't want you to know, I'm not sure if I should..."

"It's too late now, April. There is something, I knew it, so tell me what it is." April glanced over her shoulder through the kitchen window. The noise seemed to be growing. April grabbed September's arm and dragged her down the garden path towards the shed.

"Let's go down the garden like we did when you were little," April said. They went behind the shed. There was an old wooden bench there where April used to take her when she was a toddler, out of sight of the house, so April could light up a fag without Mother seeing and getting annoyed. She took another drag, and then leaned her head towards September.

"Now you've got to keep this to yourself, at least till I'm well away from here. I don't want Mother going on at me like I was still a kid."

"Okay, I won't tell anyone, whatever it is."

"Oh, everyone else knows, except, perhaps, Gus. He's a boy, he doesn't count. But if Mother doesn't want you to know then keep quiet when I've told you."

September stared at April.

"Right, I've said I won't say a thing, but tell me. Now!"

April peeped around the corner of the shed then leant close to September.

"You were twins," she whispered. September was confused.

"What do you mean?"

"There were two of you. Two girls but the first one out was dead. They thought you were too, but obviously they were wrong."

"So I am the seventh child."

"Yeh, I suppose so. Because Mother was so upset Dad let her call the other one, Mairwen, a good Welsh name. It's just blessed Mary really."

"But the baby was dead. How could she be baptised?"

"Chapel has its ways."

"But why has no-one told me before?" September shook her head in disbelief, "I shared a womb with her."

"Don't ask me. I suppose when you were small they didn't want to trouble you with the knowledge of a dead twin and then I suppose it just went on."

"What went on?"

"Well, you know, you had your problems..."

"Problems?"

"I don't know. Mother told me you were being bullied, school was difficult, that sort of thing."

September understood what April meant. She'd been no good at anything and then took to eating to be happy which had only made the bullying worse as she got fat. Mother and Father had always been kind and gentle with her, always concerned, always there. She realised why Mother was always looking in on her.

"I think Mum is still upset."

"Why?"

"Well, when I casually asked if there had been another child, she cut me off."

"Why did you even wonder about it?"

"Oh," September realised she couldn't tell April the truth, it was too ridiculous, "I suppose I just had a feeling, like twins are meant to have."

April nodded as if she understood.

"Look we had better get back," she said, "and remember, don't mention this till I'm well away."

They crept back into the house, drawing a suspicious look from Mother, but soon they were both caught up in the party.

It was late, gone midnight, when September finally closed the bedroom door, except it wasn't just her room tonight. Julie was home too, already undressed and climbing into the top bunk. Of course Julie wanted to chatter, about the party, the family, how annoying Mother and Father could be, what a great holiday she'd had, how exciting it would be going back to college after the vacation. September undressed and pulled on her sleep T-shirt, barely listening and just offering a grunt when it seemed to fit in. She put out the light, got into the lower bunk and waited for Julie to stop talking. Eventually there was just the soft sigh of her breathing.

September lay awake thinking what she had been thinking all evening. She was the seventh child, as the Mordeyrn had said she was, but not just that, she couldn't stop the picture of a dead baby being drawn from the womb filling her head. Her dead sister, her twin, half of her. Absentmindedly she rubbed her birthmark and listened carefully. The house was quiet. The guests had either left or settled for the night. September stretched out an arm from where she lay in her bed to the bottom drawer of her desk. Very slowly she pulled it open, scared of waking Julie. She reached in and drew out the locket. It felt warm in her hand, not the cold metal she expected. She flicked the front and back open and looked in wonder at the stone. It was clear and dark.

September knew what it meant. She slid her legs out from under the duvet and slowly stood up. She reached across the desk and tugged on the curtain. The curtain parted a crack and she gazed out at the clear sky. There was no Moon of course but the sky was filled with stars.

September looked from the night sky to the stone in her hand, dark but warm as if it was alive. She started to raise the stone but stopped. Did she have to go to the Land? Couldn't she just stay here and forget all that nonsense about evil and the powers of metals and the planets? But the Mordeyrn said that they needed her. What would it be like to have the powers that the Mordeyrn said she would possess? Surely she could return at any time? Perhaps if she went just for the night again to see what was happening, then return home again like she did before.

She heard a snort from the top bunk but Julie settled again.

"If I don't try, I'll always wonder," September whispered. She lifted the stone, peering at the stars through it. The stone seemed to magnify and concentrate the star light. The stars looked much brighter than they did just looking out of the window.

The light hit her in the face like water from a hose. Her head jerked back and she was losing her balance. The bedroom filled with a torrent of blue-white luminescence. The walls, the beds, the desk were hidden from view. She fell backwards.

6

The light did not banish the dark. Still small and distant, the globe of light cast no shadows and the dark filled the immeasurable depths. She was borne towards the light by the hate of the unconscious souls that surrounded her. While the malevolence of her companions was unthinking she found herself developing an awareness and form. As well as eyes to see, she felt corporeal. She was whole, a personality, a being. As yet she did not know who or what she was and anger and malice remained her whole existence but she could feel pleasure in the thought of bringing destruction down on those who opposed her, whoever or whatever they may be. She was able to reflect too that there was something other than pure hate that was drawing her towards the light.

The glowing ball was growing and now she could see its incandescence was not homogenous. It was a hollow sphere and the light emerged from specks that covered its surface. The object of her hate was within the sphere. Time began to have meaning. The migration of the betrayed souls was becoming a stampede. Soon a torrent of hate would descend on the occupants of the sphere of lights. She realised that her uniqueness gave her a power to direct the vengeance. She would be the guiding force of malice.

7

September felt the damp under her hands and bottom. She was lying on her back on grass. It's happened, she thought, I'm here. She felt elated and sick at the same time. She pushed herself on to her bare feet and slowly stood up straight. She felt her stomach, her breasts. Yes, she was back in the Land with her slim, fit body. She looked around. The scene was the same as the first time she had come. Once again she stood on the ridge with the grassy hill falling away from her in front and behind. Once again she was dressed in an ankle-length white linen dress and her hair had become long. The Moon was high in the direction that she assumed was the west and casting a pale blue light. The Moon? What did it mean that there was a Moon in the sky here and now while at home it was in shadow? Time was measured in the phases of the Moon. She was sure it meant something. She drew her gaze away from the silver orb.

She turned to face the east and gasped. The copse at the top of the hill which had been made up of rings of trees surrounding the altar had gone. Well, not gone exactly, she could see the massive tree trunks lying on the ground. Just a few of the smaller younger trees remained behind the altar. September gathered up the hem of the gown and hurried up the ridge to get a better look.

As she approached she could see that the fallen trees were laid out as if they had been blasted by a huge explosion exactly above the altar. Was that what she had seen in her dreams? Many of the trunks lay, scorched, pointing the way to the centre. A smell of burnt wood still hung in the humid air. She picked her way across the singed branches finding it difficult to fight her way through. As she approached the centre she could see the white stone altar lit up by the moonlight but she paused in shock when she saw that it was cleaved in two as if by a huge axe. There was a figure sitting at the base of the altar. She pushed desperately through the last few metres of prickly branches, thankful that the long dress protected her legs.

She must have been making a lot of noise because the figure stirred as she entered the clearing. He stood up and ran to her.

"You have come, you have come," he called as he came, then flung his arms around her and hugged her. September staggered and responded half-heartedly. She recognised the young man as one of the metal bearers she had seen on her previous visit, but which metal she could not recall. He pushed himself away from her.

"I'm sorry, Cludydd, I am overcome with joy. We have waited so long for your return."

"It's only been a couple of weeks," September said, confused.

"Not for us. It has been two years since you visited us. We have watched and waited for you ever since. I am so pleased that you have come during my period of duty. I, Berddig, cludydd o alcam, welcome you."

"You have sat up here every night waiting for me?"

"Well, not me. Many of the people of Amaethaderyn have willingly given up their nights to keep the vigil."

"But what has happened here, Berddig? The Mordeyrn called this place your refuge." September looked around at the scene of destruction, the noble trees snapped off at their bases as if they were twigs and the altar riven in two. A great sadness at the destruction filled her.

"The Malevolence grows," Berddig said sadly, "Let us set off to the village and I will try to describe what has happened." He took her hand and guided her along a path that had been made through the fallen trees. They reached the open hillside and headed down the grassy slope into the broad valley. September looked to see where she was putting her feet while Berddig strode on through the night.

"After you and the Mordeyrn defeated the Draig tân," he began, "we had some months of peace, but the Mordeyrn warned that the evil was growing and that we should prepare for more attacks. In the spring the first Draig tân appeared. The Mordeyrn destroyed it with his golden plate but then two more came."

"Three comets, all at once?" September was amazed, "That can't be natural."

Berddig looked at her as if she had said the obvious.

"Of course not. The Draig tân are the weapons of the Adwyth."

"Yes, I see. Didn't he need my help to destroy the comets?"

"They came in the daytime when the Sun gives the Mordeyrn his full power. He dispelled the second Draig tân but it took a lot of his strength. He was too drained to protect us from the third."

"Oh!"

"It burst over the Cysegr – you can see what it did. But it also spread pestilence over the valley. Many cattle have died and some of our people too."

"Oh dear. I wish I had been here to help," although the thought of the destruction scared September and she didn't know what she could have done to stop it.

Berddig stopped mid-stride, turned and smiled at her.

"We would have appreciated your presence but the Maengolauseren did not bring you. You are here now. There will be many more occasions when your power will be needed."

September felt disturbed by Berddig's words. There was a knot of fear in her chest, fear of danger and fear of not knowing what she should do.

"What about the Cemegwr? Don't they help you when the Malevolence comes?"

Berddig snorted, "The Cemegwr! That old myth. Oh, some people still believe that they created everything but hardly anyone believes that they are here now watching over us."

They fell silent and September contemplated what Berddig had said. Perhaps belief in the Cemegwr was the same as belief in God at home – just held by a few of the remaining faithful. The hillside had levelled out and now they were walking across a meadow towards a line of trees that marked the river bank. She looked out across the river. It was wide at this point, the opposite bank just a dark line in the night. Ripples of water caught the moonlight and she could see that the river flowed sluggishly. It was a peaceful scene and for a moment September forgot about the Malevolence and the threat it posed. The gently moving water was calming. They reached the bank and Berddig left her, telling her to stay still until he called. He disappeared, another shadow amongst the trees. Then Berddig called out and September saw him gesturing to her from a few metres along the bank. He was standing in a flat bottomed boat, rather like a large punt, and gripping a thick rope that was wound around a sturdy tree trunk. The other end disappeared into the river some metres from the shore.

"Come and get in. This is the ferry that will carry us across to Amaethaderyn." He held out a hand to guide her from the bank into the boat. It was broad enough to be steady in the water and she was able to take a seat on one of the cross benches without worrying about her balance. Berddig moved to the other end of the boat and pulled on the rope. The ferry moved out into the river. As he tugged, more of the rope rose from the surface dripping water. September watched with interest as the young man hauled the boat across the river. As they approached the middle of the stream the current began to tug at them. September could see that Berddig was having some difficulty.

"Can I help, Berddig?"

"Thank you, yes. This boat is big for one person to haul. We have a team of boatmen when the village travels across for gatherings at Cysegr. Stand behind me and pull on the rope."

September gingerly groped her way to the front of the boat. She stood up behind Berddig placing a hand on his shoulder to steady herself and then began tugging on the rope. With the power of two people the ferry quickly moved out of the faster flowing stream and approached the bank and another line of trees. The hull grated on the gravel of the riverbed and September grabbed hold of Berddig to stop herself toppling over. He turned to her.

"Thank you, Cludydd. Let me help you ashore." He stepped onto the bank and held out his hand for her to follow him. It made her feel grown up to be treated in such a courteous way and nothing like the silly girl she felt at home.

He took a thinner rope tied to the front of the boat and fastened it around the nearest tree.

"Not far now," he said, "the village is just through the trees, by the lake." He set off at a fast pace along a well worn path with September trotting to keep up. The trees were widely spaced so the moonlight made the way easy to follow. In a few moments they emerged into a clearing and September saw ahead of them a cluster of round buildings. They were dark shadows in the night but she could see that many were ruined, their roofs fallen in and walls flattened.

"This is your village?" She asked. Berddig paused and looked at her. There was a deep sadness on his face,

"It is not as it was, I am sorry."

"What happened?"

"A month ago we were attacked again, this time by Adarllwchgwin."

"Adarluck what?"

"Adarllwchgwin. Giant birds ridden by red-skinned servants of the Malevolence. The birds carried huge rocks and flaming bushes in their talons which they dropped on the village. Houses and workshops were damaged and many men, women and children were killed by the rocks and the fires."

September was horrified.

"I saw it in my dreams but didn't understand. I didn't think it was real. What about the Mordeyrn? Couldn't he stop them? And what about the other, what do you call them, with the metals, don't some of them have powers to defend you?"

"The Mordeyrn tried as did the Cludydd o plwm and haearn and arianbyw. I fought too using my skills and the power of alcam to support the warriors. They did well, bringing down some of the Adarllwchgwin, but there were too many and they were too powerful. A group of the evil birds attacked the Mordeyrn. Their riders carry three-pronged spears that throw out cosmic fire. The Mordeyrn tried to defend himself but the golden plate disintegrated in the onslaught."

"The Mordeyrn's gold plate was damaged?"

"Destroyed."

"But what happened to him?"

"He was winded and without the plate his power is limited, but he lives. The attackers left then but many homes were damaged and people died or were injured."

There was a call like an owl that disturbed the silence of the night. Berddig answered with a similar cry. Very quickly as they moved amongst the buildings, there were other voices and the sounds of people stirring. Men, women and children emerged from the huts, pulling on jackets, rubbing eyes, peering into the dark. They gathered around them. In the moonlight that illuminated their faces September could see weariness, sadness, fear but there was also joy and expectation directed towards her. Berddig stopped the people from pressing close.

"My friends, as you can see, the Cludydd o Maengolauseren has returned to us. She will help us in our fight against the Adwyth, but now it is late and we are tired. Return to your beds, we will meet in the daytime and welcome the Cludydd in our accustomed manner." Berddig urged people to return to their homes and gradually the crowd dispersed. A tall white haired lady came forward. September recognised her as the silver bearer.

"Cludydd. I am delighted that you have come amongst us. I am Arianwen, Cludydd o arian," she said and nodded her head.

"Hello," September relied, "I remember you from the last time I came. You gave me the cover for the stone."

"That's correct, Cludydd. It was a great honour for me."

September felt embarrassed and foolish beside this graceful woman.

"Please call me September, or just Ember, I am not sure about all this cludith stuff." Berddig and Arianwen smiled at her.

"I am sure you are tired and confused," Arianwen said, "let us find you a bed and give you time for some rest." She and Berddig led September amongst the round houses.

"We had a house prepared for you," Berddig said, "but the Adarllwchgwin burnt it to the ground."

"So I invite you to my home," Arianwen said. They stopped at one of the buildings. In the moonlight they were all dark shadows and September could not see any difference between them. Arianwen pushed on a low, wooden door and invited September to enter in front of her. September saw the whole room in one glance because of a small fire that burned in the middle of the floor. Smoke rose and disappeared somewhere in the thatched roof. The round walls enclosed a space about six metres across. There were mats scattered on the floor and a cluster of three chairs filled with cushions. The fire only really illuminated the centre of the house. Against the circular walls were the dark forms of other pieces of furniture, including a low, single bed.

"Please sit down," Arianwen said, pointing to the chairs by the fire. September sat in a wicker seat. The late night walk had made her feel weary and the cushions felt soft and comfortable. Arianwen went to a table set against the wall of the house and poured liquid from a jug into a cup. She brought it to September. "Are you thirsty after your journey?" she asked.

September found that she was and recalled the refreshing clear water she had drunk on her previous visit. She took the cup and drained it.

"Thank you, I didn't realise how thirsty I was."

"I will leave you now," Berddig said, "I will see you in the morning when we will discuss what we must do." He knelt at her feet, took her hand in his and kissed it. September felt embarrassed again.

"Why do you do this?" she asked.

"Because I am grateful that you have come to us," Berddig said, "and because I know you will help us."

"But you're treating me like a princess, bowing and kissing my hand."

"I do not know what a princess is but you are the Cludydd o Maengolauseren. I, we, respect you and honour you."

"But I don't deserve it. I haven't done anything." September felt Berddig's attention as a great burden on her.

"Not yet perhaps, but you will. The Maengolauseren gives its bearer power and strength. You will deserve all the honour we give you. Now you must rest." He stood, nodded to Arianwen and left.

September felt a tear trickle down her cheek. Arianwen noticed and came to her side, kneeling and placing an arm around her shoulders.

"What is it, my dear?"

"Everyone expects me to be some kind of hero, but I don't know what to do. I'm not special, I'm not strong, or clever," September sobbed into Arianwen's sleeve.

"Oh, that young man. He doesn't understand," Arianwen said as she hugged September, "he doesn't realise what a burden we are placing on you. Of course you don't know how you can help us. But he is correct; the Maengolauseren has selected you and brought you to us. You will discover how to use its power as you did when you helped the Mordeyrn destroy the first Draig tân. But all that is in the future. For tonight you need to rest because there is a great deal that lies ahead for all of us."

Arianwen stood up, took hold of September's hands and drew her to her feet. She guided her to the bunk set against the wall of the hut. It was covered with a woollen blanket.

"This is your bed for tonight. Sleep well," Arianwen said. She pulled back the blanket revealing another beneath. September sat and swung her legs onto the bed. The mattress was firm but comfortable. She rested her head on a soft cushion. Her mind was fuzzy with tiredness but full of all that she had seen and all that had been said. Arianwen rested a hand holding her silver amulet on her forehead.

"Sleep, child, sleep," she said softly.

8

It was the unfamiliar noises that woke September. Voices nearby calling out and talking, sounds made by animals and of large pieces of timber being hit with heavy mallets, the clang of metals, and the birds. There was the sound of chickens clucking, ducks quacking, songbirds singing, rooks cawing and many other screeches and tweets that September couldn't identify. There were smells too, wood fires and food cooking, animal odours and scents of plants hanging in the air. She opened her eyes and recalled at once that she was not at home in her own bed but lying in a wooden bunk snuggled in wonderfully soft, woollen blankets on a mattress of goose-down. She stirred, stretching and yawning.

"Ah, you have awoken," Arianwen approached the bed. Her kind, lined face with its curtain of silver-white hair looked down at September. "You slept well."

September realised that she felt thoroughly refreshed and eager to see what the day had in store. Her muscles felt taut and ready for exercise. She was quite surprised as she recalled her tears of the previous evening.

"Yes, I did, thank you. Is it late?"

"Well the Sun has been up for a couple of hours, but no, you are not late. There are many things for the people to do to rebuild our village but for you there is just rest until we meet."

September felt an urge to go to the loo. She sat up and swung her legs off the bed.

"I need to wash and um..."

"Attend to your needs?"

"Yes."

"Go out of the door and circle around the house to the left till you find a small wooden building. That is the lavatory. You will find all you need there."

September got to her feet and opened the door. The bright

sunlight dazzled her at first but as her eyes adjusted she took in the sight of the village at work. Men and women hurried past Arianwen's cottage carrying wooden posts and baskets; others were working on the ruined huts, removing timbers and thatch. Many of the people looked at her as she emerged from the hut. They smiled at her but seemed to understand that she was not ready for conversation. They resumed their errands or jobs. The day was warm and September felt beads of sweat under her linen dress. She followed the directions and found the washroom.

Inside there was a wooden box with something resembling a toilet seat over it. There was a supply of tufts of grass in a basket beside it. There was also a washbasin and a stand holding jugs of water and a small stove with a kettle of water warming on it that made the temperature inside quite stifling. September couldn't see any way of locking the door, so finally gave up in desperation, hauled up her dress and sat on the loo. Having relieved herself and got over the experience of wiping herself with handfuls of grass she considered how she should wash herself. It was obviously a communal washroom and anyone might come in, but she felt sticky and needed a shower. At home she was nervous of taking off her clothes and showing her rolls of blubber to other people but here she felt different. She had a confidence that she did not feel at home so she stood up and pulled the linen dress over her head. If anyone came in now it was tough. She poured the hot water from the kettle into the basin and refilled it with cold water from one of the jugs. She added cold water until the temperature felt right and began splashing water onto herself. There was a bar of hard grey soap beside the basin. September expected it to be useless but it lathered easily and gave off an aroma of the woodland. She noticed that the floor was made of earthenware tiles laid so that the water she poured over herself drained into a gulley that ran out of the washroom. At last September felt clean.

While she dried herself on the soft woollen towels that she found hanging next to the stove she puzzled over her body. It was her, but not her. She still had her birthmark; the red, crescent-shaped mark on her right hip. Her muscles and breasts were firmer than usual, her skin more taut, there was no spare hanging flesh, and of course her hair was much longer than back home. She hadn't had waves of white hair over her shoulders and down her back since she was a little girl. Without a mirror she was not sure what she looked like but she imagined that she must look quite striking. It was as if her body was tuned and ready for the purpose that Berddig and the Mordeyrn had spoken of but which she could only guess at. She took the pendant in her hands and opened it up. The starstone was transparent but dark. She held it up to her eye and looked into it. Tiny lights flashed and moved but she could see no image. She closed it up and let it fall between her breasts. She pulled the dress over her head and felt clean and comfortable. The dress itself though was annoying. She was not used to such a long and loose garment that tripped her up. She returned to the house and opened the door to welcoming smells.

"Do you feel better?" Arianwen asked.

"Yes, but what about replacing the jugs of water?"

"Oh don't worry. Attending to the lavatory is one of the jobs we take turns to carry out. Someone will be in there very soon checking on what needs to be done. Are you ready for some breakfast?"

"Oh, yes please." September realised that it had been at her birthday party the previous evening that she had last eaten. That seemed so long ago and far away. She looked on hungrily as Arianwen placed bread and cheese and poached eggs on a wooden plate and handed it to her. Briefly she remembered her diet but the food looked so tasty and satisfying that she gobbled it up quickly. She saw Arianwen looking at her with a smile on her face.

"You certainly were hungry, Ember, would you like some fruit now?" She offered a bowl filled to overflowing with strawberries, raspberries, oranges and other fruits that September didn't recognise. She took a selection, relishing their varied sweet, juicy flavours. There was a cup of the fresh water to wash it down and September, sitting in a chair felt full and satisfied. She fingered the shapeless dress.

"Do I have to wear this?" she asked.

Arianwen looked confused, "What else would you wear? All women wear similar dresses."

"I'm used to shorter, lighter, skirts and blouses, and trousers."

"Men wear trousers."

"Is that a law which must be obeyed?"

"No, it is customary, but not a rule." September would have enquired further but the door opened and Berddig entered. His face opened into a broad smile.

"Cludydd, you look much refreshed. Are you ready to meet?"

"Arianwen has been very kind."

"Good, well come then. There is a lot to discuss."

September followed Berddig out of the house with Arianwen behind them. As they walked along the paths between the buildings, people paused in what they were doing and hailed her with greetings and good wishes. September felt uncomfortable being treated like royalty again and blushed as she responded to the calls with small waves of her hand. Now it was daylight she could see more of the layout of the village. Not that there was a clear plan. The round mud-walled, thatched buildings were not in neat rows but clustered haphazardly, close together on the bank of a reed lined lake. Behind the village was the edge of the woodland, about three hundred metres from the water's edge.

Berddig led them into a space with a circle of wooden benches around an open hearth. Three people rose from their seats as they arrived. They were familiar to September from the night time gathering at the Refuge but she couldn't remember who was who. She needn't have worried because each approached her with arms outstretched. Two were women, dressed like September in ankle length white gowns. One was a tall mature blond while the other looked barely older than September. The last member of the trio was a grey haired man with a slight stoop wearing a long grey robe, who spoke first.

"Welcome Cludydd. I am Padarn, cludydd o plwm."

"Ah, yes, I remember," September said shaking his hand.

"This is Eluned," he introduced the younger of the women, "the cludydd o arianbyw. She may look like an innocent young girl but her powers can deceive you." The young woman stepped forward and kissed September on the cheek.

"Ignore, Padarn," she joked, "he's envious because he's not young anymore."

"Jealous, perhaps, but not envious of the future that awaits you young people," Padarn said gravely, "and this is Catrin, cludydd o efyddyn."

The tall, graceful woman also stepped forward and grasped her hand.

"We are delighted to have you amongst us, Cludydd."

"Oh please, don't call me that. My name is September."

"As you wish," Padarn said, "Now where is Iorwerth?"

A burly young man ran into the space and stopped in front of September. She was impressed that he did not look at all heated by his run.

"Am I late? I am sorry if I am, there's so much work at the forge," he said.

"No, we were just introducing everyone to September," Berddig said.

"Ah, September is your name," Iorwerth said bowing deeply, "the Cludydd o Maengolauseren."

"Just call me September. You must be the cludydd o..." September couldn't remember what all the metals were.

"Haearn."

"Oh yes, that's the easy one, iron. And plwm is lead, but arianbyw and efyddyn, I can't remember.

"Quicksilver, mercury," said Eluned.

"Copper," Catrin added.

Berddig spoke, "Right, well now that we are all here we must begin. Let us be seated." He gestured to September to a place on the circular bench. They all sat close to each other, in an arc of the circle on both sides of Berddig. There was a pause as each shuffled into a comfortable position. September felt strange sitting amongst these people. They were so welcoming and friendly but she knew they expected a lot of her. While the introductions had taken place villagers had come into the clearing and stood behind the bearers watching and listening. The sounds of sawing and hammering stopped. It seemed that everyone in the village had come to see the Cludydd and hear the speeches, whatever there was to discuss.

"I'll get the formal bit over first," Berddig said in an aside to September and then continued in a firm voice, "We are delighted to welcome the Cludydd o Maengolauseren, September, amongst us. The Adwyth has grown in power since her first appearance to us and we all know the destruction and death that has occurred. That will not end now that September has joined us, but with the power of the Maengolauseren we can and will defeat the Evil."

The other bearers nodded and there were mutters of approval from the watchers. September felt lost. How could she help? What power did the starstone give her?

"We are meeting here today," Berddig continued, "to decide what must be done, but first I feel I need to explain to September how we make our decisions here." More people had arrived pressing into the circle. Some sat on the circle of benches, facing the cludyddau.

Berddig faced September and spoke in a voice that although it was meant for her ears was clearly heard by the assembled crowd.

"If the Mordeyrn was here he would be leading the meeting but as he is not I take his place. This is because as cludydd o alcam I have certain skills that I have acquired during my training and through the power of the metal. The people respect the cludyddau because of the gifts that the metals give us. But those gifts also bring responsibilities, to our people and our land. We are not rulers; everyone here has a say in what we do and amongst us are many skilled people – woodworkers, moulders of clay, farmers, herdsmen, fishers, nurses, teachers, bakers, cooks. All have a role in our lives and all have duties to each other. So today we welcome you, Cludydd o Maengolauseren and invite you to join with us."

There was a murmuring of approval around the throng which had grown still more as Berddig spoke. September had tried to follow what he had said. It seemed that the village was run by all the people with no-one in overall authority but that the bearers were held in particular regard because of the powers they apparently had, drawn from the metals they wielded. It seemed too good to be true. Back home, September recalled, even discussions in class at school broke down into ferocious arguments and they had trouble deciding anything. She had always kept quiet thinking she had nothing worthwhile to say and anyway, the others told her to shut up if it looked as though she was going to open her mouth. Perhaps Berddig did have magical powers of persuasion.

Berddig turned to address the throng.

"Obviously our first duty is to continue the repairs to the village. There will be further attacks by the servants of the Malevolence and we must be prepared for them." Iorwerth clenched his fist and looked fierce but said nothing.

Berddig continued, "I told September last night about the great disaster that occurred when we were last attacked. The destruction of the Mordeyrn's golden plate, his instrument of power." A moan arose from the crowd. September looked at the sea of sad faces.

"That was a great setback for us," Berddig went on, "The Mordeyrn provided us with the power and the will to take on our attackers. Without his power and his knowledge and wisdom we are much weakened."

"Where is the Mordeyrn?" September asked and raised her hand to her mouth realising that she had spoken. She expected someone to tell her shush but they didn't. All the faces were grave.

"He left us soon after the attack. He is journeying to the Arsyllfa, the great observatory in the Bryn am Seren, to discuss with the astronomers and the other learned people how to regain his power and what we must do to fight the Malevolence. He left word that when you arrived among us you were to follow him."

"Oh," September gasped, "is it far to this Observatory?"

"Indeed it is. It is many days travel westwards along the Afon Deheuol, our great river and then up into the highlands to the hill of stars."

"That's it then," said Iorwerth, "What more do we need to discuss? Let's get on with our work."

September was quite sure that there was a lot more to talk about before she set off on a long journey.

"But why do I have to go? Can't I wait until the Mordeyrn returns?"

"The Mordeyrn has asked you to follow him," Arianwen said.

"But I thought you said that everyone has a say in what

happens," September was feeling aggrieved and scared of taking on a long journey in a land that she did not know.

"That is true," Arianwen said soothingly, "but the Mordeyrn is wise and can foresee what must be done."

"The Mordeyrn may not return here for a very long time. He may not return at all," Berddig went on, "He wants you with him so that he can help you develop your powers. The members of the Arsyllfa will also help you."

September could see the sense in what Berddig said, but it didn't stop her feeling scared about a long journey. Berddig went on.

"What we do need to decide, Iorwerth, is who should guide and protect September on her journey." Iorwerth shrugged in agreement.

"One of the cludydd?" Padarn asked, "although I think I am too decrepit to make the journey."

"I'll go," said Catrin.

"No," Berddig replied. "We need you here to communicate with other parts of Gwlad and to keep in touch with the Mordeyrn as he travels. In fact we cannot spare any of the cludydd. All are needed here to restore and strengthen our defence against the manifestations of evil."

"I know who it should be," Iorwerth said, "Tudfwlch, my apprentice. He is young but is learning the arts of using haearn and he is a skilled warrior. He may even have the skill to become a cludydd one day."

"A good suggestion," Berddig said and the other cludydd nodded in agreement, "Is Tudfwlch here?" There was a disturbance in the crowd and a young man pushed to the front. September thought he looked no more than her age, a smooth faced but strongly built youth with unruly dark brown hair.

"I am here and ready to escort the Cludydd," he said proudly. The people cheered and he blushed. "That is if the Cludydd wishes it," he added. September still was not at all sure she wanted to go anywhere but Tudfwlch looked friendly. She hadn't had many friends in recent years, and certainly no boys had shown any eagerness to protect and guide her, but she felt more sure of herself in this new body so she smiled at him and he nodded his head.

"Good, Tudfwlch," Berddig said, "but you have not travelled from Amaethaderyn once in your life. A guide will be needed. Someone who has travelled along the river and knows its moods and dangers."

There was a sudden cry from the back of the crowd. People pointed into the sky.

"Adarllwchgwin!" they cried. People started to push and jostle away from the clearing. Some fell and were in danger of being trampled until others came to their aid and lifted them back to their feet. The meeting was breaking up as everyone hurried off in different directions. September looked around herself wondering what was happening. Iorwerth and Berddig were peering into the sky above the far side of the lake.

"Three of them," Iorwerth said, "coming this way fast."

"We must prepare our defence," Padarn said, rising to his feet and hobbling away to the buildings."

"Come, September," Arianwen said, taking her hand and pulling her to her feet, "we must get you away from here."

"Yes," Berddig said taking his eyes off the approaching trio of birds, "You look after her Arianwen. Take her into the woods. Eluned, Catrin, you know what must be done." The other women hurried away.

"I will organise my warriors," shouted Iorwerth as he ran off. September looked into the sky.

"Aren't they just birds?" she asked but knew straight away she was being silly. The people knew what was coming. Her birthmark was itching.

"No, they're not," Arianwen said tugging at September's arm. "They are huge fierce birds ridden by wickedness. Come, we must get out of sight."

The Adarllwchgwin were closer now and September at last was able to appreciate their size. They were over the lake and only moments from the village. She saw that they were like eagles but the size of a horse with wings ten metres across. Each carried a flaming bush in its huge talons and was ridden by a crimson-skinned being. The three birds made a squawking noise that filled the sky. They were over the lake and diving towards the village.

At last fear gripped September and she responded to

Arianwen's tugging on her arm. She followed the silver haired woman away from the meeting place. They hurried between the round huts turning this way and that. September soon had no idea of their direction. Behind them there were shouts and screams. September slowed and looked over her shoulder. The birds were over the village now. One after another they released their burdens of fire and the thatched buildings exploded in flame. The riders urged their mounts on and aimed the three-pronged spears that they held. Gouts of vivid red light shot from them to unseen targets on the ground. The birds flew on towards September.

"Hurry," Arianwen urged, "we must get under the trees." September turned and ran after her. They reached the last of the houses, but there was still a gap of a hundred metres or so given over to allotments before the line of trees. Arianwen ran through the beds of lettuces and onions. September followed, finding the cultivated soil slowing down her flight. Her birthmark was burning like fury. Her left foot sank into the loose earth and her right foot caught in the hem of her dress. She fell and rolled over on to her back. Now she saw the three eagles coming straight towards her. Their huge hooked beaks opened and emitted a deafening screech; their small, red eyes were fixed on her. She saw their feather covered legs, as broad as an elephant's, with their unencumbered talons poised to grab and tear. Their great wings spread wide to soar towards her and the riders held their tridents raised.

September realised that all three of the Adarllwchgwin were coming for her. She was their prey. But why? Fear gripped her and her mind was blank. Her birthmark hurt as if someone was stabbing her with a knife. The pendant somehow was in her hand with the catches undone and the stone exposed. She raised it up. The stone glowed with a fierce blue light. What now?

The leading Adarllwchgwin reared up over her, preparing to grab her with its talons, its rider leaning to the side to aim his trident. Its outstretched wings filled the sky. The sulphurous stench of its breath blew over her.

What had the Mordeyrn said when he repulsed the comet? Unbidden the word came from her unconscious memory.

"Ymadaelwch!" she screamed. A violet cone of light leapt from the starstone enveloping the hovering bird. For a moment the Adarllwchgwin was caught like a moth in torchlight and then there was a huge crack of thunder as if the sky was parting and it was gone. The blast of air pressed September into the earth and caught the other two birds by surprise. They tipped sideways and their wings touched the ground. They crumpled and fell to the earth. The riders clung on and urged their mounts to right themselves but now September saw other figures running from the buildings.

A white tiger loped across the tilled soil, its jaws wide and roaring. It leapt at one of the birds, tearing at its neck with its knife-like teeth. The bird twisted and fought to get away but the tiger hung on, gnawing at the bird's throat. Its rider struggled to direct its trident at the tiger. Red flashes shot from its prongs but they missed the attacking animal and struck the earth harmlessly.

A band of men carrying spears lead by Iorwerth whirling his great sword attacked the other fallen bird and the red figure that clung to its back. With each stab of their haearn tipped weapons there was an eruption of rust-red light and the bird and rider screamed in agony.

Two more powerful detonations ripped through the air and the scene was obscured with a curtain of smoke.

September lay in the earth unable to move, the pain in her hip fading, just looking around her. As the smoke settled she saw that the Adarllwchgwin had disappeared and so had the tiger. A naked female figure stood where the bird had fallen. September saw that it was Eluned. The warriors also stood still holding their spears upright. Some wiped dust and sweat from their faces. Iorwerth wiped his sword against the hem of his tunic. Eluned waved to September and ran off back to the houses.

"Cludydd, are you injured?"

September turned her head to see that Arianwen was standing over her, a look of concern on her face. September realised that she was in one piece with nothing hurting.

"No, I'm fine; I tripped over this stupid dress," she said pulling at the hem so that she could regain her footing. She stood up.

"Did I see that tiger become Eluned?"

"Trawsffurfio, the ability to transform. It is the power of arianbyw," Arianwen said, "but you defeated the Adarllwchgwin, you wielded the Maengolauseren."

September looked at the stone which she still held in her hand. Though clear it was now dark again. "I don't know how I did it. And it is daytime, how could it work at all?"

"It draws power from all the objects in the sky – stars, sun, moon. With wise use it can be harnessed at any time. You have shown that the Maengolauseren has indeed chosen correctly, for even without training you can call on its powers."

September shook her head in disbelief.

"But what happened to the birds and their riders? They just disappeared."

Arianwen put an arm around September's shoulders and guided her towards the waiting warriors.

She explained, "The manifestations of the Malevolence are elemental in form. The Adarllwchgwin are creatures of air. When they were defeated their forms returned to the air. Similarly the Draig tân are the embodiment of fire. There are other monsters the evil can conjure from earth and water."

As they drew near to the waiting men September was greeted by cheering. Iorwerth came forward and held out his left hand to shake hers.

"A magnificent victory," he said grinning, "Aldyth has pierced the flesh of evil," he added waving the long sword in his right hand.

Berddig ran up panting. He saw September and stopped, breathing deeply and looking relieved.

"What happened?" he asked.

"The Cludydd destroyed one of the Adarllwchgwin and brought down the other two. Then we despatched them," Iorwerth replied. Berddig looked questioningly at September who shrugged her shoulders.

"I don't know how, it just sort of happened."

"The starstone will always oppose evil. As the bearer you will discover how to control it. But come; let us get back to our meeting. This shows how important our plans are."

They walked back between the buildings and September

was dismayed to see dead and injured villagers lying on the ground. More buildings had been damaged and smoke was still rising from some hit by the flaming bushes and the cosmic fire of the Adarllwchgwin. The pride that she had felt at her victory, however accidental, drained from her. Berddig hurried her past the fallen while Arianwen turned aside to tend to the wounded. They reached a hut where Berddig stopped. Iorwerth marched on with his band of warriors, leaving September alone with Berddig.

"Come into my home," he said, opening the door and ushering her inside. It was furnished simply and similarly to Arianwen's. Berddig indicated a chair and went to pour two cups of water. September relaxed and drank, suddenly feeling exhausted. She was used to running away and hiding from her tormentors, but those at home just called her names. She wasn't familiar with fighting giant birds that were out to kill her. Berddig settled himself into a chair.

September spoke, "I think there is something you haven't told me."

"There are many things, I am sure," Berddig replied.

"Oh, I know there's lots I don't know, but there is one thing in particular."

"What is that?"

"Those birds, those adarluck things were after me weren't they?"

Berddig frowned and covered his mouth with his hand. He seemed to be deciding how to respond. Finally he spoke.

"You're right. It is as the Mordeyrn feared. He said that you may be a target of the Malevolence as he was himself. The attacks on Cysegr and on the village were directed at the Mordeyrn and now they are drawn to you."

"So you want rid of me as soon as possible."

Berddig shook his head, "I don't want you to leave us but it is true that the sooner you begin your journey the less likely it is that Amaethaderyn will be attacked again."

September was thoughtful. The realisation that as well as being the hope of the people she was also the target of the evil filled her with fear but she knew that she had to leave so that the villagers could continue their lives in safety.

"Will I be attacked on the trip?"

"Probably, but if you move quickly and with the minimum of fuss and energy and use the Maengolauseren as little as possible, then you may be difficult for the manifestations of evil to track."

"Then I should leave as soon as possible. Is Tudfwlch ready?"

"I am sure he is, but you still need a guide, and transport and supplies. Tomorrow or the next day will be soon enough. Relax today, talk to the other cludyddau, meet the villagers. They want to congratulate you after your victory over the Adarllwchgwin."

"It doesn't feel like much of a victory with people dead and injured, all because I'm here."

"If you hadn't been able to use the power of the stone then it could have been much worse, particularly if you had been lost. We have all heard the Mordeyrn's warnings that the strength of the Malevolence is increasing and that terrible things will happen unless he and the other members of the Arsyllfa find ways of defeating the Evil. You are an important part of that hope."

The door opened and the black haired young woman entered, now dressed once again in her white gown.

"Ah, Eluned. Well done," Berddig greeted her, "You destroyed one of the Adarllwchgwin."

The young woman grinned, "Yes, I sank my teeth into its neck and it dissipated. But it was September who brought them down."

"Well, why don't you take September and convince her that she has done good deeds today. I have to get arrangements made for her journey."

"I'll be delighted," Eluned took September's hand and drew her from the chair, "there's so much to show you.'

9

Eluned guided September through the bustling village. It was as if the attack by the Adarllwchgwin had not happened. Chickens ran hither and thither and flocks of small birds flew overhead. September realised that during the attack the birds had disappeared but now they had returned as noisy and busy as before. They made slow progress because every few steps a villager would stop them, thank them for defeating the attackers and wish them well. September was taken aback. She was not used to people appreciating her or thanking her for something she had done. Back home it was mostly, "Get out of the way" or "That's not how you do it" or "Oh, don't bother I'll do it myself". It was a strange feeling not being useless.

By the time they reached the bank of the lake, September was feeling dazed. Eluned took her arm and pointed out the reed bed that stretched out into the water, the reeds that the villagers used to thatch their homes. September could barely see over the tips of the tall flat leaves to see the clear water beyond where flocks of ducks and geese were noisily taking off and landing on the water. Eluned turned to the left following the bank and soon they had left the village behind. They skirted the edge of the gardens where vegetables and fruits grew. Sparrows and starlings pecked at the ground. Then they were into the woodland with the trees growing right to the bank. The rooks squawked at them and other woodland birds called to each other.

"There are so many birds," September noted.

"That is how the village got its name," Eluned said, "Amaethaderyn, farm of birds."

It was easy to find a path though the trees as the undergrowth was sparse. September realised why when she saw dark brown cattle moving amongst the trees stopping now and then to tear at some grass or nibble at a sapling.

Despite the shade, she was beginning to feel warm. It was not yet noon and yet the air felt hot, surprisingly so for late September. For the first time, she had hardly had an opportunity before, September began to wonder where in the Land she was. Although the trees and plants looked sort of familiar she wondered whether Amaethaderyn was in a similar part of the Earth to her home. Was the Land even on Earth? It was another puzzle to add to all the others that were building up in her head.

It had been difficult to talk as Eluned led the way through the trees but after a short while they reached a patch of the bank where trees did not grow. Eluned flung herself down on the soft grass and beckoned September to do the same.

"This is one of my places," Eluned said, "I come here for a bit of peace."

"Don't other people come here?" September hadn't thought they had come that far from the village.

"Oh, they do, but when I'm on my own it just feels so calm and soothing. Don't you think so?"

September looked out at the smooth water, barely troubled by a breeze and the surrounding trees standing guard. There was the smell of the water and the grass that they sat on and other unfamiliar smells from the trees and plants.

"Yes, I see what you mean, but, well," suddenly the realisation that she was far from her own home, in unfamiliar surroundings, got to September. The sob started as a lump in her chest and rose up until it burst out of her mouth. "Oh dear, I'm sorry," she said through tears, "everything is so different, I don't know why I'm here, what I'm supposed to do or what would happen if those dreadful big birds got me..."

Eluned shuffled close and put her arms around September's shoulders.

"Oh, Cludydd, I'm so sorry, I didn't think. I've never been away from here. I hadn't thought what it must be like for you drawn from your own world to defend us from the Malevolence." She hugged September tightly until the tears ceased to flow. "I see it must be confusing, having just arrived, the gathering and then the Adarllwchgwin attacking."

"Everyone has been very kind," September said weakly, "but I'm just feeling lost."

"I'll try to answer some of your questions," Eluned offered, "but first, let's have a swim. It's been a hot, tiring morning." She released September, stood up and in one sweeping movement pulled her dress over her head. She dropped it on the grass and ran toward the bank. September barely saw her naked back before she leapt into the air and dived into the water a couple of metres from the shore. September was unsure what to do. She wasn't used to swimming in lakes and she never took her clothes off so that others could see her rolls of fat. But she didn't have fat here and Eluned seemed so comfortable with her nakedness and swimming in the water. September did feel hot and sweaty. She made up her mind, got to her feet and struggled to tug her dress over her head. She wanted to feel the water on her skin too. In just a few moments she stood on the bank looking down at her unfamiliar body, then at the water, deciding whether to jump, dive or step in gingerly. There was a huge whoosh and a silver-skinned dolphin leapt from the lake in front of her. It crashed back down into the foaming water and swam towards the bank, it circled around in front of where September stood, bobbing its snout, then raced away. September stared after it. Before her eyes there was another eruption of water and there was Eluned treading water.

"Come on, the water's lovely," Eluned cried. September decided to half step, half jump and found herself immersed in the cool water. It was nothing like as cold as she feared, practically the temperature of the swimming pool where she had been for her compulsory swimming lessons in school. She felt comfortable and relaxed. She wasn't a strong swimmer but the new-found strength in her muscles gave her confidence. She struck out to join Eluned. Something clicked in her mind.

"The dolphin. That was you?" September asked. Eluned nodded and swam away. September chased after her.

"Can you really change into a tiger and a dolphin? What did Arianwen call it? Traws... something." September called out. Eluned rolled over in the water and faced her.

"A tiger when I want to be fierce, a dolphin when I want to

swim, a monkey that climbs through the trees and a fox that hunts by night. Trawsffurfio. It is the gift of arianbyw." She held up the small crystal phial she wore on a silver chain around her neck. September noticed that the phial contained a silver liquid – mercury.

"But that's magic," September exclaimed.

Eluned looked confused, "I don't know the word 'magic'. When I was a child I was tested and found to have an affinity for the power of arianbyw. For many years I have been training to use the metal's properties and the power of Mercher," she pointed into the sky, "I hope that one day I will be able to adopt the shape of any animal I wish, as the Prif-cludydd can." She rolled in the water, kicked her feet and surged away. September thrashed away with her arms trying to keep up. She didn't catch up until Eluned stopped.

"Prif-cludydd?" September repeated.

"The chief, the most accomplished, the senior bearer of the metal in all of Gwlad. Each metal has one."

"Where are they?"

"Oh, I don't know. The Prif-cludydd o arianbyw visited here when I was very young. I don't know where he lives but I expect he's at the Arsyllfa now. He must be quite old. " September had come to think of the few villagers she had met as being the only people in the Land. Now she was beginning to realise that the Land was a bigger place and that there were a lot more people in it.

"What about the others, are they Prif-cludydds?"

Eluned laughed, "Oh no. Iorwerth, Arianwen, Berddig, Padarn, Catrin. They are all wonderful cludyddau but if they were here they would be the first to admit that there are others in Gwlad who can wield their metals with more strength and skill."

"What about the Mordeyrn?"

"Ah, now he is different. He is the Prif-cludydd o aur. We have been so fortunate to have him live amongst us, but the loss of his golden plate is dreadful. He was so ill after it was destroyed but he set out on his journey immediately." Eluned dived and September gasped as in a blink she changed into the dolphin. It swam around her, its tail washing powerful currents against her legs. Then it headed back towards the bank. September swam as fast as she could to try to keep up with it but to no avail.

Eluned was already sitting on the bank squeezing the water out of her black hair when September reached the land. She climbed onto the bank and sat beside Eluned. Sitting there, naked in the warm air, felt natural and relaxing.

"Berddig said it was many days of travel to the observatory," September said thoughtfully.

"Yes, it's a long way," Eluned agreed, "even using the river and travelling all day."

"So the Land, Gwlad, is pretty big?"

"It's all the land of the world," Eluned nodded, "I'm sorry but as I've never been away from Amaethaderyn I don't know a lot about the rest of Gwlad."

"But there are other villages, towns even? People living in different parts?"

"Oh yes. I can tell you what I was taught about the seven regions of Gwlad."

"Seven regions?" September noticed the important number again.

"Yes, we're in the Southern River region, people that live within reach of the river and use it for travel and trade. South of here are the great plains where the nomads who ride horses live. Their lands end in the desert. To the north is the other great river, it's cooler than our river. Both rivers end at the coast in the east where people grow rice and catch fish in the ocean. North of the northern river is the great forest where the woodfolk live and then further north still is the Mynydd Tywyll where the miners and metal workers live."

"What's beyond the mountains?"

"Nothing."

"Nothing!"

"Well, not nothing, but no-one lives there. It's too cold and covered with ice."

"So, um, let me see. What did you say the regions were? The Plains, north river and south river, coast, forest, mountains. That's six regions."

"That's right. The seventh is the western hills, the Bryn am Seren where the Arsyllfa is."

It was a lot to remember and September wasn't sure that

she had all the positions of the regions sorted but she had something of a picture of Gwlad. She realised that Eluned had described not just a country but a continent. But it was the number seven that intrigued her.

"Seven regions, seven metals, seven objects in the sky. Why is it always seven?" Then she remembered what she had discovered; was it really only last night? "And I'm the seventh child of my mother."

"That's what the Mordeyrn said you were," Eluned agreed, "The Cludydd o Maengolauseren is always the seventh child."

"Yes, but I didn't know that until yesterday," September said, "Last night at my birthday party I found out that I had a twin I didn't know about."

Eluned was excited.

"A twin! Twins often share their powers."

"But my twin is dead. She was dead when she was born just before me."

Eluned clapped her hand to her mouth.

"Oh, oh. That's awful."

September wondered at Eluned's reaction which seemed more than just sympathy.

"Well, I was shocked, since Mum had kept it from me, but it happens."

"No, you don't understand September. Dead unborns go to the place above the stars where the Malevolence resides. Being a twin you will have a link to the evil." September saw horror on Eluned's face. September thought she was being superstitious.

"That's nonsense. She's dead. That's it."

Her birthmark started itching; September rubbed her hip. Eluned noticed what she was doing.

"Do you have a mark on you?"

September rolled over displaying her hip and her buttock to Eluned.

"Yes, I've always had it. It's a birthmark. It just irritates me now and again."

Eluned's expression had changed to one of awe.

"It's a rich pink colour and shaped like the new Moon. It must have formed when you were in your mother's womb with your twin sister. It is a sign."

"A sign?"

"Yes. A sign of your connection to the heavens, the Maengolauseren and to your twin."

"It's just a birthmark," September dismissed Eluned's ramblings.

"No, September, it could be important. Never forget your twin." Eluned got to her feet and pulled her dress over her head, "We should continue our walk."

September dressed too and dropped into step beside Eluned. They walked in silence for a few minutes. Eluned seemed to be thinking and not wanting to chat. September didn't mind because she was contemplating what Eluned had said. She had hardly had time to take in the knowledge that she had a twin sister in the womb, now Eluned had suggested that her dead twin may not be lost completely, that some part of her still existed somewhere beyond the world. What sort of personality could she have? Dead before being born, she had no experience in the world. Would her only knowledge be of the Malevolence, above the stars – whatever that meant?

"Eluned," she said to her companion as they weaved in and out of the trees lining the lake.

"Yes, Cludydd," Eluned turned and smiled at her.

"What can you tell me about the Malevolence? I don't really understand what it is."

Eluned frowned and her face darkened, "It's not something we like to discuss. It just is and it brings unhappiness."

"But the Mordeyrn said it exists above the stars but has no leader."

"That's correct. It is responsible for all the sickness, disease, bitterness and jealousy in the world. It is within us and around us but its origin is beyond the sphere of stars."

"You're saying that anything bad that happens, any bad things that people do, is caused by the Malevolence."

"Yes. Without it people cooperate and are happy and fulfilled, but when the Malevolence attacks, people become suspicious and greedy. Whole villages can be destroyed because people stop trusting each other and become selfish."

"But there are also the other things – the Draig tân and the Adar-whatever – they're real, not just characteristics of people?"

"The manifestations of the Malevolence appear when its strength grows. That is happening now – the Mordeyrn can explain why, I don't understand enough about the movements in the heavens. It explains why you answered the Mordeyrn's appeal and have come amongst us. The Maengolauseren is awoken by the growing power of the Malevolence."

"So the Malevolence is getting stronger, causing people to become bad, and stop working together; these monsters appear to attack the good people and the only answer is that this stone brings me here." September lifted the pendant from her chest and dangled it from her finger and thumb."

"That's it," Eluned nodded, "We can fight the manifestations with the powers the metals give us but they are not strong enough and there are not enough of us adept in their use. The Mordeyrn and the other leaders and the Prif-cludyddau are going to meet to decide how they can help you."

"Help? I need more than help. I need to know what it is I have to do and how to do it. That's before I work out whether I can. I've never done anything like this. I've never done anything."

September stopped walking and stood on the bank. They were on the opposite side of the lake to the village. The thatched roofs were visible above the reeds with several plumes of smoke rising into the sky.

"What about the Cemegwr? Why don't they help?"

"Well, a few people think that they can but even if they did exist and were responsible for making the world like it is there has been no sign of them since. They have never come to our assistance before. The Cludydd o Maengolauseren is the only help we have ever had at the time of the Conjunctions. You are our hope, September."

"I'm not sure that I will be able to do whatever it is you think I can do," September said with a sad note to her voice.

"Don't say that," Eluned came to her side and wrapped her arms around her, "The Maengolauseren is very powerful, it will guide you and give you the strength to do whatever is necessary. After all, you have already destroyed a Draig tân and an Adarllwchgwin. The Mordeyrn and the others will help you."

September felt a little encouraged by Eluned's support but she still feared what was to come.

"But first I have to travel to meet them. A long way so everyone says."

"Yes. An adventure. I wish I could come too."

"So, do I." September returned Eluned's hug.

The roar of a torrent shattered the peace; a fountain of water erupted from the lake and fell on them with the force of a water cannon. With her ears ringing, water drenching her dress and running from her hair down her nose, September saw a great horse rise up from the lake on its rear legs and loom over them. It spread vast, bat-like wings as water cascaded from a body which was the blue-green colour of the lake. The wings flapped sending a gale of wet air blowing over them. The horse stamped its feet on the surface of the water sending waves crashing against the bank and it tossed its massive head and mane, baring huge yellow teeth and letting out a roar that shook the trees. A gale of sulphurous breath blew over them. September was frozen and stared at the scene as if watching a movie but her birthmark burned as if it was on fire.

Beside her, Eluned was not turned to stone. She stripped off her dress and dived into the lake. Moments later September saw a flash of silver leap from the water and clamp itself to the horse's neck. The monster roared in anguish and shook its head wildly but the dolphin clung on, tearing a gash in the huge beast's neck. Desperate to remove the irritation the horse twisted its neck. It couldn't bring its teeth close to the dolphin but again it shook violently. The dolphin tore a strip of flesh from the horse's neck and fell into the water. The monster, turquoise blood pouring from its wound, searched for its tormenter pummelling the water with its hooves and churning the waters of the lake. Bearing its teeth, it reared up on its hind legs again, poised to fall on its prey.

September's heart pounded. Eluned, her new friend, had leapt to her defence and now needed her help. But what should she do? Released from her inability to move but barely thinking, September lifted the pendant from her chest, unclipped the case and held the stone in front of her eyes. Through the clear jewel she saw the forelegs of the horse begin to fall. Consumed by fear and fury, she wished the horse could be destroyed in an explosion of fire.

Blue light blasted from the Maengolauseren, surrounding the head and body of the great horse. For a moment the great winged horse was a silhouette. Then it exploded with a clap of thunder. Flaming gobbets of skin and muscle and bone rained down around September turning to gouts of filthy water as they reached the ground. The remainder of the body fell back into the lake with an immense splash and merged with the water creating breaking waves which crashed against the shore. The ripples rapidly decreased in height until the waters of the lake were smooth again.

September dashed to the waters' edge searching for the dolphin and saw Eluned's pale, naked body floating a few feet from the bank. September leapt into the water and waded out. The water was up to her breasts when she reached the girl who was floating motionless and face down. September turned her over and began to tow her to the shore not knowing from where she had found the skill or the courage to effect a rescue. When she reached shallow water, September lifted Eluned up in her arms surprised at how light she was. She dragged her feet from the mud of the lake and took a few steps onto the bank. She laid Eluned on the grass and knelt to listen to her chest. Eluned's heart was beating slowly and shallowly and her breath rattled faintly in her throat. September picked her up again and set off as fast as she could for the village, finding her way between the trees but keeping the lake close by.

Before she had taken a hundred paces, September was panting and Eluned had become an intolerable weight in her arms. Her pace slowed, each step becoming a trial. A few more tens of steps and her arms were numb but still she struggled on. Suddenly she was surrounded by men and women brandishing axes, knives and wooden staves, and there was Iorwerth, with Aldyth raised in front of him. September's knees gave way and she sagged to the ground with Eluned limp in her arms. Without a word said, Eluned was taken from her and September herself was lifted up and carried at speed to the village.

She soon found herself again in Arianwen's cottage. Arianwen was bent over the still body of Eluned that lay on the couch. September sat in one of the chairs, her sodden dress cooling against her skin, other villagers fussing around her. Berddig burst in.

"What happened?" he demanded, looking at everyone in turn.

September pointed towards the bed where Eluned lay.

"Eluned stopped the thing from attacking me," she said tearfully, "but the monster flung her off."

"I was at the river, I didn't see," Berddig said.

"The Cludydd destroyed the Ceffyl dwr," Iorwerth spoke from beside September, "I heard its roar from my workshop. When I stepped outside I could see it on the other side of the lake. Then there was a flash of the Maengolauseren's light and the monster blew apart. We ran around the bank to find the Cludydd carrying Eluned. She is sorely injured."

Berddig ran to Eluned's bed and bent down beside Arianwen. He turned his head to September.

"Is Iorwerth correct? You destroyed the Ceffyl dwr with the power of the Starstone?"

"I don't know what that horse thing was and I don't know what I did," September said, shaking her head, "But the blue light came from the stone again and blew the thing to pieces. But I was too late. It had already thrown Eluned off. I thought she was dead."

Arianwen stood up.

"She will survive, child, thanks to your power and quick thinking. She is sleeping now but her injuries are severe. Her ribs are broken and her back is strained. It will be some days before she is leaping around again. I have done all I can for her for now. The healing power of arian will do its work. Now what can I do for you, Cludydd?"

"I'm fine, just this stupid dress got soaked."

"Take it off and I'll find something else for you to wear." Arianwen went to a wicker box and drew out another white dress. September pulled the wet cloth over her head and pulled on the replacement.

"Are you sure Eluned will be alright?" she asked, "As soon as the horse thing appeared she dived into the lake and attacked it. It was huge but she leapt out of the water and bit its neck. But then it flung her off. Every time the Malevolence attacks, people help me and get hurt. What good am I if I attract this evil thing and you all get injured?"

Berddig shook his head, "The Mordeyrn warned us that you would be a target for the Adwyth but we never realised that the attacks would be so frequent or so soon after you arrived among us."

"Eluned thought that my twin might have something to do with the bad things."

Berddig, Arianwen and Iorwerth stared at September.

"Your twin?" Berddig said at last.

"I didn't know," September went on, a sob growing in her throat and tears in her eyes, "but the Mordeyrn was right, I am my mother's seventh child; her sixth child was my twin sister and she was dead when she was born. I found out last night at my birthday party."

"This is troubling news," Arianwen said, "Our souls enter our bodies at birth from the core of Daear. The soul of your sister would have been despatched beyond the stars and is trapped in the realm of the Malevolence. Nevertheless, the bond between twins is strong and so you may have some link with your sister and the Malevolence."

"That's something like what Eluned said, but it all sounds like nonsense to me. My mother may believe in souls and devils and things but I don't. At home there is nothing beyond the stars, except more stars, not some evil thing." September paused as a thought came to her – what do I mean, at home? Where is home?

"We know little of your world," Berddig said, "but the Cludydd o Maengolauseren always has a foot in both worlds. Your actions have an influence here and there. A connection between you and your twin could have an influence on the Malevolence."

"Only the Mordeyrn and the other members of the Arsyllfa may know what this means," Arianwen said.

"So we'd better get you on your way so you can meet them," Iorwerth said bluntly.

Berddig spoke immediately, "Now, Iorwerth, we must prepare the Cludydd for the journey. She will leave soon."

September felt herself getting annoyed. These people were making plans for her.

"Look all I want is to go home. I don't care about your Ars whatever or what the Malevolence is." Then her eyes fell on the still body of Eluned and her anger disappeared. "I'm sorry, I didn't mean that. Eluned got hurt trying to protect me and I don't want that to happen. If this thing," she held up the pendant containing the Starstone, "won't let me go home then I guess I have to do what I can. But I'm not wearing these stupid dresses to go on a long journey." She grabbed a handful of the white loose dress and shook it.

Arianwen smiled indulgently, "We'll do what we can to make your journey pleasant and your stay in Gwlad as safe as possible."

"Now rest while we make things ready," Berddig said. "We'll eat together and give you guidance for your travels."

Berddig and Iorwerth left and Arianwen went to Eluned, rested a hand on her forehead and checked her pulse. September rested in the chair and found her eyes becoming heavy.

10

September awoke to bustling in the cottage. Villagers were moving in and out carrying trays and bowls which were placed on a low table that had been set up close to the fire. September could tell by the light that came through the doorway that the day had moved on and that evening had come. She yawned, stretched and stood up. The villagers nodded their heads to her and gave her space.

"Ah, you are awake, Cludydd," Arianwen appeared from the shadows, "You have had a well-deserved sleep. You will need your energy for the journey, I think."

"Yes, I feel better now," she looked across to the bed where the still form of Eluned lay, "How is Eluned?"

"She is asleep now. It is best while her injuries heal, but do not fear for her. She is a strong young woman and soon she will recover completely. What about you?"

"I think I need to freshen up a bit." September left the hut and found her way to the wash-house. When she returned to Arianwen's house the villagers had left but the table was filled with a huge assortment of things to eat – salads, bread, cheese, cooked meats, jugs filled with liquids. Arianwen had been joined by Berddig and Padarn, the old lead-bearer, and were deep in discussion about something. Iorwerth followed September through the doorway, and Catrin, the wielder of copper was behind him.

Arianwen welcomed them all.

"Come in everyone. Find somewhere to sit." Extra chairs and cushions had been brought in so that space in the cottage became difficult to find. As everyone sat down, the door was pushed open again and young Tudfwlch appeared with a much older man behind him. Berddig leapt to his feet and welcomed them both.

"September, you have met Tudfwlch but this is Cynddylig. He'll guide you on your journey. There's nothing he doesn't know about the river and its surroundings." The old man grunted and reluctantly held September's hand.

"Hello. I'm pleased to meet you," she said trying to sound as polite as she could but the look in Cynddylig's eyes told her he wasn't about to idolise her like some of the villagers.

"Ah, well, best to get you as far away from here as possible," he muttered.

"Come, let us eat," Arianwen said. "All this food and drink has been prepared for us, we should not let it go to waste."

The guests made a move for the buffet table, but September held back and looked at Eluned on the bed where she still lay motionless. Arianwen stood at September's shoulder.

"We are not disturbing her. If she awakens during the evening then that will be good. Go and eat."

September felt her chest lighten and she moved to join the throng filling wooden plates with the delicious food. Soon they were sitting in clusters eating and drinking and talking light-heartedly. September found Tudfwlch sitting at her feet. He looked up at her, his eyes shining.

"You destroyed a Ceffyl dwr," he said.

"What do you call it?" September asked.

"Ceffyl dwr, the water horse."

"Oh, that's right, that's the name Iorwerth and Berddig gave it. It just came out of the lake."

"They are a water manifestation," Tudfwlch explained, "but they are unlike real horses."

"The wings were a bit of a giveaway, as well as the size of the thing," September giggled.

"Yes, but they move fast despite their size and they can easily trample you."

"How do you know this? Have you seen one before?"

"Oh no. The manifestations of the Malevolence are described in the old stories. It's only recently that they have begun to appear again."

"Now that I've arrived they're all coming back."

"Well," Tudfwlch looked a bit embarrassed, "there is a connection between the growth of the Malevolence and your coming."

"Yes, I know and it seems that people are getting hurt and their homes destroyed because of it." She glanced across at the still form of Eluned.

"That is true, but your presence among us gives us hope that the energy of the Maengolauseren combined with our skills, wielding the metals, will be enough to combat the evil."

"You sound as if you're certain."

Tudfwlch smiled, "I am. You have already shown the power that you can project."

"I have?"

Berddig knelt beside her.

"Of course you have. On your very first visit you helped the Mordeyrn stop one Draig tân. This morning you brought down an Adarllwchgwin and this afternoon you destroyed the Ceffyl dwr."

September thought about what Berddig had said. She recalled her feelings in those three attacks; disbelief when the fiery comet appeared in the sky followed by fear as she realised that it was a real threat; terror when the birds and the riders attacked the village and came after her; surprise and then fear and anger when the flying horse had risen out of the lake and hurt Eluned. But on each occasion she realised that the stone that hung round her neck had removed the threat. She lifted the silver pendant from her chest. It was true, she was the wielder of a powerful weapon.

"But if you are right, Berddig, and I do have this power, why does everyone leap to my defence. Why did Eluned dive into the lake to attack the horse as soon as it appeared? Why didn't she wait for me to blow the thing apart?"

"Well, it's what we are trained for – to fight the Malevolence and all its manifestations. You are untrained in the use of the Maengolauseren, you know nothing about the Malevolence, so we don't know what you will do when faced with danger. You've shown already that you are a worthy bearer of the stone. You have the instinct to use it to defend yourself and us. But we and you have to be on our guard and ready or else the Adwyth could overcome you without you knowing it. You don't know yet how you can use it to fight the more subtle wiles of the evil or how you can protect everyone in Gwlad from the Malevolence. Only the Arsyllfa can teach you."

"So, I have to go on this journey."

"I'll be beside you," Tudfwlch said, smiling broadly, "together we'll take on whatever the Malevolence can throw at us."

"I hope we can avoid too much of that," Berddig said sombrely, "I am afraid that despite the Mordeyrn's warnings we did not realise how much the Malevolence would be drawn to the Maengolauseren and its bearer. If you are to make the long journey safely then we must shield you from the evil power."

"How are you going to do that?" September asked.

Berddig got to his feet and clapped his hands.

"Friends, I think it is time to prepare the Cludydd for her journey." The talking stopped and everyone else looked to the tin-bearer. There was a shuffling and moving of chairs and stools to form a circle facing September. Berddig addressed everyone.

"We have been discussing how the Cludydd's presence in Gwlad has itself attracted the attention of the Adwyth and called forth the manifestations that we have witnessed. The Mordeyrn requested that we prepare a shield that will make the Cludydd all but invisible to the evil. It has been a difficult task and I wish it had been ready for the Cludydd's arrival, but Padarn has it now."

The old lead-bearer got to his feet and went into the shadows at the walls of the cottage. He returned with a cloth draped over his arms. He walked right up to September and laid it in her lap.

"It is my pleasure to give you this cloak, Cludydd. Wear it at all times and you will disappear from the Malevolence's perception."

September looked at the silver-grey cloak in her arms. It was made of tiny links of metal each one sparkling in the light of the fire.

"What is it made from?" September asked.

"A mixture of plwm and alcam," Padarn replied, now returned to his seat, "Plwm provides the shielding from the evil energies and indeed reflects all light and heat and repels forces. The alcam strengthens and reinforces the powers. Berddig and I have worked long to create the ideal combination and to channel the powers of the metals and planets. Casting the rings and fashioning them into this garment also took our apprentices a great deal of time."

"Put it on. Let's see it." Berddig said.

September stood up letting the folds of the cloak fall out. Plwm and alcam, lead and tin. Mixtures of metals. September vaguely recalled chemistry lessons at school. Wasn't the solder used by electricians a mixture of tin and lead? Or was that zinc and lead? She wasn't sure. But solder was a very soft metal wasn't it? There were other mixtures of metals, weren't there? Her brain hurt from the effort of remembering lessons poorly learned. Now she wished she had listened more carefully or had more talent for recalling facts. A memory came to her of Mother taking her around some old house. There were lots of silver plates displayed on shelves; well September had thought they were silver, but Mother seemed to know a lot more. They were made of pewter she said, an alloy of tin and lead.

Pewter. That was it. But an alloy of tin and lead should be heavy, surely. She could barely feel the cloak in her arms. Each link was so tiny and thin that the total amount of metal making up the cloak was very small indeed. She unfolded it and threw it over her shoulders. It covered her from neck to feet, and there was a hood that she pulled up over her head. She could barely feel it.

Arianwen and Catrin clapped their hands.

"It is wonderful," Arianwen said, "It shimmers and catches the light so much that your shape can hardly be made out."

"It is so light," September said, "I can't believe that it's made out of tin and lead."

"Berddig and Padarn are very skilled bearers of alcam and plwm," Catrin pointed out.

"It is as well that it is light and easy to wear," Berddig said, "as you must wear it at all times to stay out of the Malevolence's focus."

"There won't be any more attacks by those monsters?" September asked.

"Well, I can't promise that you won't meet any manifestations of evil on your way but they will not be drawn to you."

"Won't it be hot wearing this heavy dress and the cloak?" September asked again.

"I'll find more suitable clothes for you to travel in," Arianwen said.

"And the cloak will keep the heat of the Sun off you," Padarn added.

September sat down again fascinated by the patterns of light made in the folds of the metal fabric.

Catrin stood up, crossed to where September sat and knelt at her feet.

"Berddig and Padarn have given you their gift. This is mine," she opened a leather pouch slung over her shoulder and took out a small, shiny, orange object. She held it up for September to hold. September took it and examined it. It was made of copper shaped into a small curved horn. It was perfectly smooth. September admired the curves and the colour.

"Thank you," she said, "but what is it?"

"A speaking horn. By the power of efyddyn you are linked to anyone else who possesses one. You speak at this end," Catrin indicated the narrow end with a mouthpiece like a trumpet, "and listen at the other end." September held the copper instrument to her face and found that when the mouthpiece was against her lips the open end of the horn was next to her right ear.

September searched the horn for controls, "How do I connect it to the person I want to speak to?"

"Just speak the name of the person and they will hear you – if they have their horn with them."

"Thank you," September said, "Will I be able to speak to all of you when we are travelling?"

Berddig laughed, "I'm afraid not, these speaking horns are very special. Few have been made."

"I have the only other one in the village," Catrin said.

September held the horn out to her.

"If it is so precious surely the village needs it?"

"We have discussed it," Arianwen said, "we all agree that you need it to communicate with the Mordeyrn on your journey. It will take you many weeks and the Mordeyrn will be able to help you along the way."

"He has one of these things?"

"Yes. As Mordeyrn and Prif-cludydd he has to communicate with people across Gwlad."

"You've spoken to him since I arrived?"

"Briefly. He is travelling as fast as he can so has little time to talk. He suggested you follow him as soon as you can."

"Take the horn," Berddig encouraged September, "it will be of use to you."

"Thank you. You are so kind and I'm worried about leaving you without a way of contacting each other."

"We'll manage," Padarn said, "One is all we need to find out what is going wrong in the world."

September replaced the horn in its pouch and rested it in her lap thinking that it was the strangest mobile phone she'd come across.

"Now you might think that Tudfwlch is my gift to you," Iorwerth guffawed, and clapped the youth on his back almost knocking him from the stool he was sitting on, "You look after the Cludydd, lad."

Tudfwlch recovered, "Of course. It's an honour to be the Cludydd's protector," he winked at September, "it will be an adventure won't it."

"I'm not sure." September had not decided if she was looking forward to the journey even with the cloak to protect her and the horn to keep her in touch.

"Ah-hm," Iorwerth tried to regain their attention, "but here there is something just for you." He produced, from where September wasn't quite sure, a bundle of cloth. He unrolled it and there in his hands lay a knife in a leather holster. September stared at the weapon. She estimated the blade to be about twenty centimetres long and five wide.

"Take it, girl, it's yours," the iron bearer insisted.

Gingerly, September lifted the leather-bound handle and held it in her hand. Carefully she slid the cover off the blade. The knife was heavy but she realised that it was exceptionally well balanced. Gripping it firmly the blade seemed to be an extension of her hand. She admired the surface of the blade which had a blue sheen. The edge looked so sharp she was afraid to even touch it.

"I know you have the Maengolauseren to defend yourself

with but everyone needs a good sharp knife when they're travelling." Iorwerth said.

"It's wonderful," September said, astounded by the functional beauty of the knife, "Did you make it?"

Iorwerth raised his head proudly, "Yes, forged in my own fire. There's no sharper blade on this stretch of the Southern River. And it possesses the power of haearn. It will slice through any manifestation of the Malevolence."

September carefully pushed the blade back into its scabbard.

"Thank you," she said, resting the knife with the speaking horn in her lap.

"You already have my gift," Arianwen said.

"I do?"

"Yes, it's around your neck. The chain and locket which holds your starstone."

September drew the ornate silver pendant from inside her dress.

"You made this?"

"I did. When the Mordeyrn said he was going to summon the Cludydd o Maengolauseren he said such a thing would be needed and so I made it ready for your appearance."

"Thank you, it's beautiful." September caressed the heavy locket.

"And don't forget that as it is made from arian it has its own powers. It is not just a holder for the starstone."

"Powers?"

"It can heal injuries and relieve ill health. Just hold it against the affected part."

"Thank you Arianwen. I'll treasure it." September felt quite overcome by all the kindness that she had received. There were tears in her eyes.

"You're crying," Arianwen said.

"I'm sorry," September sobbed, "I should be happy with all these presents. You've been so kind to me but I know you are expecting me to do amazing things and I don't think I can. I'm just a silly, fat girl back home who doesn't do anything special."

Arianwen placed her arms around September's shoulders and leaned forward to hug her.

"Now, child. We know you are inexperienced and confused. You have been plucked from your own world which we have little knowledge of. We can understand how you feel but those feelings will pass. You are not silly. The ability to bear the Maengolauseren does not rest on whether you are fat or slim."

"Do not be afraid," Iorwerth said, rising to his feet and clenching his fists, "The prophecies say that a new Cludydd will appear when the Malevolence grows in strength and the bearer of the starstone will have the power to defeat the evil."

"What Iorwerth means," Catrin said in a more soothing voice, "is that we have faith in you and that the Maengolauseren will guide and protect you."

"That's correct," Padarn added, "and the time will come soon, when you will learn the powers of the starstone and no longer have need of us or any other citizen of the Land to assist you."

September sniffed. She still had no idea what she was supposed to do but the support and tender words of the cludyddau cheered her. She smiled thinly.

"Thank you. I will try to be what you want me to be."

"We are sure you will, Cludydd," Arianwen said resuming her seat.

"Now," Berddig said, as if returning to the business of the evening, "Tudfwlch has his orders to protect you. Cynddylig will guide you to the Arsyllfa. Your boat has been prepared and stocked with all that you will need for your journey. Of course, food and water you will have to collect as you travel but you will pass other villages and they will offer you assistance. It is just your other needs that we must see to."

It seemed that a lot had been going on that September did not know about. She felt a bit hassled.

"I don't want to travel wearing these long dresses," she said, repeating herself, sure that a bit of irritation had entered her voice.

"Don't worry," soothed Arianwen, "you will have the light clothes that you need for the journey along the river, but you will need sturdier clothes and shoes for when you reach the Bryn am Seren."

A moan came from the bed set against the wall of the

house. Arianwen ran to Eluned.

"Ceffyl dwr. Cludydd," Eluned's voice was weak.

"It's all right, Eluned. The Ceffyl dwr is gone," Arianwen rested a hand on Eluned's forehead.

"The Cludydd, she's in danger," Eluned spoke more strongly. September got up, placed the knife and horn on the seat and ran to the side of Eluned's bed.

"I'm here, Eluned. I'm safe. You're back in the village."

Eluned's eyes opened. She saw September and tried to sit up. Pain made her wince and she fell back on to the mattress.

"Rest my dear," Arianwen said, "your back is injured. You need to lie still."

Eluned puffed out a breath and seemed to awaken. She looked up into Arianwen's gentle face and then saw September looking worried.

"Ah, you are safe. I'm glad," she sighed, "what happened to me?"

"You dived into the lake and became the dolphin, then threw yourself at the horse monster," September explained, "but it shook you off." She described briefly how the horse had been destroyed and how the villagers had come to rescue them.

"Thank you, September. You saved my life."

"No, you saved me. If I hadn't been frozen with fear I could have blown up that stupid horse and you wouldn't have got hurt."

Eluned looked confused.

Arianwen rubbed her silver amulet against Eluned's forehead.

"Sleep now my dear and you will recover soon."

"I'll see you tomorrow before I leave," September said.

"Ah, your journey," Eluned said, struggling to keep her eyes open as Arianwen's soothing began to take effect, "I must give you my gift." She tried to raise her arm to her neck, the effort giving her obvious pain. She gripped the phial of mercury on her necklace, "Please, take this."

Arianwen reached under her neck and pulled the leather thong over her head. Painfully Eluned lifted her hand holding the phial towards September.

"I can't," September said.

"It's for you."

"But how can I use it? I can't change into a tiger or a dolphin. What did you call it – trawsffurfio. You said you were born with the skill and trained for years."

"No, you won't become another creature but it will change you and any material it's mixed with – make hard metals soft, heavy things float – anything you wish. I want you to have it, to remember me on your journey."

September reached out and took the small crystal tube from Eluned's hand. It was cold and although just a couple of centimetres long felt heavy in her hand. Eluned's head sank back against the cushions, her eyes closed and her breathing became gentle and even.

"She will sleep well now. Perhaps tomorrow she will be able to sit up." Arianwen said.

"Will she get back to how she was? I mean, be able to change and things?" September asked.

"Oh, yes. She'll soon be leaping about and swimming. She's a strong young woman. Like you, September."

With no pockets in her dress or the cloak, September put the necklace bearing the phial of mercury around her neck then felt she had to get away for a moment, be on her own.

"Excuse me, I need the loo," she turned away from Arianwen and ducked out of the door. It was dark outside and the village was quiet except for the murmur of conversation behind her. The Moon was just rising above the trees, almost, but not quite full. I've been here a whole day, she thought. She took out the pendant from under her dress and the cloak, undid the clasps and opened it up. She held the starstone up to her eye. It was clear and dark. She lined it up with the Moon and saw the image slide into view, but that was all. No rush of light, no disorienting shift. She lowered it. The Land and the village were still around her. Apparently it was her destiny to stay and carry out whatever the task was before her. She closed the locket, hiding the stone from view and hid it once again inside the cloak. She hoped that Padarn was correct and that the cloak would prevent the creatures of the Malevolence from finding her.

She hurried to the washroom and then returned to Arianwen's cottage. The other cludyddau, Tudfwlch and

Cynddylig, were on their feet and saying farewell.

"Goodnight, girl," Cynddylig growled. "Be ready to travel come morning."

"Sleep well," Tudfwlch said as he skipped out of the door. The others wished her a pleasant night and left. Arianwen was busy piling up the empty wooden dishes.

"I'm afraid it's the chairs or the ground for both of us tonight," she said.

September realised that she was exhausted after the long day and all the confusion and strange happenings. She lifted the knife and horn from where she had left them and held them to her chest.

"I think I could sleep anywhere," she said.

Arianwen laid cushions around the fire and brought blankets.

September laid herself down, placed her gifts under a pillow and curled up with the silver cloak wrapped around her. Despite the strange bed she felt her eyes closing moments later.

11

There was shouting and screaming, the sound of feet running, of destruction. Was she dreaming? September opened her eyes. She was awake but it was dark. The dying embers of the fire provided no illumination of the hut. The noises were real. Outside, people were panicking, running hither and thither. Arianwen stirred beside her and was on her feet immediately.

"The Malevolence, it must be the Malevolence," she said. "What form of evil is attacking us now?" Barely had she spoken than there was a hammering on the wooden door and a young man entered brandishing a short iron sword.

"Pardon, Cludydd," he said, wild eyed and breathless, "Iorwerth sent me,"

"Calm down, Meuryn, tell us the news. What is happening?" Arianwen replied.

"The village is being attacked, Cludydd."

"I gathered that. By what, where?"

"Gwyllian, three or four of them, all over the village."

"Gwyllian?" September asked. What were they?

"Dark spirits in the form of old women not long in the grave," Arianwen said.

"Dead people? Like zombies?" September said, shivering and scared.

"I do not know the word zombie, but Gwyllian are not dead, for they have never lived."

"But, what can they do?"

"They are manifestations of earth. Not the soil that brings forth new growth but the decay and decomposition of the cesspit. Anything and anyone that they touch turns to decrepitude. You must not get within their reach."

The noises outside the cottage were continuing. People were running from the hideous creatures. There was a distant sound as if of thunder or a wall crashing to the ground.

"What is Iorwerth doing?" Arianwen asked.

"He and his warriors are rousing people and getting them away from the Gwyllian," Meuryn said.

"Are they coming this way?"

"It is not clear, Cludydd. They are going from house to house but do not seem to have any intention other than to destroy us all."

"Ah, good. You see September, you are hidden from them. The cloak hides you from their senses so they do not know where you are. You will be safe here for some time yet."

"I must do something," September said, scrambling to her feet. She had not suddenly found courage but knew that the Starstone had the power to destroy the manifestations of evil.

"No, Cludydd. We have been foolish in allowing you to wield the Maengolauseren like a beacon since you have arrived. We did not realise how quickly the Malevolence would react to your presence amongst us. But now you have the cloak we must avoid revealing you."

"But can't the stone destroy these Gwyl-things?"

"Yes, but at the risk of drawing yet more evil. We can manage. Iorwerth will organise our defence." The cries of distress and the padding of feet on the hardened earth suggested that the fight was not yet won.

"Meuryn, stand at the door," Arianwen said, "tell us what is happening." The young man did as he was told. With his sword held ahead of him he stood in the doorway.

"People are running from the edge of the village," he said, "they are carrying babies, but it is dark, it is so difficult to see what they are running from."

"Pick up your possessions, Cludydd," Arianwen said, "We may have to flee."

September picked up the iron knife in its scabbard and the leather pouch holding the copper horn from the floor beside her cushions. She slung the strap over her shoulder and grasped the knife in her hand.

A creaking and rumbling sounded as of a tree falling. More shouts and cries were raised, louder and more anguished. More distant there was another loud crash.

"It's a Gwyllian," Meuryn shouted.

"What's it done?" Arianwen asked.

"I saw it. It lifted a hand to touch a house. The walls crumbled to dust and the wooden beams and the rushes on the roof decayed instantly and collapsed. The house is destroyed."

"How close?"

"Not far. The Gwyllian is moving to the next. I can just see her ghostly figure in the moonlight. She will be here soon."

"I think we must move, Cludydd," Arianwen said, "We must not become trapped. We will get to the centre of the village and meet up with Iorwerth. I'll lead, Meuryn you follow and protect the Cludydd."

"But what about Eluned?" September cried, remembering her friend still asleep in her bed.

"She cannot walk," Arianwen said, "It's you we must protect. We must hope that Eluned will survive."

"I can carry her," Meuryn said, sliding his sword into his belt and going to the bed. He lifted up the slight body of the cludydd. She stirred and moaned.

"Be careful," Arianwen said. "Her spine is still tender."

"I have her," Meuryn said.

"We must move."

Arianwen led September from the cottage. Meuryn followed with Eluned in his arms. People were hurrying past carrying or dragging children with them. September glanced behind her just in time to see another round house collapse into a heap of dust. She saw the bent, skeletal figure of what appeared to be an old woman in long, filthy rags. Its arm was stretched out and a long finger pointed at the remains of the building. Slowly it turned and took stiff, infirm steps towards the next dwelling. The Gwyllian did not seem to notice the three of them escaping.

They rounded the next hut and almost collided with Iorwerth and Catrin.

"Hah! You are safe," Iorwerth said.

"For now," Arianwen replied, "But there is a Gwyllian causing great destruction just behind us."

"We know." Iorwerth said, "It is the last. We have destroyed three more on the other side of the village. Come on Catrin."

Iorwerth and Catrin pushed past them. Iorwerth had the

great sword Aldyth drawn and raised and September saw that
Catrin carried a tall copper pole with a ball at one end and a
spike at the other. September and Arianwen followed the
other cludyddau. They turned the corner and there in the
space outside Arianwen's house was the Gwyllian. Its foetid
odour of decay drifted towards them. September covered her
nose and mouth with her spare hand. Now she was able to see
the figure more closely.

It did indeed have the look of an ancient woman who
should have been dead even if she had never been alive. It
was clothed in the remains of a grey dress that had decayed
to hanging threads. A few wispy white hairs straggled from
its head. Skin that wasn't hanging in flaps from its face and
neck, was drawn tight around the skull. The empty eye
sockets looked towards them and the figure staggered a few
steps in their direction. It raised a thin arm and stretched out a
bony finger with a long curled nail.

"Keep out of its reach," Iorwerth warned, "One touch and
you will be turned to dust. At least the Gwyllian do not move
fast. Catrin, use your powers."

Catrin stepped forward and lifted the pole onto her
shoulder like a javelin. The spike pointed towards the
Gwyllian which advanced step by faltering step towards her.
Catrin muttered some unintelligible words. It became even
darker and September looked up to see clouds building and
obscuring the Moon. Moments passed during which the
Gwyllian approached to within a couple of metres of the
impassive woman. There was a flash of lightning followed by
the crack of thunder. It happened so quickly that September
almost failed to see what happened, but it seemed that a
jagged bolt of lightning struck the balled end of Catrin's pole
which, lit up like an orange fluorescent lamp. Then electric
blue light burst from the spike and struck the Gwyllian. Then
came the thunder and the apparition disintegrated into a cloud
of dust which drifted to the ground in a heap.

"Well done," Iorwerth shouted and the other people around
them cheered and clapped. Catrin lowered her pole, turned
and smiled triumphantly at them. The Moon emerged from
the clouds and once again the village was bathed in pale
moonlight. September heard Arianwen let out a huge sigh.

"Let us see what the damage is," she said, "It seems my house is still intact. Meuryn, take Eluned back to her bed."

Meuryn trudged off with his burden as Berddig appeared breathless and concerned.

"Is the Gwyllian defeated?" he asked, "Is the Cludydd safe?"

"Yes, Berddig, as you can see we are standing here, taking stock," Iorwerth replied chortling, "Catrin wielded her electric pole which despatched the manifestations."

Berddig looked relieved but not overjoyed.

"That is good, but a number of our community have died and many have had their homes and workshops destroyed. I had hoped that with the Cludydd clothed in the cloak we would not attract the Malevolence again so soon."

"The Gwyllian did seem disorientated," Catrin said, "Their attacks were indiscriminate. They were unable to sense the Cludydd."

"That's true," Iorwerth agreed, "they just set upon anyone or anything that was in their path."

"So why did they come? Was it just one of the evil's random attacks?"

"Perhaps, Berddig, it was the disappearance of the Cludydd that stirred the Adwyth," Arianwen said. "Like when one candle amongst many is extinguished, its absence disturbs the pattern and draws your attention."

"You may have a point, but the candle that is the Maengolauseren is so much brighter than those of the rest of us, cludyddau included. Since she arrived the starstone has been a bright signal that drew the Malevolence like a moth to a lamp, especially when it was used."

September had been listening to the conversation and understanding more fully the danger she represented to the people of Amaethaderyn.

"Um, I think the attack by the Gwyllian, may have been my fault," she said quietly and fearfully. They all looked at her.

"What do you mean Cludydd?" Arianwen asked.

"Well, just before we settled down, I came outside."

"Yes, I remember. Go on."

"Well, before I went to the loo, I saw the Moon in the sky and I wondered whether I might be able to go home."

"Ah," Berddig said, nodding slowly.

"Go home?" said Iorwerth.

"You took the starstone out, didn't you," Arianwen accused.

"Yes," September said faintly, "I took it out from under the cloak, opened it up and looked through it at the Moon. But nothing happened. The stone was clear but dark."

"Nevertheless, its power was revealed," Arianwen said.

"Like a flash in the dark," Iorwerth said, "a signal to our enemy."

"I'm sorry," September cried, "I didn't realise." She felt wretched; she had been stupid, again, after being told that the cloak was to hide her and the starstone from view.

"We don't know it was that brief revelation of the stone," Berddig said, "after all it had been just a short time since we gave the Cludydd the cloak to cover it and herself. We should have had the cloak ready as soon as the Cludydd appeared amongst us. We are as much to blame as the Cludydd."

The others nodded and agreed. Arianwen rested a hand on September's shoulder.

"I'm sorry Cludydd. I shouldn't have accused you of attracting the Gwyllian. As Berddig says they could have been arising from the earth before you were presented with the cloak, and in any case you were not to realise the dangers of revealing yourself. Come, return to your rest. There is still your journey to commence tomorrow."

"I must assist the people who have lost their homes and console those that have lost family and friends," Berddig said hurrying off.

"And I must check that Tudfwlch has the guard keeping watch," Iorwerth said, "just in case we have more visitations."

"I too should help in any way I can," Catrin, added about to move off.

September spoke to her. "That pole is some weapon."

"It is, although the powers of efyddyn are not often used for destruction. Good night Cludydd." Catrin marched off holding the pole as a staff.

As September and Arianwen walked the short distance to her cottage, September looked around. It was dark and the moon did not provide much light, nevertheless, September was appalled at the devastation that confronted her. It seemed that most of the buildings from Arianwen's home out to the edge of the village had been flattened. All that remained were heaps of dust and rubble with the reeds used as thatch reduced to compost and the timbers left as crumbling, rotten splinters of wood. People were searching in the debris for possessions, a cooking pot, a tool, a water jug. It was her fault, September thought, she had been thoughtless and stupid to take the stone out from under the cloak, despite Berddig kindly diverting the blame from her. I must remain covered from now on, she vowed.

"Come in," Arianwen said, holding the door open. Inside Meuryn was kneeling beside Eluned's bed. Arianwen bent to look at the girl. She caressed Eluned's forehead with her amulet.

"Is she alright?" September asked.

"Yes, she is sleeping normally now. Meuryn was very gentle in lifting her."

"I'm glad." September sank onto her cushions laying her knife and pouch by her side.

"I must go and see if there are any of the injured that need my help," Arianwen said, "Meuryn, stay and look after the Cludydd and Eluned." The young man nodded and Arianwen left them.

September wrapped the silver cloak around herself and settled onto the cushions. She turned away from Meuryn because she didn't want him to see her sobbing herself to sleep.

12

The dark was behind her. Above, below, left and right of her were immense balls of light separated by vast stretches of space. This is what the speck of light, the sphere of glimmers had become and now she knew where she was – the sphere of stars. Within the sphere was more darkness but it had a different quality, for everything inside the sphere of stars had virtue. There hanging at the very centre was a globe of blue and green and white, and around it revolved the seven wanderers, each in its crystal sphere, the outermost hardly any distance from the sphere of stars. One of the orbiting bodies was a bright, hot ball of fire that gave light and succour to the other seven objects within the universe.

She was at the boundary between the realms of good and evil but it was no barrier. The wretched souls of hate streamed past her bound for that green-blue orb, there to achieve their purpose and wreak vengeance. She knew that was where life existed born of the tender love nurtured by the planets. She shared the anger of the souls and soon would follow them to foul and destroy the sickening idyll, but she was not quite ready.

In her long journey across the nothingness outside space and time she had developed. She now had form, a body, a head, arms and legs and was able, given the opportunity, to sense light, sound, odour and taste. She wasn't sure why she had those limbs or senses, perhaps it was some remnant of the existence she had before, not that she recalled any such past, nevertheless perhaps they would be of use when she took her rightful place in the universe.

Now however, she knew what she was. Like the determined souls that flocked towards the world, she was one of the unborn, a life snuffed out before it had independent existence. She knew too that she was special, that some connection gave her the ability to think, to plan, to control.

No unconscious servant of the Malevolence she. Her destiny was power not simply mindless destruction. But destruction, or the promise of it, nevertheless gave her pleasure. She would guide the assault of the Malevolence on the planets and their people. She would unite the powers of the souls and bring victory at last to the dark and destroy the light. And she would enjoy the task for she was Malice.

Part 2

~

Journey

13

The waters of the Afon Deheuol flowed swiftly past the small boat, but the trees that bordered the river moved more slowly. The craft was fighting a strong current but it did so silently and as far as September could tell without any source of power whatsoever. She sat in the middle of the vessel, which was really a large canoe, while Tudfwlch crouched in the bows looking ahead. Cynddylig was in the stern, his right hand gripping the tiller. Overhead the sun was approaching its zenith and the sky was clear and blue. The air was very warm but wrapped in her silver cloak, September felt cool – Padarn had been correct that the metal reflected the sun's rays.

Although they had been travelling for little over an hour, September was already bored. The river banks were unchanging and the trees blocked views of the countryside on each side. Conversation had ceased as the two men settled to the journey and there was nothing for her to do. Feeling drowsy, September recalled the preparations for setting off.

Arianwen had roused her shortly after dawn. She had washed herself and returned to the cottage to find a new set of clothes laid out for her, not the long, white dress that was always tripping her up, but a pair of calf length trousers and a long sleeved tunic top, both in a light beige colour.

"They are made for the men, but should fit you," Arianwen said with a tone of mild disapproval. September couldn't understand how the women put up with wearing the full dresses when the trousers and tunic would make it easier to move. Underwear didn't seem to be in fashion however so she dressed quickly keeping the silver cloak around herself the whole time.

"I think you will need this," Arianwen said, handing September a leather belt.

"Thank you," September said, buckling it around her waist. She found that the scabbard of the knife Iorwerth had given her fitted onto the belt and the pouch with the small copper horn presented to her by Catrin slid onto the belt as well. With Eluned's phial and the starstone around her neck, she had all her possessions on her body.

Arianwen brought breakfast – bread, cheese, fruit – and while September was eating, Berddig appeared.

"Ah, I'm pleased to see you are ready," he said, "your boat is prepared and Cynddylig is impatient to make a start."

"Is he?" September asked, "He didn't seem too keen last night."

"Oh, don't worry about him. Cynddylig is a bit different to most people; he sees doom and gloom when others find hope."

"He doesn't think I can stop the Malevolence, does he?"

"He doesn't have the faith in our powers of resistance to evil that most of us have. None of us know for certain, and we realise that we have little else to help us withstand the Malevolence, but the old stories tell us that the Maengolauseren is a powerful tool in resisting it and the Cludydd, whoever she is, has always protected us."

"I wish I knew more of these stories and what I am supposed to do."

"There will be time on your journey. Tudfwlch knows the tales – it is part of his training, and no doubt Cynddylig will have things to tell you. Now are you ready to leave?"

September swallowed her last mouthful of bread and lifted her cup to down the last swig of cool, fresh water.

"Yes, I think so."

Arianwen held a large woven sack closed by a draw-string.

"I think you will need this," she said.

"What is in it?" September asked.

"A change of clothes for your journey and for when you reach the Arsyllfa, and there's a blanket for the cold nights."

"Thank you. I hadn't thought much about what I will need."

"Of course not child. You have barely arrived and we are packing you off to face whatever destiny holds for you, and for us," Arianwen looked serious, "I, we, will be thinking of you every day and sending our thoughts to support you in the trials that lie ahead. When all this is over, perhaps you will return to us here at Amaethaderyn, and we can be together in happier times."

September felt a tear in her eye. She had hardly known this woman for more than a day and yet she felt as close to her as to her own mother. Arianwen opened her arms and September stepped forward into a hug.

"Thank you," she sobbed, "I will try and do whatever it is that I'm needed for."

"We know you will."

They separated and September crossed to the bed at the side of the cottage where Eluned lay. Her eyes were open and she smiled at September.

"Good luck, Cludydd," she whispered, "May all the stars and all the planets help you in your task."

September's eyes filled again. Eluned was her friend, perhaps her best friend but they had enjoyed so little time together. She leant forward and kissed the mercury bearer on her forehead.

"You get fit quickly. I'd like to see the tiger and the dolphin again if – when – I come back."

Eluned smiled, "We'll have lots of fun."

September picked up the bag by its strings and hefted it over her shoulder. She, Berddig and Arianwen left the cottage and stepped into the bright, warm morning.

It was a short walk to the riverbank and many other people seemed to be making the same journey. When they reached the waterside September saw that a large crowd had assembled. The people made a path for them to pass through.

"Is everyone here to see me leave?" she asked Berddig.

"Of course."

"Glad to see me go, I expect, after all the trouble I've caused." There were signs of the damage caused by the Adarlwchgwin and the Gwyllian all the way through the village.

"That's not the reason. Everyone knows how important your journey is. All their hopes for the future lie in the conference at the Arsyllfa. Don't look so worried. Your strength is in the stone. It will give you all the power you need. Here now, let's get you and your bag on board."

September turned from Berddig and the crowd and saw the boat bobbing gently at the bank. It was smaller than she expected for a long journey, little more than a canoe with seating for three or four people. There were already a number of sacks, leather bags and small wooden barrels filling the available space so September's sack made little difference.

Tudfwlch welcomed her brightly and helped her step into the middle of the boat. Then he took up a position in the bow. September looked to the stern where Cynddylig was fiddling with a grey metal box attached to a wooden tiller. She was determined to be friendly to the older man.

"Good morning, Cynddylig."

"Hmm," was the only reply. It seemed he was too engrossed to be polite.

"What is that box you are looking at?" she asked, trying to engage him in conversation. She had a little more success because after a moment he looked up at her.

"It is our source of movement, girl," he said.

"Oh, an engine." It didn't look much like an out-board motor to September, not that she had ever had the opportunity to look closely at one, "it turns a propeller that pushes the boat forward," she said to show that she wasn't completely dumb and that she had some understanding of such things.

"Yes," Cynddylig said returning to inspect the motor. September was confused because she had seen no other signs of machines run by engines in the village. All the work seemed to be done by the people themselves and wood was burned to provide heat.

"What fuel does it use?" she asked.

"Fuel?" Cynddylig looked at her with a sneer, "nothing is burned to make the boat move. We would need a boat twice the size if we had to carry wood to burn."

"What makes the boat move then?" September asked.

"The power of Haul of course."

"Haul?" September was confused. She had heard the word but had forgotten what it stood for. Cynddylig pointed to the sky.

"The Sun," he said.

"Oh, you mean it uses solar power," September was proud that she thought she understood but as she looked around she saw something was missing, "where are the solar panels?"

"I don't understand what you are saying," Cynddylig growled and returned to studying the motor, or whatever it was.

"I think I should explain," Berddig said. September had forgotten that he was behind her as she had got into the boat and he had overheard the conversation. "I presume that you do not have artefacts of such ingenuity in your world," he continued, kneeling beside the boat.

"No, I don't think so" September shrugged.

"The engine, as you called it, is the peak of skill of the prif-cludyddau o haearn and aur."

"You mean the Mordeyrn and Iorwerth."

"The Mordeyrn, yes, he is the greatest bearer of gold, but not Iorwerth. He is powerful but not even he has the skill to construct this device. It is the work of the Prif-cludydd who lives with the metal miners in the Mynydd Tywyll. He wrought the iron into intricate shapes that turn the fins that push the boat through the water. The Mordeyrn provided the tiny nugget of gold that focuses the power of the Sun and causes the engine to work."

"It sounds pretty special," September was over-awed by Berddig's reverential explanation. She couldn't understand at all how a piece of gold could act as a solar power source – it was just magic, like so many things in the Land.

"It is. Our village has but two of the devices to drive our boats and many villages have none at all."

"So once again, you are giving up something valuable and precious to the village to send me on my way."

"As we have said before, Cludydd, you are important to us and we must ensure that you get to the Arsyllfa as soon as possible. Without the engine you would take many more days of paddling against the flow of the river. It is for all of our benefits that you should take the machine."

"Well, thank you again, Berddig."

"By the power of the Cemegwr! Are we getting started today, or are you going to waste more time in chatter?" Cynddylig said. Berddig looked startled then stood up.

"You are correct, Cynddylig, you should set off. Cast off Tudfwlch." The young man undid the rope holding the bow of the boat into the shore while Cynddylig did the same with the stern rope. The crowd standing on the bank cheered and waved. September waited for a roar of the motor as Cynddylig got them started but there was no noise of an engine; there was no sound at all except for the swishing of the propeller. The boat moved smoothly away from the bank and into the stream with no sign of effort. September waved to the people while feeling amazed at the magic of the fuel-less engine.

Although the current of the river was strong the crowd was soon disappearing behind them as the little craft slipped quietly through the water. For a few minutes they passed fields and gardens on the banks of the river. September looked towards the opposite bank and beyond to the hill of the refuge and its blasted copse of trees, but then the trees crowded together at the water's edge and her view was lost. She made herself as comfortable as possible sitting on a wooden cross-member, resting back against the bags that filled the hull. Tudfwlch too, wriggled into a position to look ahead along the river. She glanced back at Cynddylig who was sitting stiffly, staring ahead with his hand on the tiller. And so they began their journey.

September stirred herself. There was no change to the scenery but she needed some diversion. She knew she couldn't spend the whole journey asking "Are we nearly there yet?" because she knew they weren't. Her recollection of the conversation with Berddig before they had left had given her an idea for some entertainment.

"Tudfwlch?"

"Yes, Cludydd," the young man did not stir from staring ahead.

"Everyone expects me to defeat the Malevolence because that's what happened before. Is that right?"

"We don't expect it but you are our hope, perhaps our only one."

There was a grunt from behind her but no further comment.

"Berddig said you had stories which explained why you

have this hope."

"That's right. Everyone is familiar with the stories of the fight against the Malevolence but those of us training to be a cludydd have to learn the tales in detail."

"Well, we have a long journey ahead of us and I'm going to be pretty bored if it goes on like this, why don't you tell me some of the stories? They may help me to understand what I'm supposed to be doing here."

Tudfwlch turned to face her and smiled broadly.

"It would be a great pleasure to tell you the tales, Cludydd, but I shall have to watch the river while I do."

There was another grunt from behind September but Cynddylig kept his silence.

"That's fine, I can hear you. Let's start."

"Ah, now that's difficult. Where shall I begin?"

"What's the problem?"

"Well, you see there have been several times when the power of the Malevolence has grown, many lifetimes apart. The early stories are confused and difficult to understand and make more use of the old tongue."

"Tell me the more recent ones then. How about the last time the Malevolence appeared?"

"That's a good idea, although even that was a long time ago." Tudfwlch coughed to clear his throat and knelt more upright on his seat of sacks. He took a deep breath and spoke in a loud and almost melodic voice as if reciting something he had heard many times.

"It was a time of sadness and anger in the Land. Man fought against man, woman against woman, and vicious monsters arose to kill, destroy and bring pestilence on the people. Men and women despaired that the Adwyth was growing in power. That's the name for the Malevolence in the old tongue, Cludydd."

"I know," September said. Tudfwlch went on.

"They thought it would gain control over everyone and everything that lived in the seven regions of Gwlad. Then the Prif-cludydd o Aur, the Mordeyrn of Coedwig Fawr, the Great Forest..."

"Where's that?"

Tudfwlch stuttered, his recitation broken.

"Uh, um, north of here. The forest lies between the northern river and Mynydd Tywyll. It is a vast area of tall, dark, pine trees. The people live there by cutting down the trees for timbers for the miners and charcoal for the metalsmiths in the mountains."

"I see, and this Mordeyrn was not the Mordeyrn I've met."

"No of course not. This was years and years ago. Our Mordeyrn's name is Aurddolen. The Mordeyrn's then was Heulyn, the ray of Sun."

"I see. Go on."

"Um... then Heulyn remembered the stories of yore and cried out to the heavens to send us our saviour once again, the Cludydd o Maengolauseren. For seven days and seven nights he stood on a great stump of a tree in the middle of the forest and voiced his appeal. And on the seventh night, when the moon was overhead she appeared. Clad in white with hair as white as the snows of the north, she ..."

"Snow? You mean her hair was white, like mine?"

"Yes, Cludydd, she was indeed white of hair and pale of complexion. She appeared holding the Maengolauseren in her hand. She was young and beautiful ... yes, like you Cludydd... but she was confused. She had no knowledge of the Land and was unfamiliar with the ways of the people of the Land..."

"Hold on. You're saying that this woman, who looked something like me arrived in the Land, summoned by this Heulyn, just like the Mordeyrn summoned me. And she came from my world?"

"Perhaps. She was certainly not of this world but she came bearing the stone which you now carry."

"How do you know it's the same one?"

"There is no other starstone of the same size and power."

"Right, I see."

"Shall I continue, Cludydd?" Tudfwlch asked glancing at September.

"Yes please, but call me September."

"Yes Clud...September. Heulyn instructed the Cludydd o Maengolauseren in her powers and very soon her skills were tested. Just a few days after her arrival amongst the people of the Land the forces of the Malevolence attacked. A Draig tân descended from the heavens and hordes of Adarllwchgwin hurled stones and fire at the people of Coedwig Fawr. There was great destruction and many died or were injured but the Cludydd triumphed. She fought off the beasts and destroyed the Draig tân. The Mordeyrn Heulyn realised that this victory was not enough however. The Malevolence had not been weakened, just held back for a time. Heulyn knew that the people of Gwlad and in particular the bearers of power must work together. He called the Prif-cludyddau to a conference in the Mynydd Tywyll and guided the Cludydd o Maengolauseren there himself. Their journey was beset with attacks from the evil; monsters of the earth, air, fire and water and also people who had turned to evil. I won't go on with the tales of the journey, September."

September was roused from the ancient times to respond to Tudfwlch's last comment.

"Why not?"

"It is very long and while exciting to children to hear about how the Cludydd defeated the servants of the malevolence it is, um, a little repetitive."

September realised that wasn't quite what Tudfwlch meant. They were on a journey to meet the Prif-cludyddau, she was the bearer of the starstone, and the Malevolence was at large. They too may be attacked at any time.

"But perhaps there are clues as to how I should deal with the Malevolence and its servants?"

"Ah, yes, that is true," Tudfwlch said, pondering, "I will tell you the stories later – we have plenty of time. I wanted to get to the part where the Malevolence was defeated."

September was still thinking over the story.

"You say this earlier Cludydd was attacked all along her journey?"

"That's right. The Malevolence sensed her presence and her importance and attackers manifested from the soil, the air, the rivers and lakes all along their route."

"She didn't have a cloak to hide her from sight?" September indicated the silver garment that enrobed her.

"No, that is a new invention of Berddig and Padarn suggested to them by the Mordeyrn."

"But it hasn't been tested except for last night?"

"How could it? It needs you and the Malevolence for its fitness for purpose to be proved."

"Ah, yes."

"We will have to wait to see if it works but the Gwyllian last night were unable to perceive you. If they had they would have come straight to Arianwen's house instead of destroying all the other huts. I think that is a good sign, September." Tudfwlch's voice had a merry tone to it. Remembering all the destruction wrought by the Gwyllian, September wasn't so sure. She turned to Cynddylig.

"Is Tudfwlch right? Is the cloak keeping me hidden from the Malevolence?"

Cynddylig shrugged.

"Perhaps the Cludyddau have been successful in making you invisible to the Malevolence but the evil knows that you are in the Land. We have a journey of many days. Who knows whether the robe will keep your whereabouts secret for all that time."

September was not cheered by Cynddylig's words but she realised that it was not in the character of the man to be encouraging. Perhaps he was being realistic and not defeatist. She turned back to Tudfwlch.

"There's something else. They didn't travel to the Arsyllfa?"

"It did not exist in those times. Although the Arsyllfa seems an ancient institution to us today, and indeed it is many hundreds of years old, it was only after the last rising of the Malevolence that it was established and the observatory built in the Bryn am Seren. After the Cludydd defeated the Malevolence it was Heulyn's life's work to set up the Arsyllfa to prepare for the next coming of the evil. But I'm getting ahead of the story."

"No, wait. You're saying that things are different to the last time."

"Well, the Arsyllfa was established to collect knowledge of the Malevolence, to observe the heavens which control the waxing and waning of its power and to dispense instructions for preparations throughout Gwlad."

"Why was nothing done before?"

Now it was Tudfwlch's turn to shrug.

"We are an independent people, scattered across the Land. We work hard to maintain our homes and families. It is not easy providing sufficient food, and clothes, and tools. Each village largely looks after itself, with just a few people travelling from one to another."

"Is there no government?"

"Government?"

Tudfwlch didn't appear to understand the word.

"Leaders, laws, taxes. All that stuff." September recalled her father ranting at the impositions of government.

Cynddylig spoke, "He doesn't understand you girl. You speak words that have little meaning for us, as opaque as the thoughts of the Cemegwr. Each village has its rules of life and its tithes and the cludyddau are leaders of a sort, but the whole of Gwlad has no such organisation – well, until recently."

"What do you mean?"

"The Mordeyrn Aurddolen has attempted to impose his views about the Malevolence on the other Prif-cludyddau. This conference of the Arsyllfa is his parliament of the whole of Gwlad."

"Perhaps it is needed to oppose the Malevolence," September said.

"Aye, maybe it is, but some think that it is itself the work of the Adwyth, to bind us in rules and control our deeds and thoughts."

"That's nonsense," Tudfwlch said heatedly, "you can't suggest that the Mordeyrn is a servant of evil, especially after the battle in which his gold plate was shattered."

Cynddylig dissolved into mutters and grunts. "It's what some say. I'm not saying I believe it."

"The point, September, is that the Arsyllfa, and the Mordeyrn, have known that the Malevolence was growing in power for some time. He is trying to prepare for it hence his first appeal to you. But the Land is a big place; it takes a lot of organisation to get the seven regions working to the same ends."

"OK, so go back to your story. How did this earlier Mordeyrn and the Cludydd win? What was her name by the way?"

Tudfwlch became dreamy. "The Cludydd o Maengolauseren was named Breuddwyd in her own world."

"What! That's unbelievable," September was shocked and excited.

"What is it, September?" Tudfwlch turned to see her face.

"That name, Breuddwyd, it's my mother's name. I've never heard of anyone else with it. She says it means 'dream'." Something else occurred to September. "She's a seventh child too. I've got six uncles scattered around Wales." What did this mean? Could her mother have been the bearer of the starstone at the last rising of the Malevolence? But that was centuries ago, surely it couldn't be. September recalled that the passage of time in the Land was different to her home as only a fortnight had passed for her between her visits while two years had passed for the people of Gwlad.

"You certainly bear a resemblance to descriptions of the former Cludydd," Tudfwlch said apparently unexcited, "Why shouldn't the stone be handed from mother to daughter?"

"But she never mentioned it to me."

"Did you tell your mother of your first visit to us?"

"No, but..."

"There you are then; she had no reason to tell you."

"But surely if what your story says happened to her, those great battles and things, she would have fantastic stories to tell."

"Perhaps that was it. From what you have said your world is very different to ours. Maybe your mother thought it best to keep her tales to herself."

September shrugged. She couldn't believe it, couldn't take in the possibility that her own mother, Mum, had once wielded the powerful stone that hung now from her neck.

"What happened at the end? She, this Cludydd Breuddwyd, won?"

"That's right."

"How?"

Tudfwlch took a deep breath and launched again into the story.

"Heulyn determined that the focus of the Malevolence was in the southern desert, far to the south of here."

"But they were up north in the forests."

"Yes, they embarked on a great trek, the Cludydd, the Mordeyrn and the other Prif-cludyddau. Along the way they gathered a huge army of village people who left their homes and their families to fight for good and to protect the Cludydd. After many months and many battles with the servants of the Malevolence they reached the edge of the Plains. The desert stretched in front of them. There would be no water or food for the army. The Cludydd decided to go on alone. Heulyn wanted to go on with her to defend her but she insisted he stay behind and look after the people. She left them, heading for the place and the time that Heulyn had predicted that the Malevolence would reach its greatest power. Heulyn and the army waited. Days passed and then on the night that Heulyn had foretold there was a huge eruption in the distance. The sky lit up with blue fire and after a time a great roar of noise blasted them to the ground and deafened them all. A vast cloud of dust rolled over the land burying each and every one of them and making them choke. Then there was silence. The sky went dark again and the stars reappeared. The army picked itself up and dusted themselves off. There was a feeling of release, of joy, of a weight lifted from them. Heulyn knew that the Cludydd had succeeded. The Malevolence was banished. They waited for the Cludydd to return. Days passed with no further attacks by the manifestations of evil and the villagers began to drift away, beginning the long journey home. Eventually just the Mordeyrn Heulyn remained. He walked out into the desert and arrived at a great area where the sand was turned to crystal but he found no sign of the Cludydd or the Maengolauseren. He returned to his home and set about his plans for the Arsyllfa and making preparations for the next visitation of the Malevolence. He knew that while Breuddwyd had been successful, evil will always rise again." Tudfwlch fell silent, Cynddylig sniffed, and September sat still trying to take in the story.

"She didn't die," she said at last, "she went home."

"That is what Heulyn presumed. Everyone was disappointed and hoped that she would return and enjoy the appreciation of the people. But Heulyn said that the Cludydd o Maengolauseren will only appear in the Land when the Malevolence grows strong. Only now has that time come again. You are with us September."

"Hmm, if those stories have been passed on correctly," Cynddylig growled.

September turned to face him.

"You don't believe the stories are true?"

"Oh, there's truth in them as in all old stories. I'm just not certain they are a guide to our future. They are tales told to frighten children or to teach them how to behave."

"Don't you believe in the evil?"

"Oh, there's evil, in the world."

"And what about the monsters, the Draig tân, the Adarllwchgwin, the Ceffyl dwr, Gwyllian? You've got to believe in those."

"Aye, girl, I believe there are monsters in the world too."

"So what don't you believe then?"

"I can't believe that those tales of the past have any meaning for us now."

"What about the Cemegwr? You've mentioned them twice."

Cynddylig was silent for a moment.

"You're right girl. I do call upon them from time to time, but not out of belief or faith.

"What then?"

"The oldest stories of the Land tell how this world and all the others we see in the heavens were made by the Cemegwr. They made the land and the seas and the air. They provided the metals in the ground for us to use. They created all the living things, including us."

"And..."

"That's it; they are old stories, fables. They have never appeared to help us when the Malevolence has grown strong although some people, the misguided and the gullible, say that the Cemegwr made us to oppose the Evil."

"What do you think?"

"I think that if they exist the Cemegwr are sitting on their backsides watching us and having a laugh at our futile attempts to plan for the next assault by the Malevolence. But no, I don't believe that they are out there waiting to help us or that they even exist."

"Do you believe in me?"

"Oh, you're real and you bear a stone of power, but can you rid the world of the evil? I don't know."

Tudfwlch snorted.

"Oh, come on Cynddylig. Everything that the Mordeyrn predicted has happened. He said the power of the Malevolence was increasing and it has. In the last few years the attacks have become more frequent and there have been tales from elsewhere of diseases and disputes which are the work of the evil in the minds of the people. He summoned September and here she is; the bearer of the stone who has already wielded its power."

Cynddylig shrugged.

"Let us hope then that the Mordeyrn's plans are successful."

"I have more than hope," Tudfwlch asserted, "I believe in the Mordeyrn and the Cludydd." He turned back to face the bow of the boat and fell silent. Cynddylig did not respond and returned to steering the craft silently.

September wriggled her bottom amongst the sacks making herself more comfortable. She closed her eyes to shut out the world and to be with her thoughts. Could she believe that Mother had once been in her position, had travelled across Gwlad and wielded the Maengolauseren in a fierce battle with the Malevolence? It seemed too fantastic to be true and yet here she was sailing along a wide river in a boat powered by a speck of gold and some kind of magic. Perhaps when Mother returned to her life at home she had thought that her experiences were too farfetched to pass on and had no idea that her own daughter could become part of the same saga. If only she could talk to Mother and learn more about the powers of the starstone. September realised that any conversation would probably have to wait until the completion of her task, if she was successful. She wasn't her Mother, didn't have the skills or common sense that she had; nevertheless if Mother succeeded, surely she could too. There was something else though, an added complication; her dead twin. Perhaps if her twin had been alive she might have been born after September and then she would be the seventh not

September. It was all too uncertain.

September became aware of a change in the boat's motion. She opened her eyes and realised that she must have been asleep. The sun was low in the sky and the boat was moving across the current. They were headed towards a break in the high bank, a shelving beach and a clearing in the trees. September sat up straight to get a clearer sight of where they were going.

"Ah, you've woken up. Just in time girl," Cynddylig said. September turned to him.

"Are we stopping?"

"Yes, it's time to make camp for the night. The light will be gone soon and it's not a good idea to be on the river at night even when the Malevolence is not in its ascendency."

The bow of the boat ground against the shingle. Tudfwlch leaped overboard with the rope in his hand. He splashed into the water but a few steps took him to the sandy beach. He hauled on the rope pulling the small craft ashore. September crawled over the sacks and barrels to the bow and jumped on to dry land. She joined Tudfwlch in tugging the boat further out of the water.

"That'll do," Cynddylig called, "Find somewhere to tie her to." Tudfwlch took the rope and began tying it around the nearest tree trunk. "Here, girl, catch." Cynddylig called again as he threw a sack in September's direction. She caught it in her arms and was surprised to find how light it was.

"What's this?" she said.

"Your bed," Cynddylig replied, "put it down and catch this one." September hurried to drop the sack on the dry ground well away from the water and arrived back to receive another similar package tossed from the boat. Tudfwlch joined her and together they gathered the sacks and barrels that Cynddylig threw to them.

"That's enough for tonight," Cynddylig said, looking at the half empty hull. He jumped from the bow and strode up the beach. "Now let's get this camp sorted and some food on the fire."

By the time the sun had sunk below the trees, the three travellers had made camp in the shelter of the forest edge. Tudfwlch had lit a fire of twigs and branches that he had collected and Cynddylig had set up a small cauldron over it. September could already smell tempting odours wafting from the vegetables and herbs that he had tossed into it. She had been pleased to discover that the 'beds' were sleeping bags packed thickly with wool. Tudfwlch had told her that she would appreciate the warmth because after the heat of the day the nights could be cold. Now she sat on her own sleeping bag with her silver robe wrapped around her watching Cynddylig at work. Tudfwlch handed her a wooden cup filled with water. She drank gratefully. Tudfwlch sat next to her and looked around.

"Should be safe; a quiet spot," he said.

"Have you camped here before?" September asked.

"No, but he has," Tudfwlch indicated Cynddylig, "he knows all the stopping points along the river, but this is my first time away from Amaethaderyn."

"Are you looking forward to the trip?"

"Oh, yes. I know it will be hard and we may meet difficulties, but I've wanted an excuse to travel."

"Your people don't travel much then?"

"No, the village is all that most of us know. There's just a few like Cynddylig who take away some goods and bring back other things. The cludyddau usually travel a bit, learning their skills from others and passing on their own knowledge. Perhaps I would have set off myself sometime soon to learn more of the craft of Haearn," he hesitated, "of course, Iorwerth's a great cludydd and a good teacher."

"But you'd like to get away and see more of the world," September said, "I know how you feel, I'd like to do something exciting when I'm older, perhaps even go to university." She would love to study something but she didn't know what and on her past record the chances of getting good qualifications seemed slim. She presumed she would be stuck at home looking for a boring job. She realised that Tudfwlch didn't understand what she had said, "You'd like to go away from home, a place like the Arsyllfa I suppose."

"Ah, yes. The trouble is that the Malevolence has changed things. People are more wary of travelling and meeting strangers. We're not so sure that we trust people as much as we used to. You hear stories..."

"What sort of stories?"

"Oh, groups of people, possessed by evil, attacking villages and running off with their food and wares."

"Can't people defend themselves? What about the bearers of the metals? They have powers."

"That is true but not all villages have cludyddau as skilled as those at Amaethaderyn and don't forget that in two of the attacks it was your power that defeated the manifestations of the Malevolence."

"Hmm, it comes back to the starstone, doesn't it."

"Yes, its power is so great that I feel we have no need to fear evil. Would you let me look at it?"

September reached inside her cloak and felt the weight of the stone in its silver clasp in her hand. She pulled it out for Tudfwlch to see.

"Put that thing away!"

Cynddylig's roar startled September. She released the starstone and it slid back inside her cloak.

"If that cloak of yours is to do its job you must keep the stone hidden inside it."

September saw anger and frustration pass quickly over Tudfwlch's face to be replaced by a look of contrition. She couldn't believe how stupid she had been to uncover the stone after all that happened last night.

"Of course. I was foolish to ask," Tudfwlch said, "we must do nothing to attract the attention of the Adwyth."

"That's right, lad," Cynddylig said more gently, "use the sense that Iorwerth's tried to drum into you."

September regained her composure and pressed her hand against her breast feeling the hidden pendant.

"There was no need to shout," she said.

"I'm sorry, girl, but even a moment of exposure may be enough to awaken a manifestation of the evil."

"Cynddylig's right," Tudfwlch said. "Who knows what monsters may be lurking nearby awaiting a sign."

September stood up, "I need a wash, or a bath. It was hot and sticky sitting in a boat all day." She felt a need to get away from Cynddylig for a while.

"You're right," Tudfwlch said, "Let's get into the river."

He started undoing his belt and pulling his tunic over his head. September wasn't sure whether to follow him and strip off her clothes.

"If you're going in the water, Cludydd, don't forget to keep your cloak around you," Cynddylig said, "and don't be long. The food will be ready soon."

Tudfwlch was tugging his trousers off his legs and standing naked in the twilight.

"Come on," he said, running to the waters" edge. September watched his slim, muscular body with interest and made a decision. With the body she had here in the Land she needn't feel ashamed and anyway she would still be covered by the silver cloak. She removed her belt with the dagger and pouch, contorted herself to take off her top and wriggled the trousers down. Then gripping the cloak around her she ran to join Tudfwlch. He was already splashing in the water a couple of metres beyond where the boat was moored. His white skin caught the pale moonlight and the ripples of water around him sparkled. September stepped tentatively into the water.

"It's not cold," Tudfwlch called. He was right; it was nothing like as cold as she suspected a river in Britain would be at any time of year. The water still retained the warmth of the sun that it had collected on its long, meandering journey from the mountains. Holding the cloak around her September moved further into the river until the water was up to her waist. Then she sank down immersing her body in the water. The water's touch reminded her of the differences between the body she had now and what she was familiar with at home. She felt fitter, as if her body had no excess fat and was used to much more exercise than she had at home. The body felt more mature, more looked after. She felt the same as Tudfwlch looked – a young person at the peak of their youthful health.

"How does that feel?" Tudfwlch said, swimming to her side.

"Wonderful," she replied. "It's great to wash all the sweat off."

"Come and eat, supper is ready," Cynddylig called. They waded out of the water and saw Cynddylig spooning the broth into wooden bowls. Tudfwlch pulled a couple of cloths out of a sack and they quickly mopped the water from themselves. It took further contortions to get back into her clothes but soon she was sitting with Tudfwlch and Cynddylig around the fire with a warm bowl on her lap.

Before long, September's hunger was satisfied, hunger that she hadn't been aware of until she took her first mouthful of Cynddylig's soup. The flavours of various vegetables and cheese were so enticing that she drained two bowlfuls, as did Tudfwlch and Cynddylig himself. She helped wash up and then the three of them sat in their sleeping bags around the fire. Cynddylig began to sing in a soft lilting voice. September couldn't follow the words but presumed they were of the old language that the people seemed to use for formal and cultural purposes. Tudfwlch joined in and September was enjoying just listening to the tunes.

The sound of a faint and distant horn clashed with the singing. September looked into the darkness all around but could not pick out the direction the sound was coming from. Neither of the men seemed to notice the sound and September became convinced that the notes of the horn were coming from very close to her. She looked at herself and her eyes fell on the leather pouch at her waist. Then she remembered. She opened it and pulled out the small copper horn that Catrin had given her. It was indeed the little horn that was producing the faint tones. She lifted it to her ear to listen more carefully and as she did so the music stopped.

"Cludydd. Do you hear me?" The voice was tinny and distant but she recognised the gentle, deep voice of the Mordeyrn Aurddolen.

"Mordeyrn, is that you?"

"Ah, you do have the speaking tube. Good evening Cludydd."

"Good evening."

"I am delighted to be able to speak to you and so sorry that I was not able to be present at your coming or to defend you during your first day in the Land."

"Oh, that's all right. Arianwen, Berddig and the others were very helpful." September felt strange having this conversation with the distant Mordeyrn. The copper horn was not a lot like her mobile phone.

"That is good. I presume you have begun your journey."

"Yes, we're camped for the night."

"Good. I had intended speaking to you before you left, but we had a difficult time yesterday."

"What happened?"

"We met with some manifestations of the Malevolence on the river. It took all our powers to evade them and continue on our way."

"But you escaped."

"Yes. We are safe now and tomorrow we should reach Dwytrefrhaedr. However I am concerned for your safety. The evil is growing stronger and I fear that you will encounter its various guises as you follow behind us."

"I have my cloak."

"Ah yes, the cloak of plwm and alcam. A most amazing development. It will certainly protect you but you must keep it around you and especially keep the Maengolauseren within its folds. Even a glimpse of its power may attract the wrath of evil."

"Oh yes. I'll make sure I do." September felt a rush of guilt about almost pulling out the stone to show Tudfwlch.

"But even hidden, you may still meet up with evil. The Malevolence has subtle ways as well as the aggressive monsters that you have seen already. Remain observant at all times."

"I shall, I shall."

"I look forward to welcoming you to the Arsyllfa and to having an opportunity to discuss the part you must play in helping us through our great danger. Hasten, but take care."

"We will."

"Good. We will talk again at this time tomorrow evening. Sleep well, Cludydd."

The Mordeyrn's voice faded. September looked at the little copper horn sitting in her hand wondering how such an instrument could carry a conversation over hundreds of miles. She noticed that the singing had also stopped and looked up to see Cynddylig and Tudfwlch looking at her.

"You have been speaking to the Mordeyrn?" Tudfwlch

said.

"Yes. I don't know how this thing works." September said, still grasping the horn.

"The art of the Cludydd o Efyddyn," Cynddylig said not particularly helpfully.

"What did he say?" Tudfwlch asked.

"Oh, he said that they've had to fight their way past evil things but should reach Dwytref... whatever, tomorrow."

"Ah, that's about right," Cynddylig nodded, "he has kept to the schedule he set. We have many days of travel to catch him up."

"They have met the Malevolence?" Tudfwlch was worried.

"Yes, he said we must take care as there is evil along the river and even with my cloak it may try to stop us. Oh, and he said to hurry."

"He's right," Cynddylig said, "The evil will attack anyone, villagers or travellers, hidden or not. The sooner we can get you to the Arsyllfa and into his protection the better. I think it's time to settle for the night. We must be away at dawn."

A wave of tiredness came over September. She wondered why since she had spent the day just sitting in the boat, but she was grateful for the thick, soft, sleeping bag. She shuffled down inside.

"Do you want to take first watch or shall I?" Tudfwlch asked.

"You go first, then I can be making ready for the journey on my watch," Cynddylig replied.

"Oh, do you want me to take a turn?" September asked already feeling dopey.

"No, girl," Cynddylig answered. "You do not have the knowledge of the Land. You would be waking us up at every chirp of a bird or call of an animal. Get your sleep while you can. I am sure you will need your energy at some stage."

September was happy to lay down her head. With the cloak, and the wool around her and a full stomach she felt warm and content. Soon she was asleep.

14

The gentle rocking of the boat lulled September back to sleep. She felt tired after the early start. Cynddylig had been good to his word and had roused her and Tudfwlch before it was light. They had eaten a quick breakfast of bread and cheese and then loaded the boat before the Sun rose. Now the monotony of travel on the river was making September listless and drowsy. The tall trees that crowded the banks of the wide river prevented any sight of the land and the view remained the same hour after hour.

The Sun had risen in a cloudless sky and the temperature was rising. Only September's metal cloak kept her from becoming over heated. The only thing that stopped her dropping off into a deep slumber was the discomfort of sitting amongst bundles and barrels.

Cynddylig was silent as ever, his hand on the tiller and his face a picture of concentration. September wondered whether some mental power was needed to keep the magical motor propelling them through the water but Cynddylig didn't seem keen to talk about it.

Tudfwlch sat in the bow again, ostensibly watching for dangers but he seemed mesmerised by the passing water. He hadn't spoken or moved for quite a while.

"Tudfwlch," she said. There was no reply. She said his name again, louder, and he stirred, turning to face her.

"Sorry, September, I was day dreaming."

"I thought so."

"Did you want something?"

"Other than to get off this boat? No, not really. It's not very interesting is it, and we've got days and days of it with nothing different to see."

"Well, the land will change, you'll see, and we will pass some other communities further along."

"Yes, but it's pretty boring now. Can you tell me another

story or something?"

"What would you like to hear?"

"Oh, I don't know. How about something about yourself?"

"There's not a lot to tell. I was born in Amaethaderyn, like my parents before me and their parents before them. Actually, that's not true. One grandfather came from a village further down the river. My parents are leather workers using the skins of the cattle and pigs that we have in the village. I would have joined them but when I was seven years old I showed I had the potential to be a bearer of Haearn."

"How did you find out?"

"Every year at our midsummer festival all the seven year olds are assessed by the cludyddau. My year was the first time that Iorwerth was the Cludydd o Haearn. I can remember everything that happened. I was watching him working the iron at his forge. As he hammered the metal he sang the songs of Mawrth and in no time the lump of iron became a knife or buckle. He handed me a hammer and held a piece of red-hot Haearn on his anvil. He told me to beat it into a hook. I didn't know the words but I felt I knew what to do and the metal almost shaped itself. Iorwerth was impressed and told my parents that I could be a cludydd myself, if I studied hard. My parents were pleased for me and so I joined Iorwerth as his apprentice. Now my two younger sisters will have to take over the leatherwork from my parents."

"What's the singing all about? Surely you just have to hammer the iron into shape?"

"Oh no, there's much more to being a Cludydd o Haearn than just beating the metal. The songs give the Haearn power."

"What power?"

"There are songs that help a blade keep its sharp edge and prevent it from snapping, others for making wheels run smoothly. There are songs that I haven't learnt yet for making all the parts of this boat's engine work together and harnessing the power of the Aur. Not even Iorwerth is that skilled."

"When will you be qualified?"

Tudfwlch shrugged. "When I'm needed. While Iorwerth

lives I will be his assistant, unless I travel to another village that has need of a Cludydd o Haearn."

"So, that's why you want to travel, to find a vacancy," September spoke lightly, kidding Tudfwlch, but he frowned at her.

"No, but yes. What I mean is I would be happy working with Iorwerth for as long as he lives, and I hope that will be a long time. I have no wish to leave Amaethaderyn, but I would like to travel to learn how cludyddau work in other places."

"I'm sure that would be a good idea. It seems that there is not much mixing of people from one place and another here."

"Is it different in your world?" Tudfwlch asked.

"Yes, I think it is," September suddenly felt homesick.

"Tell me about your home," Tudfwlch insisted.

"Well, everything is different. There are a lot more people for a start. We don't just have villages with a few people we have towns and cities with millions, all living close together and relying on each other for food and water and energy and, well everything."

"Millions of people? I can't imagine such a number."

"Well, neither can I really, but they are there, filling up our planet and using the resources."

"And they all travel?"

"Not all, but I suppose a lot do, for work and holidays."

"Holidays? A holiday is when everyone gets together and eats and drinks and sings to celebrate something."

"Oh, we have holidays like that but we also have holidays when we go off and sit on a beach for a couple of weeks."

Tudfwlch shook his head, "I hear your words but I do not understand what you say. Your world seems so confusing."

They continued talking for much of the day about their respective homes while Cynddylig maintained his silence. September felt that she had learned more about the slow, peaceful lives of the people of Gwlad, their spirit of cooperation and their quiet endeavours to provide the necessities of life from the resources around them. In some ways it sounded an idyllic life but September also wondered whether she would be bored without the diversions of TV and computers and visiting the shops to choose new clothes. She had tried to explain her own life but Tudfwlch seemed to have got an impression just of noise and chaos and waste, which she had to admit, was not far from the truth.

She wondered what her mother's feelings about Gwlad were, if indeed she had been the Cludydd that banished the Malevolence the last time it had arisen. September noted that her mother seemed to value everything that was good about the way of life in Gwlad and tried to maintain a steady, peaceful lifestyle despite having six children to raise. She pondered on her Mother's apparently strong Christian beliefs while the people of Gwlad believed in the power of the seven metals and the seven heavenly bodies that governed them.

As the Sun sank below the trees ahead of them, Cynddylig pointed the boat to the bank, again finding a spot where they could get ashore and make camp. September was glad of the activity after a day in the boat. She helped Tudfwlch collect dry wood for the camp fire and chopped vegetables for Cynddylig's soup. Despite being largely the same ingredients he was able to make the flavour different and appetising.

They were settling into their sleeping bags when September heard the faint sound of the horn. This time she knew where the sound was coming from and quickly got the copper instrument from her pouch.

"Hello, Mordeyrn," she said .

"Ah, please call me Aurddolen. Mordeyrn is rather too formal for these little chats. You and your companions are well?"

"Yes, it's been a very quiet day. We were on the river from sunrise to sunset."

"Good, you will have travelled a fair distance."

"It's pretty boring though. There's nothing to see. And it's going to be the same for lots of days yet, so Cynddylig says."

"That is true, Cludydd, but please do not hope for a livelier journey. I fear that you will meet enough excitement along the way. Sleep well and prepare for more travel."

"I will, and please call me September."

"Ah, yes, I must recall your familiar name."

"And what about your journey? Have you arrived at the town, Dwy... whatever it's called?"

142

"Yes, I am relieved to say we got here, this afternoon. Tomorrow we ascend to the upper town and start the trek into the hills. Good night, September."

The horn went silent before September had an opportunity to ask him what he meant by the upper town. She was a little worried by his warning of excitements to come but she found her eyes becoming heavy as she snuggled under the woollen covers.

The following morning saw them in their accustomed places in the boat.

"Today you will have something to see," Cynddylig said without enlightening September further. For the first couple of hours everything looked much the same, tree after tree lining the banks. Then September did notice a difference. The trees thinned out and there seemed to be signs of cultivation in the clearings. She even thought she saw people moving. Rounding a broad bend in the river, September had a real view for once. The river branched. There was a tributary on the left joining the main river with the arch of a bridge over it linking two clusters of buildings. As the boat carried them closer, September could see that the bridge and the buildings were constructed of wood with the walls of the one and two storey houses filled in with red mud.

"Where are we?" she asked.

"Abercyflym," Cynddylig replied, "a very old town. It's two rivers provide it with fish and the Afon Cyflym brings goods from the south."

"Is it bigger than Amaethaderyn?"

"It's difficult to say. At times in the past when there was more trade it has been an important market town, but now I doubt whether more live here than at Amaethaderyn."

"Are we stopping?" Tudfwlch asked turning to face the stern.

"No lad. We have no need of supplies yet, and we have a long way to go." September was disappointed to hear that she wouldn't have the chance to leave the boat and look around somewhere new but she understood Cynddylig's desire to press on. Nevertheless, as they drew close to the village, people came to the waterfront and waved to them. Tudfwlch and September waved back. The boat rocked as the fast moving water from the tributary flowed into the main stream.

"I wouldn't show yourself too much, lass, if I were you," Cynddylig warned.

"Why not?"

"Well, that silver robe of yours marks you out as someone special and while the Malevolence cannot see you with it around you, someone with eyes can spot you and may wonder. If evil touches their heart your whereabouts will be known."

"But the people looked normal and pleased to see us."

"Things may look normal but evil can lurk unseen until the moment arrives."

"What moment?"

"Cynddylig is making things up," Tudfwlch said.

"I am not making things up, young man. You know as well as I do that a person can be turned by the Malevolence and await its bidding."

"So it is said, but I have never seen it."

"You haven't lived, lad, nor seen much at all in your young life."

"Yes, well..."

"Wait and see. We may come upon things you'd wish you hadn't seen."

Already the village of Abercyflym was receding behind them and September looked back, struggling to take in every last detail of the place to contrast with the returning monotony of the tree lined banks.

"Do you know anyone there?" September asked.

"Yes, I do," Cynddylig's voice took on a wistful tone, "there was a young woman. Well she was young, old now, my age. I nearly settled in Abercyflym as it happens, but well, there was work to do elsewhere, so I moved on."

It was another cloudless, hot day and September was glad to wrap the cloak around her to reflect the bulk of the Sun's energy. They talked more about the villages along the river and September began to get more of an impression of Gwlad. It was a vast continent with small widely spaced communities which were largely self-sufficient, taking advantage of the resources available where they were situated. Trade was largely confined to precious commodities like metals and finished articles such as the leather goods that Tudfwlch's family manufactured.

When they camped for the night, September was eager for the Mordeyrn's call on the copper instrument so that she could tell him that they had passed the landmark that the village had been. He was pleased with their progress and announced that he was now walking into the hills and only a couple of days climb away from the Arsyllfa.

The following day dawned overcast. September was pleased as it seemed to indicate that the day would be cooler but Cynddylig was not so happy.

"Cloud means rain," he said as they settled into the day's travel. Sure enough within the hour a steady drizzle began. September drew the cloak around her with the hood pulled tight over her head and sat hunched amongst the bundles. The rain wasn't cold but the drip that seemed to find its way between her breasts was annoying. Cynddylig and Tudfwlch sat covered by waxed cloth sheets looking miserable. The pitter-patter of the raindrops on the boat and the water made talk difficult so they continued on their way without conversation.

The cloud became heavier and lower and at the same the river narrowed and took a more twisted route through the trees which grew up over low hills on both sides of the river. September peered through the mist at what looked like a dead end ahead. Only as they got close to the bank did the course of the river open up to the left or the right. September was glad that Cynddylig was steering and apparently knew the route because she was thoroughly confused by the river's twists and turns while the rain fell and clouds clung to the water.

They swung around a bend, to find their passage obscured. Looming out of the grey mist was another vessel, bearing down on them at a speed that exceeded the flow of the water. Tudfwlch shouted, September screamed and the little boat lurched as Cynddylig flung the tiller over. The approaching boat was ten times their size, a barge, churning up a bow wave of white water. In what felt like a lifetime but was actually just a few seconds they moved out of its path but the danger was not yet over. As the boat slid past them, its sides just a few metres away, September peered up at the towering bulk of the vessel. Its wide wooden planks were stacked one above the other up to the sky but in fact it was just three or four metres from water level to gunwales. Their small craft bucked as it passed over the wash. For a moment September thought they may capsize but with the danger of a collision averted Cynddylig steered into the waves and the boat began to cut through the crests instead of rolling off them. As they passed the stern of the larger vessel, September looked up and saw crewmen looking down on them waving excitedly but then the craft's speed carried them onwards and there was no opportunity to exchange so much as a word. She watched as the barge rounded the bend and disappeared from view.

"What was that?" September shouted to Cynddylig.

"Ah, one of the great vessels of the river," he called back, "It carries trade goods from Dwytrefrhaedr to the coast and back again. I think that was the Gleisiad."

"What does that mean?"

"It is a fish that swims up river from the ocean to the higher reaches. Red of flesh."

"A salmon?"

Cynddylig shrugged and concentrated on getting them back on course. Tudfwlch settled back down beneath his sheeting and September pulled her cloak tight.

Shortly the rain eased and the clouds lifted and parted. The Sun shone and their moods lifted. September turned to speak to Cynddylig.

"I didn't see any sails on that boat. What pushes it through the water?"

"The same as this vessel."

"What, a gold nugget and an iron motor?"

"The very same although somewhat bigger than the engine we have. It's the Sun that gives Gleisiad her power."

"Are there many boats like the Gleisiad?"

"Not as many as there once were, not that there were ever many of her size. I suppose there are still two or three doing the coast run."

"That's not many boats for a country this big."

"There are more, smaller, vessels like this."

September looked around her.

"This hardly carries much for trading and the Gleisiad, although she looked frighteningly huge when she was about to run us down, wasn't a ship. But why are there fewer boats like that one?"

"There's less trade these days. People are scared by talk of the Malevolence attacking vessels and turning people to theft and murder."

"People are less prepared to entrust their wares to travelling tradesmen," Tudfwlch added.

"What about the crew of the Gleisiad?"

"What about them, lass?"

"Were they as surprised to see us as we were to see them? They were waving but they didn't seem happy."

"It was raining and they had nearly run us down," Tudfwlch said.

"Aye lad, but the girl's right, there was something else in their signals. A warning perhaps."

They fell silent, pondering what they had seen, trying to elicit meaning in the gestures the crew had made to them. September was trying to imagine a fleet of the sun-powered vessels sliding effortlessly up and down the river and what it would be like when one called at the villages along the banks.

At last they stopped to make camp and they performed their now accustomed tasks. Cynddylig looked into the sack of root vegetables.

"It will be good if we can re-stock some of our supplies tomorrow," he said.

"Oh, how are we going to do that?" September asked.

"We should reach another village, Glanyrafon, tomorrow. I know a few people there. I am sure they will help us. But you will have to be discreet. I don't want other people to know who you are."

"That's a bit difficult when I'm wearing this cloak all the time. As you said, it marks me out as someone special."

"Yes, well keep out of the way when we land and we'll think of something. I don't really want to stop and meet people, just in case we attract too much interest, but the Glanyrafon people are good folk. There won't be any stops after there."

After they had eaten, September spoke to the Mordeyrn through the horn. There was more to talk about this evening. She told him about their near disaster with the Gleisiad.

"Those vessels move at speed. We passed her only a few days ago."

"It's a shame I couldn't travel on a big, fast boat. I would have caught you up more quickly."

"I understand September, but unfortunately there are few vessels of the Gleisiad's class in Gwlad these days and none were available to help you."

September went on to tell him about Cynddylig's plan to stop off at the next village.

"Ah, tell him to take great care but I am sure it will be safe. We didn't stop at Glanyrafon but it is your last chance to pick up provisions for some time."

As September settled down she wondered how far they had travelled in the four days since they had left Amaethaderyn. Three days of travelling from dawn to dusk. Cynddylig was rather vague about distances and September couldn't gauge how fast their little boat moved, but it was considerably faster than walking pace. Two or three hundred kilometres perhaps. September knew there were many hundreds of kilometres still ahead of them.

15

She waited in the dark while the souls around her poured into the universe to perform their tasks of hate. Many were deflected by the planets moving in their orbits and flung back into the dark above the stars, but others reached their goal to bring disease and dissension or to stir the elemental forces to fight and destroy. Malice watched and waited. A path was opening up to the green-blue world at the centre of the sphere of stars that would allow her and the evil around her unimpeded access. She could be patient despite the anger and hate gnawing at her. Her time would come when she would control the actions of the Malevolence, direct them to the targets she chose and bring this world of tender goodness to its knees.

Malice had wondered what had brought her to this place. Her soul had not been created here, and she had no bond with the unthinking wraiths that vented their hate on the world within the stars, but now she understood. She had been drawn here by another to whom she was bound and who had an existence in both universes. This other was a wielder of power, power that she wanted for herself. Who or what the other was she had yet to discover but when her time came to enter the universe and wreak her vengeance, then she would know and all would learn to fear her.

Meanwhile, Malice waited and watched and learned and seethed with hate.

16

The next morning was bright, birds were singing in the trees, and although he wouldn't say when he expected them to reach the village, Cynddylig seemed eager. Perhaps it was another ladyfriend he expected to find, September wondered. Tudfwlch too seemed keen to visit a new place. The river was still much the same, a wide, green expanse of flowing water with tall trees along the banks. It was mid-afternoon when September noticed the same changes as she had noticed when they had approached Abercyflym. The trees on the south, left-hand bank thinned out and there were signs of agriculture, but much as she searched the clearings she could see no sign of people working on the land. The trees on the bank gave way to wooden buildings clustered around a short pier. Cynddylig steered towards the village and Tudfwlch stood in the bow grasping the rope. There was no one by the waterside and no call went out to show they had been seen.

"Is everyone in the fields?" September asked. Cynddylig didn't answer but slowed the boat down to bring her alongside the wooden jetty. Tudfwlch jumped off and tied the rope around a bollard, then reached out to help September out of the boat.

"I don't like this silence," Cynddylig said, pulling the tiller off the motor and stepping ashore with it in his hands.

"Neither do I," Tudfwlch agreed, reaching into the bow of the boat and lifting out his sword in its scabbard. He tucked it into the belt around his tunic.

"Shouldn't someone have noticed us by now?" September asked.

"Yes," Cynddylig said, "That's what worries me. Stay close."

They walked along the jetty to the bank. There was a row of a dozen small houses along the bank but a dusty street went inland from the end of the jetty. It too was lined with wooden shacks, with wooden doors and shuttered windows. They approached the corner house. Cynddylig went up to the door and rapped on it with the handle of the tiller. The sound echoed eerily. September realised that there was no noise at all. There were no birds in the sky or sitting on the roof-tops or pecking at the grit in the street. Just silence.

Cynddylig pushed on the door and it swung open. September looked into a living room with a table and stools. One of the stools was tipped over. There were plates and bowls and a jug on the table. Cynddylig stepped back into the street.

"Let's try somewhere else," he said.

They walked three abreast up the street, away from the river. Tudfwlch went and banged on the door of the next building. Again the sound disturbed the unnatural peace but there was no response. He opened the door and a similar sight confronted them; a table set for a meal but stools overturned and no sign of any occupants. The same was the case at the house opposite and the next and the next. In some there were signs of the owners' occupation, a loom, a carpenter's workbench, a cobbler's last, but no workers. All had left their tools behind. They moved slowly up the mud-paved street growing more agitated as they found home after home deserted and signs of a hurried departure. September began to notice a smell, a foetid, noxious odour which grew stronger the further they moved along the road.

They were approaching the last house in the street and then there was an open space with a low fence around it, a village green or meeting place. The smell had grown stronger and September covered her mouth and nose with her cloak.

"I think I can see the villagers," Cynddylig said, taking a few steps forward to the fence at the edge of the field.

"Where?" September asked, looking to the trees and bushes beyond the field.

"There." Cynddylig pointed into the field. With their khaki and beige clothes and covered with a thin layer of sandy dust September's eyes had not recognised the lumpy surface of the field for what it was – bodies, dozens of them. They stepped up to the fence but did not go further for fear of stepping on a body of a man, woman or child, each fallen where they had been struck down. September didn't want to look but her eyes were drawn from one to the next, each showing a huge bloody wound. Some had limbs or head almost severed from their bodies, others great gashes in their torsos. September felt sick, was sick. She retched, spilling her breakfast and lunch over the dusty grass. Tudfwlch placed an arm across her shoulder while Cynddylig crouched down.

"Who? How? Why?" September gasped between spitting the foul, acidic fluid from her mouth. She rubbed her hip. Her birthmark had started to itch.

"What brought them out here, all together?" Tudfwlch asked, "They must all have rushed from their houses at once."

"Someone must have raised the alarm and they all ran here, to their meeting place, to find out what was happening" Cynddylig said, "and then they must have been surrounded and slaughtered. They were dead before they knew what was happening."

"Why?" September repeated.

"There's no reason. Just the Adwyth. I told you it turns one man against another."

"But murder, a massacre? It must have been a gang of terrorists." September was still unable to fully grasp the horror that faced her. The itch had grown to an annoyance.

"No, they wouldn't have all left their homes and assembled here if they were being attacked by outsiders. People they knew lured them here."

A cry came from the trees to their right and a band of men and women came running towards them. They too were dressed in the typical clothes of the villagers.

"Oh, there are still some alive," September said.

"But we won't be if we don't leave." Tudfwlch shouted, "Run!"

September looked again and saw that each and every one of the villagers, fast approaching them, carried a weapon – a sickle, a machete, a short sword, a hammer. Their cries were not ones of welcome but of attack.

September turned to run with Tudfwlch and Cynddylig down the street towards the river. She took two steps and caught her feet in the low hem of the cloak. She tumbled to the ground. Tudfwlch turned back and grabbed her arm.

"Come on, they'll kill us without a thought," Cynddylig shouted, pausing in his flight. September gathered up the cloak around her waist and ran with Tudfwlch. They were halfway down the street, with the jetty and their little boat in sight, when another group of villagers appeared around the corner and ran up the street towards them. They too brandished weapons. September and her companions shuddered to a halt.

"We're going to have to fight," Tudfwlch said, drawing his sword.

"Aye, lad, it looks like it," Cynddylig placed a firm grip on the tiller.

"Should we go into a house?" September gasped, her heart racing.

"They'll have us trapped, if we go inside," Tudfwlch said. He dragged September into an alcove between two of the houses. Cynddylig and Tudfwlch stood side by side in the narrow gap facing onto the street.

The two bands of villagers joined up and with an incoherent roar launched themselves towards their targets. Just one or two at a time could attack swinging their weapons wildly with those behind pushing forward. Cynddylig fended off their blows with the long tiller while Tudfwlch cut and thrust with his sword. Each strike drew blood. The first two attackers fell but they were dragged aside and two more stepped over them to renew the assault. September cowered behind her pair of protectors stunned by the ferociousness of the attack. The faces were contorted into caricatures of humanity. They wailed and growled and screamed as their weapons rose and fell. The clash of iron on iron and the screams as the attackers were pierced by Tudfwlch's blade deafened and scared her. One after another was felled but their attackers just stamped over the fallen to take up the fight. Slowly, step by step Tudfwlch and Cynddylig were forced backwards. They were weakening, struggling to block the blows of the attackers.

It was as if a calm had settled on her. She no longer heard the screams and shouts. The flailing arms were just a blur. September realised that Tudfwlch and Cynddylig were protecting her yet she had the means of their defence. With Tudfwlch's broad shoulders pressing against her she struggled to reach inside her cloak. Her fingers found the locket and she drew it out. She undid the clasp revealing the starstone. She raised it up in her hand above the heads of her defenders. What could she say? She had no idea of spells or commands. There was just one thing she wanted.

"Be gone!"

Perhaps it was being in a narrow gap but the quality of her voice was changed, like singing in the bathroom. Instead of just a shout or scream, her voice resounded. Her words filled the air. A dome of blue light formed over the three of them and then expanded like the air bag in a car, inflating in an instant. Everything in its path – the buildings around them, the attackers – were blown away. There was a noise like a long roll of thunder directly overhead. September, Cynddylig and Tudfwlch fell to the ground in a heap of limbs.

Dust slowly settled on them and there was quiet. The three of them struggled to their feet and looked around. Everything in a circle around them as far as the waterfront was flattened. The beams and planks used to construct the buildings were broken into splinters. Amongst the ruins were the scattered bodies of their attackers, dismembered and bloody.

Cynddylig wiped a sleeve over his dusty face.

"Well! I'm a Cemegwr! That's some power you have there, lady," he said, "I think you should put it away now."

September noticed that her right hand was still gripping the stone. She closed the case and slid it back inside the cloak.

"I didn't know..." she said, not sure what she was trying to say. She had no plan so had no idea what would happen when the power of the Maengolauseren was unleashed against people.

"I am just thankful you did something," Tudfwlch said, "I don't think I had the energy to hold them all off."

"Let's get away from here," Cynddylig said, stepping gingerly across the debris and heading towards the jetty.

The boat bobbed on the river as if nothing had happened, but when they were aboard and looked back they could see a huge circle of destruction.

"What about all those bodies in the field?" September said.

"Nothing we can do," Cynddylig said, fitting the notched and scarred tiller back on the rudder, "We'll have to leave them to the birds and the worms." He reversed the boat away from the pier and turned upstream.

In a few minutes the ruins of Glanyrafon were out of sight. Despite the afternoon heat September shivered. She wrapped her arms around herself and hunched herself down amongst the sacks.

"What happened there?" she asked.

"The work of the Adwyth," Cynddylig replied.

"But how?"

"Some of the villagers, those that attacked us, fell under the evil influence and lured their fellows to their deaths."

"Why did they become evil?"

Cynddylig shrugged. "There are many ways that the Malevolence can get into a person's blood and turn them."

"Did you see the people you were expecting to meet?"

"Gwilym and Dona, my brother and his wife? No, they were not among the attackers."

"Your brother?"

"Yes. I haven't seen him or Dona for years. Won't now. I expect they're lying hacked to pieces in the meeting field. At least that's better than dying as a slave of the Malevolence."

September realised that the attackers were dead because of her.

"I killed all those people," she said.

"They would have killed us."

"Yes, but perhaps if I had known how to use the stone better I could have stopped them attacking us and got rid of the evil in them."

"No, lass. Once the evil is inside a person they change forever. Their mind is eaten away by the evil and they become an extension of the Adwyth. If anything, killing them saved them from themselves."

September wasn't totally convinced. "But why is it that I don't think to use the stone until I'm being attacked? You and Tudfwlch were fighting to protect me."

"I don't know how the power of the Maengolauseren works, lady. Perhaps it requires strong emotions before its power can be directed."

"The only emotion I have had so far when I have used it is fear."

"There you are. Perhaps the Mordeyrn and the Arsyllfa will help you control your emotions and thereby direct the Starstone to your bidding. I am just grateful that you used it today. I'm sure Tudfwlch is too."

September turned to face the bow. Tudfwlch had been silent since they had left the village.

"Tudfwlch, are you feeling alright?"

He turned slowly to answer. His face was pale and his clothes were splashed with blood. She thought that it was the blood of the attackers but then she saw that he was holding his right hand and blood was dripping from it.

"Oh, Tudfwlch. You're injured. Why didn't you say?"

"It's only a small cut in my hand. It's a bit sore. Worst thing is it's my sword hand."

"Lass, come and take the tiller. I've got some cloth somewhere that we can wind round Tudfwlch's hand to stop the bleeding."

September scrambled over the bags and barrels to take Cynddylig's place in the stern.

"Just hold her steady and pointed up the middle of the river," he said as she settled, nervously gripping the tiller in her right hand. Cynddylig crawled forward, pausing to open a bag and take out some cloth which he tore into strips. Tudfwlch offered his hand and Cynddylig bound it tightly with the cloth.

"There lad. That should stop the bleeding. You fought skillfully back there. Iorwerth has taught you how to wield a sword well." Tudfwlch produced a thin smile then returned to silently watching the water go by. Cynddylig scrambled back but took the seat on the right of the tiller.

"You carry on lass. You're holding her line well. Have you handled a boat in your world?"

"Not really. We had a day sailing with one of my uncles but he wouldn't let me steer. He probably thought I'd crash the boat. It's the sort of thing that usually happens to me." She was pretty useless at everything, September reflected, but here speeding along the river she felt different, more confident.

"Ah, well, I'll keep an eye on the engine while you keep us straight."

September was surprised how quickly the time passed while she was concentrating on holding the course of the boat. That and Cynddylig's tales of boats he had known and trips he had made kept her mind off the events at Glanyrafon. With the Sun dropping into the river, Cynddylig slowed the boat.

"I think this will be our berth for tonight," he said. "Steer into the left bank, lass." He pointed and September saw the patch of beach he was directing her towards. Quite confidently she steered the craft towards the shore. Just before they grounded, Tudfwlch raised himself, climbed over the side and waded through the water hauling the boat onto the shingle.

They made camp and September busied herself getting the wood for the fire as Tudfwlch seemed a little lethargic.

"Are you feeling okay, Tudfwlch?"

"Hand's a bit sore," he said. September felt there was more.

"You're worried about something." There was a pause before Tudfwlch spoke.

"Well, it's like this. I've never killed anyone before. Never used my sword to injure another person. I was scared September and I'm supposed to be protecting you." The memory of those desperate moments filled her mind, the evil ones pressing on them with blades slashing. She recalled Tudfwlch parrying the strikes and making every one of his thrusts count.

"You did protect me. You fought well. I'm very grateful."

"But, I can feel my sword slicing through flesh, the blood, the tissues spilling out. I'm not sure I can go through that again."

"I hope we don't have to, but you did what you needed to do." She recalled what Cynddylig had told her, "They weren't people anymore, Tudfwlch. As Cynddylig said, they were slaves of the Malevolence." Tudfwlch nodded in agreement and collected his bowl of steaming broth from Cynddylig.

They ate in silence coming to terms with the day's events.

September was relieved when the Mordeyrn called. She felt she needed to tell the story, to share it and distance herself from it. The Mordeyrn was appalled by her tale.

"I was worried that a single servant of the Malevolence in the village may have become aware of your presence but I had not anticipated a whole village being wiped out by the evil. I must congratulate you all on extricating yourselves from the situation."

"Cynddylig and Tudfwlch fought them off until I used the stone."

"Ah, yes, the stone. I know you had to use its power but it must have been like a beacon to the Malevolence. It will feel your presence in the Land and focus its forces on the region through which you are travelling. You must keep the stone hidden to avoid providing any more clues to your whereabouts."

"Oh, I will."

"I hope you can avoid any further encounters with the servants of evil. Tomorrow I will arrive at the Arsyllfa and there at last I will have the assistance and the resources to provide you with some guidance on your journey."

"Thank you, Aurddolen." September was not too sure what the Mordeyrn would be able to do from his observatory in the hills, hundreds of kilometres away.

"Cast away thoughts of today's events and sleep well."

Sleep well she didn't. All through the night she was troubled by visions of hordes of weapon waving villagers pressing on her and no sign of Cynddylig, Tudfwlch or anyone to help her. There was just a feeling of someone or something unseen watching her. At last when it was just turning light she heard Cynddylig stoking the fire and preparing breakfast. She struggled out of her sleeping bag and shivered in the cold morning air. Having dealt with her morning necessities, a ritual after a few days of living rough, she rubbed her birthmark which was still itching a little, then went to help Cynddylig. Tudfwlch was lying in his bed, still but moaning.

"Tudfwlch, it's time we were on our way," Cynddylig called. There was no reply. Cynddylig went and knelt by his side, "What's wrong lad?" Tudfwlch turned his face towards the older man.

"He looks feverish," Cynddylig said to September, "let's have a look at that hand." September joined him beside Tudfwlch as he drew his injured hand from within the sleeping bag. September could tell from the smell that things weren't right. Cynddylig unwound the bandage, unsticking it from the putrescent flesh.

"It only looked like a nick when I bound it yesterday," Cynddylig said angrily, "It's badly infected."

"What can you do?" September asked.

"We need arian, and the cludydd."

"Well, I have silver," September said, "it was Arianwen's gift, the silver locket and chain which holds the Starstone."

Cynddylig brightened.

"That's something. We don't have the words to invoke the power of Lleuad but the arian will do some good. But how do we use it without revealing the Maengolauseren?"

September thought for a moment then reached inside her cloak to the back of her neck and lifted the chain over her head. She held the locket and chain in one hand beneath the cloak and leaned over Tudfwlch. She took the yellow pus-ridden hand in hers, grimacing as she did so, and slid it inside her cloak. She wound the silver chain around the hand and pressed the locket to the wound.

"What do I do now?" she asked.

"I don't know. Hold it there and just imagine the hand healed I suppose."

September summoned up an image of Tudfwlch's young, smooth hands.

"I'll load the boat. You stay there." Cynddylig continued. He rose to his feet and busied himself with breaking camp. September found that to keep Tudfwlch's hand under her cloak she had to kneel awkwardly. Her back started to ache.

After what seemed like many minutes Cynddylig returned.

"Right, let's see what it looks like."

September loosened the chain and released Tudfwlch's hand. It slipped out of her cloak and she gasped. It was unmarked; there was no sign of infection, no sign of a wound at all.

"You're some healer," Cynddylig said, "Let's get him up

and on to the boat." They dragged the sleeping bag off Tudfwlch and helped him to his feet. He was still weak and groggy and leaned heavily on Cynddylig as they staggered to the boat. September replaced the locket around her neck then picked up Tudfwlch's belongings and followed behind.

The Sun was already above the trees in the east as they set off, with Tudfwlch slumped in the bow.

"Will he be better now?" September asked.

"I should think so. You've healed his hand, so I expect he will recover quickly."

17

The day passed slowly and the heat of the Sun was tiring. The scenery was unchanging and today there was no light-hearted chat from Tudfwlch. He remained slumped in the bow, occasionally muttering. Cynddylig allowed September to steer for a time while he made Tudfwlch swallow some water and got out some of their stored fruit and cheese for lunch. It was a sombre company that made camp that evening. Cynddylig and September helped Tudfwlch ashore and rested him on his sleeping bag, and then she collected the firewood while Cynddylig cooked supper. Tudfwlch had roused enough to eat the broth but then sank into a deep sleep.

September explained Tudfwlch's symptoms to Aurddolen when he called.

"It is worrying that he remained ill after you healed the wound. Some of the infection must have gone to his head. Let me know how he is tomorrow and I will get some advice on what you can do to help him."

"You have arrived at the Arsyllfa?"

"Yes. I am relieved that my journey is over and long for your arrival amongst us. We have much to do. Already I have had reports of how the power of the Malevolence is growing across the Land. We have need of your power, Cludydd."

September was rather embarrassed and nervous of his enthusiasm for her involvement. She still had little idea what she could do against the growing evil even now that she knew that her mother had defeated it once. She bade her farewells and settled down to sleep, her birthmark still irritating a little.

September was very relieved to find Tudfwlch much improved in the morning. If not back to his normal self, he was up and greeted her with some of his previous warmth.

Soon they were on their way, and they had not been travelling for more than a couple of hours when they approached another settlement. Cynddylig made no move to stop steering down the centre of the river. Some fishermen wading in the water close to the bank waved to them and others standing on the shore by a cluster of wooden huts also greeted them. September returned the waves.

"At least they seem unaffected by the Malevolence," Cynddylig said.

"We're all affected by the evil," Tudfwlch said in a gloomy voice.

"I don't know what you mean, Tudfwlch," September said. "Those people don't seem to be possessed by evil."

"Their time will come," Tudfwlch persisted.

"Now who is the pessimist!" Cynddylig said with a forced jollity. Tudfwlch didn't reply but returned to watching the water.

That evening September told the Mordeyrn that Tudfwlch seemed improved if a little subdued.

"Perhaps the reality of his responsibility has come upon him," Aurddolen replied, "he has had to use his skills with Haearn to protect you and it is a new experience for him."

The next day began much the same with the familiar chores of preparing breakfast, loading the boat and cleaning their campsite, followed by the monotony of the journey. How long has it been now, September wondered. She had difficulty working out how many days they had been on the river which meandered lazily through the vast forest. Was this the seventh or the eighth day since they left Amaethaderyn? Whatever, they were over a week into their journey, perhaps a third of the way to the Arsyllfa. Their food stocks were growing low.

They were on a straight stretch of the river. It seemed to vanish into the distant heat haze. The trees lining the bank were two parallel lines of green and brown meeting somewhere near infinity. As September stared ahead it seemed that there was something in the water ahead of them not quite blocking the way but certainly sticking out from the bank into the middle of the river, but it was still too distant to distinguish clearly.

"Can you see what it is?" September asked.

"My eyes aren't what they used to be," Cynddylig said, "but there's definitely some obstruction. Can you make it out Tudfwlch?"

Tudfwlch shrugged and said nothing.

"Is there a village here?" September suggested.

"No, nothing on this reach."

"Well, I wonder what it can be?"

"We'll find out soon enough, lass."

Minutes passed and the boat swiftly reduced the distance to the barrier.

"It's a boat," September cried, "a big barge, like the one we passed."

"What are the crew doing?" Cynddylig said, shaking his head.

September struggled to understand what she saw. "The back of it is very low in the water. It must be heavily loaded."

"It's not that, it's sunk," Tudfwlch said, in matter of fact voice, "it's been wrecked."

Now they were close enough to see details. The bow of the barge was driven up on to the bank, but it was listing and the stern was only just above the water level. Cynddylig slowed down to avoid approaching too close to the barge.

"I recognise that boat," Cynddylig said, excited, "it's the Dyfrgi. It called into Amaethaderyn a couple of days before you arrived. What has happened?"

Cynddylig held the boat motionless against the current as they examined the barge. There were great holes in the planking along the side. The roof over the cabin at the stern was charred, and the huge tiller was broken off and leaning against the stern.

Tudfwlch suddenly raised himself up in the bow and shouted.

"Anyone on board?"

"Quiet Tudfwlch, sit down," Cynddylig ordered turning their boat downstream.

September turned to speak to him and to carry on looking at the wreck.

"What's wrong Cynddylig? Why shouldn't Tudfwlch call

out?"

"Can't you see girl. The boat hasn't just run aground by accident. It's been wrecked. It must be the work of the Malevolence."

"But there might be people injured on board. We could help them."

"No, lass, it's no use any of us going on board. The crew are dead. Anyone left alive is a servant of evil. After what happened at Glanyrafon you can guess what it might be like inside."

September shuddered but wondered how the crew of the barge had met their fate.

"They were a lovely group of people," Cynddylig went on, "Men, women and children lived on board Dyfrgi, trading goods up and down the river. It was always a feast day when they called at Amaethaderyn." His voice tailed off sadly. Tudfwlch snorted, and September turned in time to catch a strange grimace of a smile on his face before he turned away from her.

"What are we going to do?" September asked.

"We've got to move on," Cynddylig said, "we'll have to pass her, but I'll keep as far away as possible." He pulled the tiller towards his chest and the boat resumed its course up the river. Cynddylig headed towards the left bank away from the hulk of the Dyfrgi which stretched over half way across the river. The current had grown stronger as the flow of the river was forced to divert around the wreck. The little boat struggled and their progress slowed.

As they crept nearer to the stern, September saw the boat's name written in large white letters across the wooden planking.

"What does Dyfrgi mean?" she asked.

"It's the name of an animal." Cynddylig replied.

"A fish?"

"No, it has four legs and lives on land, but swims and catches fish for its food. A lively, jolly creature."

September thought for a moment, and wondered.

"An otter?"

"I do not know what word you would have for it."

September continued to examine the barge. A movement

caught her eye.

"I saw something," she said, "Look there, by the tiller." A figure had appeared, a woman with long blonde hair, wearing a loose, white gown. The figure raised a hand pointing to them and called out. The voice came to September like a deep moan.

"Is it one of the crew?" she asked, "Perhaps they're hurt?"

"I told you, if they're alive we don't want to get close to them. Keep your hand on your stone, but keep it hidden – for now."

September moved her hand beneath her cloak grasping the locket. They were inching past the stern of the barge now, the fast flowing water splashing against the sides of their little craft. The figure was gazing down on them, appealing with her arms outstretched.

"Tudfwlch," Cynddylig called, "Stir yourself. Get your sword ready."

Tudfwlch didn't stir.

"Why? What could I possibly do?"

"What's the matter? What's happening?" September cried out. Cynddylig struggled to hold the tiller as the boat was hit by swirls and eddies.

"It's not a member of the crew. It's a Pwca!" Cynddylig gasped.

"A what?" September said, but as she looked the figure changed. It seemed to melt like a candle to take a new form. Where a moment before had stood a fair woman, now there was a black, long necked bird. It launched into the air from the stern of the barge and swooped towards them. It soared over their heads and dived into the river fifty metres ahead of them.

"It's gone," September said, relieved but the itch on her hip which had grown more painful, remained.

"No," Cynddylig cried, steering away from the point where the bird had disappeared.

A great fountain of water erupted and the huge head of a serpent rose out of the water. Its neck grew and grew. The head reared over them, its small eyes glowing red. A vast mouth opened revealing a forked tongue which flicked in and out between rows of needle-like teeth.

"Tudfwlch," Cynddylig appealed, but the young man cowered in the bow. The head lunged down at them. Cynddylig rammed the tiller over and the boat swung around. The serpent's head smashed into the water where the boat would have been. The muscles in the neck tensed and hauled the head up with water and mud pouring from its mouth.

"Cludydd, it's got to be you," Cynddylig cried. September awoke from her stunned gaze at the monstrous snake. She pulled the Maengolauseren from under the cloak, snapping the locket open as she did so. She stretched her arm out, holding the stone up as the serpent's head bore down on them again. I will destroy it, she thought.

The stone did nothing. The boat rocked violently as Cynddylig thrust the tiller over again. The serpent's head swooped over the bow of the boat just a couple of feet above Tudfwlch's head. He ducked.

"You could have had it then, Tudfwlch. Cursed Cemegwr!" Cynddylig called, "Where is your sword, warrior?"

The serpent was recovering for another attack while September stared at the stone in her outstretched hand. How could she make it work? What did she have to do? She remembered the faces of the evil villagers and her fear as they slashed at her companions, and she recalled what she had done to defeat the Ceffyl dwr after Eluned had tried to save her.

The eyes of the serpent were fixed on her as it prepared to strike again. September peered through the starstone at the fiendish head, its mouth wide and the snake-like tongue flickering at her. She could feel its furnace hot breath. The image of the serpent exploding in a ball of fire came into her head. That's what she wanted to happen.

A vivid blue beam flashed from the stone to the head of the serpent, blowing it apart in a ball of violet and yellow flame. The flames roared down the neck, vaporising the flesh instantly. A crash of thunder accompanied the dissipation of the monster.

The boat bucked as waves of hot air radiated outwards from the serpent's last position. The hot wind passed over them and the river was calm again. Cynddylig straightened the tiller and at full speed put as much distance as he could between them and the wreck of the Dyfrgi.

September sank into her seat amongst the sacks, taking deep breaths and still shaking.

"Well done, Cludydd. You have saved us again."

September rolled over to face him.

"What was that thing? What did you call it?"

"A Pwca. An air manifestation of the Adwyth. It can change its form at will, as the clouds can change."

"How did you know?"

"When the figure appeared on the stern of the Dyfrgi I realised it was not one of the crew or indeed any real person. It must have been something that could take on the form of a human; hence it must be a Pwca. Its fiery breath could have destroyed us, but the stone saved us."

"Yes, but I don't know why it didn't work straight away when I opened the locket. I thought, I've got the super weapon, all I have to do is point it and the monster will be destroyed, but it didn't happen," September said sadly.

"You hadn't found the command."

"Perhaps. I couldn't think what to do until I remembered you and Tudfwlch fighting the people and Eluned leaping to attack the water horse. I remembered the fear and the anger I'd felt then."

"There you are. You need the emotions and you need your companions to be there with you," Cynddylig raised his voice, "Tudfwlch, why didn't you fight?"

September turned towards the bow. Tudfwlch was curled up in his seat.

"What good would I be? I don't have the Maengolauseren to cast violet fire and destroy all monsters. All I have is a simple sword of Haearn."

"But, you do have power," September said, "you showed how good you were with the sword before."

"Aye lad. One slash of your blade would have severed the Pwca's neck. The energy in the haearn would have done the rest."

Tudfwlch grunted and buried his head in his arms. Cynddylig shook his head.

"I don't know what is wrong with the lad," he said quietly, "it's almost as if he's jealous of your power."

"It's not my power," September said, "The stone produces the fire to get rid of these monsters."

"Don't be modest. The stone draws energy from the heavens but you are the sluice gate that controls and directs it. In someone else's hands, who knows what it might do."

The rest of the journey that day was trouble-free, even boring. Tudfwlch remained sullen and morose in the bow refusing to converse with September. Cynddylig did allow September to steer for a time but that was the only thing that distracted her from her thoughts. She felt she needed to practise using the starstone, to understand how to wield its power. Five times now it had come to their rescue to save her and her companions from attack by the forces of the Malevolence, but she had little idea about what she had done. It seemed to be a mixture of strong emotions and powerful commands like "Be Gone" were needed but it all seemed rather random. With the fear of revealing herself yet again, she couldn't even take it out to examine and try out various ideas. She wondered how well Mother had mastered the stone. Could she have told her what to do? She had never had control of anything that was potentially harmful. Mother let her use the vacuum cleaner but she managed to get that clogged up with fluff. Why was she expected to handle the energy of the starstone? Surely there were people more suited to being heroes than her.

They moored at nightfall, made camp, bathed and ate the thin gruel that Cynddylig prepared eking out their diminishing stock of vegetables. Tudfwlch still remained aloof. Was he really jealous of her or merely embarrassed that he had not done more to fight the Pwca? September told the Mordeyrn all about it when he made his regular call. He was upset to hear of the destruction of the Dyfrgi but relieved that they were unhurt.

"Tudfwlch worries me. He is a fine young man, a warrior. He should be taking the lead when you meet your foes. Keep a watch on him."

As had become the normal routine, Tudfwlch was to take the first watch of the night. September settled down as usual but made sure she stayed awake for as long as she could.

Tudfwlch sat impassively not reacting to any of the occasional noises that disturbed the night.

Day after day passed with September both familiar and bored with the daily routine. They had another day of steady rain but otherwise the sky remained clear and sitting in the boat hour after hour was hot and uncomfortable. September was grateful for the shade that the cloak provided her. The river continued to meander through the tropical forest. They passed a few communities but Cynddylig refused to pull in despite getting anxious about their food supply. He didn't want people to meet September and he was wary of any more encounters with the servants or manifestations of the Malevolence. At least they could pick up some food whenever they stopped for the night. There were usually fruit or nut bearing trees near their campsite although as it was always nearly dark when they stopped it was difficult to forage. Tudfwlch seemed to improve but he remained withdrawn and less talkative than he had been at the start of their journey.

September came to admire Cynddylig more and more for his knowledge of the river and his skill at producing interesting food from the same ingredients day after day. But the daily repetition and the unchanging scenery were getting to September, as was the constant itch on her thigh. She had tried to keep track of the days. How many was it now, fourteen, fifteen, sixteen? She reckoned they must have travelled well over a thousand kilometres from Amaethaderyn, but the view did not seem to have altered a bit.

Then there was a change of routine. It was still mid-afternoon when Cynddylig steered the little craft towards a clearing on the bank.

"Are we stopping?" September asked.

"Yes," Cynddylig replied.

"Why? There are still a few hours to nightfall."

"This is the last mooring before we reach the great lake and we have to make a decision."

"I don't understand."

"I'll explain when we have made camp."

They pulled the boat onto the beach and unloaded all that they needed for the night stop. As there was still plenty of daylight, September and Tudfwlch went collecting oranges and nuts from the wild trees that grew in the forest. When they returned they found that Cynddylig had caught some fish and was preparing the meal.

September sat on the ground while Cynddylig worked.

"What is the decision we have to make?" she asked.

"The river enters Llyn Pysgod on the west side of the lake. The lake is large and is home to many people because of all the fish that live in it. Hence its name, Lake of Fish. If we travel around the edge of the lake it will take us four or five days to reach the river again and we will not be able to avoid passing through quite a few communities. Alternatively we can set off straight across the lake. At full speed it will take us a day and half including travelling throughout the night. We will not be able to stop to eat or sleep. The lake is deep in parts and if a storm should blow up we could be in danger."

"But it cuts a couple of days off the journey to go straight across."

"That's right."

"How do we find our way in the middle of a lake at night?"

"We follow the stars."

"Well, I don't think there is anything to discuss," September said, relishing the change of routine, "we head straight across."

"I thought you would say that. What about you Tudfwlch?"

Tudfwlch looked up from his bed where he had been lying, apparently not caring to listen to the conversation. He shrugged but didn't reply.

"Seems he hasn't got an opinion," Cynddylig said, "So, we eat well now, sleep, collect firewood and get on the river at dawn. Then we should be able to moor in the gorge by nightfall the day after tomorrow."

They did as Cynddylig suggested and the Mordeyrn backed up the decision to head across the lake. September settled to sleep but was excited. At last there would be a change, something different to see. Despite the dangers Cynddylig had warned of she was eager to set off again.

18

They were surrounded by water; no land in sight except for a thin grey line on the western horizon and that had been there since they entered the lake. September was aware of how small their boat really was as waves broke over the sides soaking their bags. Cynddylig held the tiller firm, maintaining a line with the Sun directly behind them. It hardly seemed that they had only been travelling for a couple of hours.

Cynddylig had got September out of her sleeping bag while it was still dark. They had eaten and loaded the boat before the morning's first light. A short while later, less than an hour, September reckoned, with the Sun only just rising above the trees behind them, a final bend in the river had taken them out into the lake. The shore had quickly disappeared to the north and south. Cynddylig directed the boat out into the empty waters. It could have been an ocean rather than a lake. The far horizon was a grey line that may have been haze or their destination. Tudfwlch had settled morosely amongst the bags in the bow and September tried to make herself more comfortable amongst the sacks and barrels, but the boat was rocking from side to side in an unfamiliar manner. Without the protection of the tall trees they were exposed to the wind that blew from the south-west. At first it just seemed gentle and cooling as the Sun rose in a clear sky, but gradually September realised that the wind was creating the waves that broke over the side of the boat.

Now she and Cynddylig were looking anxiously at the sky. The Sun was no longer a bright orb in clear blue. Instead it glowed dimly from overcast cloud and the wind had grown in strength.

"I fear luck is not with us," Cynddylig called as another wave topped the side of the boat and soaked September's thighs. She was grateful that the cloak kept water off her as well as the rays of the Sun.

"Will it get worse?" she shouted over the moan of the wind and the crashing of the waves.

"Before it gets better, yes. Even if we don't have to face a full storm there is at least a squall on its way."

"What can I do?"

"Stay as low as you can, but bale out the water that's coming aboard."

September piled up the sacks around her to raise the sides of the boat and found the cooking pot. She started scooping up the water that was pooling in the bottom of the hull. Tudfwlch too, used a bucket to remove the water. At least the activity took her mind off the rocking of the boat that had been making her feel queasy.

The sky darkened until the sun was no longer visible at all, and the wind grew stronger. Cynddylig had both arms wrapped around the tiller ensuring that the gold powered engine noiselessly propelled them into the waves that were breaking viciously over the bow. September and Tudfwlch baled faster.

Then the rain came. Great huge drops of cold water, falling from the dark grey sky. They hammered on September's head and rivulets of water ran down the cloak into her lap, dribbling inside to soak her tunic and trousers. The boat was rapidly filling and as fast as she filled her pot so more water ran into the bottom of the boat. There was nothing to see to the left, right, forward or behind and she had no idea whether they were still moving forwards or backwards or in circles.

Tudfwlch crawled over the bags and barrels towards her.

"If you were really the Cludydd o Maengolauseren, you would do something," he shouted over the roar of the wind and rain.

"What do you mean?"

"The stone can command the weather."

"Do you mean this storm is caused by the Malevolence?"

"Maybe, maybe not, but the bearer of the stone has power over nature."

"I don't know what to do?"

Tudfwlch was in front of her, their faces barely centimetres apart. His eyes glowed with a strange light and his mouth was twisted into an unusual grimace. September tried to push herself away from him.

"What are you doing, Tudfwlch? You need to keep baling," Cynddylig shouted over the noise of the storm."

"You don't know anything, do you," Tudfwlch sneered at September, "You're not the seventh child of the Cludydd Breuddwyd. You don't deserve to bear the stone." He grabbed her arm.

"What do you mean, Tudfwlch? Get off me."

"Give me the stone. I will show you what I can do with it." He lunged forward, pushing her onto her back. She fought to get up but was caught amongst the bags and sacks.

"I want it," Tudfwlch screamed. His hand reached inside her cloak. September felt his cold, wet hand groping between her breasts. She struggled to get free but Tudfwlch was pressing down on her. She felt his fingers grip the pendant. He tugged and the silver chain snapped.

"I have it," Tudfwlch's cry pierced the roar of the storm, "Now the Adwyth cannot be defeated." He raised himself up, and held the silver locket bearing the Maengolauseren in his upraised hand. September found herself free to move again. There was something pressing against her side. Her hand investigated. It was the knife that she carried fastened to her belt. She slid it out of its scabbard.

"Give the stone back to me," she appealed to Tudfwlch.

"Never! Its power is mine now," he snarled, his eyes glowing red. The stone remained unlit. Tudfwlch looked at it then thrust it up again towards the sky.

"I am the cludydd now," he shouted above the roar of the storm.

September pulled her hand from under her cloak and punched upwards. The knife of Haearn, crafted by Iorwerth and imbued with the power of Mawrth, slid through the threads of Tudfwlch's tunic and pierced his abdomen. A look of shock passed across his face, he looked down at the handle of the blade, still held by September's hand, thrust into his side. September bent her arm and the knife slipped out. The red light in Tudfwlch's eyes dulled as blood poured from the wound, running down his thigh to mix with the rain and the pool of water in the hull of the boat; and then he toppled sideways. The boat rolled over a wave and Tudfwlch fell overboard. The Maengolauseren fell from his weakening grasp as he hit the water and sank out of sight.

"No! No!" September screamed, "Cynddylig stop the boat." She had no idea whether Cynddylig obeyed her or was already reacting but she felt the motion of the boat change. Now they were at the mercy of the waves. The boat rolled and yawed violently. September looked over the side but Tudfwlch had disappeared as indeed had the stone in its silver casing.

September sobbed, "What have I done?"

"You had no choice," Cynddylig called through the wind and rain, "Tudfwlch was possessed by the Malevolence." Almost as he spoke the storm seemed to pass over. The wind died away and the rain faded to drizzle. The boat's motions settled. September sank into the bottom of the boat, crying. Everything had gone wrong; she had lost the starstone and killed her friend. Her body shook and tears filled her eyes as she saw again the last crazed look on Tudfwlch's face as he tore the locket from her and what she had done to him. The knife was still in her hand. She dropped it and it clattered amongst the spars at the bottom of the boat.

"Cludydd! Cludydd! By the Cemegwr!" Cynddylig's calls penetrated her self-pity.

"What?"

"Get up. You must find the Maengolauseren."

September sat up and peered through tear-filled eyes. The clouds were clearing, the Sun was already shining and the wind had dropped to a drying, warm breeze.

"How can I find it? Tudfwlch dropped it in the lake when he fell." Another bout of shoulder-shaking sobbing took hold of her.

"Of course you can find it. You are linked to the stone. It will find you if you search."

"Do you mean it?"

"Of course."

Perhaps the stone wasn't lost for good. Perhaps it would rise into her hands if she just got into the water. She stood up and took the cloak off; after all, there was nothing to hide anymore. She removed her belt and the sopping wet tunic and trousers and kicked off her sandals. She stood up straight, naked, suddenly aware that Cynddylig could see her. She turned to look at him. He was watching her but not with a leery look.

"I know what you are thinking, young lady. I have seen a naked young woman before, many times, but my years of yearning are over."

She realised how silly it was to feel modest at this desperate time. She held her nose in her right hand, put a foot on the side of the boat and stepped into the lake. The water of the lake enveloped her. She kicked her feet, not touching the bottom, and then she was rising back to the surface. Her eyes opened; the hull of the boat was nearby. She broke the surface and shook her head to clear her ears and nose. The water was colder than the river had been but not uncomfortable. She looked around. Apart from the boat and Cynddylig sitting anxiously in the stern there was nothing else to see. There was no sign of Tudfwlch and certainly no sign of the stone and its silver chain.

September had never been a strong swimmer and she had always hated being under water. She had floated easily enough; her fat acted as a buoyancy ring. Now she felt different, determined, unafraid of the depth of water beneath her. She took a deep breath and dived. The water was murky and visibility quickly dropped. She kicked her legs to push herself deeper but the pressure of the water pushed her back to the surface. She broke into air again and clung on to the side of the boat, breathing deeply.

"I can't reach the bottom."

"The lake's a good ten arms' reaches deep," Cynddylig said stretching his arms wide to demonstrate. That's about twenty metres or more, September calculated; I can't dive that far.

"What can I do? The stone must have sunk to the bottom."

"It will find you."

"Yes, but it can't move on its own. I've got to get to it." She hung onto the boat, "Help me get on board please, Cynddylig."

He got up from his seat and came to the side of the boat. He placed his hands under her armpits. She saw the muscles

177

in his thin, leathery arms tighten and he hauled her up. She hooked a leg over the side and pushed herself upright. They stood in the boat with her dripping breasts rubbing against his tunic. He looked down at her.

"What's that you have around your neck?"

She lifted her hand to feel and found the phial that Eluned had given her. It had been there alongside the Maengolauseren for over a fortnight and she'd barely thought about it.

"Eluned gave it to me. It contains mercury."

"Arianbyw."

"She said that although I couldn't change into another animal like she can, it would change me and any material in any way that I wished."

Cynddylig released her and September sat amongst the drying bags. The old boatman returned to his seat by the tiller.

"Perhaps it could help you now."

"I don't know. To reach the bottom of the lake I'll need to be able to push myself down."

"You'll have to hold your breath a long time."

"I need to be a mermaid, don't I?"

September had an image of her lower body turned into the silvery body of a fish. Anything you wish, Eluned had said. Well, it was worth a go. She stood up and searched for the metal cloak. She found it and wrapped it around her middle.

"What are you doing?" Cynddylig asked.

"Trying something."

The cloak hung like a long skirt from her waist and folds of the metal cloth covered her feet. She took the phial from around her neck and loosened the tiny cork. She held the small crystal bottle at her waist and carefully tipped it. A drop of silver liquid formed at the spout and fell onto the metal cloth. It broke into tiny spheres that ran over the metallic threads then disappeared. She closed her eyes and summoned up the image of herself as a mermaid. Cynddylig gasped and she felt the cloak tighten around her legs and hips. Her feet felt strange and she half fell, half sank onto the baggage.

"I don't know how it happened, but something has,"

Cynddylig said. September opened her eyes and looked down at herself. The cloak had certainly changed. Now her lower half was encased in smooth silver which ended with a broad fin covering her feet. She put the stopper back into the phial and replaced it around her neck.

"I'm not sure how long this will last or even whether it will work," she said hauling herself to the side of the boat, "but I'll give it a try." She filled her lungs with air and slipped into the water.

With a flick of her tail she dived, descending rapidly. There seemed to be no pain in her chest as she held her breath and she felt no panic. The water grew dark and cold but still she dived, her eyes open, searching for the bottom. She started to circle as she descended, extending her search.

The light appeared before she saw the dark, muddy bottom of the lake. It was a tiny pinprick of blue, deeper still and some distance to her right. Without hesitation she swam towards it. The light grew in intensity illuminating the surrounding silt. There were creatures down here, a starfish, a crab, a few small fish, curious about the strange glowing object. Now she was full of joy. She reached for it and picked up the silver locket and chain and its glowing stone. With the pendant held firmly in her hand she waved her tail and turned upwards. She rose like a bubble in a bottle of lemonade, faster and faster until she broke the surface. The boat was a few metres away. Cynddylig was sitting in the stern, his arm around the tiller and staring intently into the water.

"I have it," she cried joyfully, waving her arms. She swam smoothly to the boat. As Cynddylig leant down to grab her, a shiver passed down her spine and she felt different. She had feet again and her silver skin had become the metal cloak which dragged in the water. Cynddylig hauled her on to the boat and hugged her.

"You were gone so long, I was worried,"

"So long? It hardly seemed a minute. I had no difficulty holding my breath."

"You were gone for many, many heartbeats. I do not know how you didn't drown. Eluned's powers are evidently strong."

"Yes, Eluned has saved me again. Look, I have the stone.

You were right; it was signalling to me." She opened her hand. The stone no longer glowed and was hidden inside its casing. "But the chain is broken."

"Let me see. I have some tools for looking after our engine, which may be of use."

They sat together in the middle of the boat, the locket firmly in September's hand while Cynddylig used a small pair of pliers taken from a leather wallet to mend the broken links of the chain. In moments he had it fixed and September gratefully hung it round her neck.

"Now my girl, we must move. We don't want to spend two nights on the lake." Cynddylig moved to the stern and took hold of the tiller. Silently the boat slipped through the water with the Sun now overhead in a cloudless sky. September dressed herself in her clothes which had dried and wrapped the cloak around herself. Then she sat in her usual seat. Her discarded knife lay in the hull. She picked it up and looked at it then she looked ahead. The bow was empty. The memory of what had happened returned and she put her head on her knees and cried.

"What's the matter?" Cynddylig asked.

"I killed Tudfwlch," she cried, turning her tear stained face to the stern, and waving the knife at Cynddylig, "He was my friend and I killed him."

"It wasn't your friend. It wasn't the Tudfwlch you knew," Cynddylig said sternly, "I should have recognised the signs, the change of personality, the misery, the defeatism, the unwillingness to help. He had become a servant of the Adwyth."

"But did I have to kill him?"

"Yes. It was lucky you had a blade of Haearn to hand. If you hadn't killed him he would have done for you and me."

"But how did it happen? How could he become evil? He wanted to help me so much."

"He did and that's the Tudfwlch we must recall. It must have been the cut on his hand. We thought the arian had healed it but the evil must have got inside. He wasn't the same after Glanyrafon was he?"

"No, you're right. First he was sick, then he seemed, well, different."

"The power of the Malevolence was growing inside him, like a maggot in an apple, destroying him and taking over his body."

"Couldn't we have done something?"

"Well, I've seen enough evil in my time and after what happened to the people of Glanyrafon I should have recognised the changes that were taking place in him; but, no, there was nothing we could do. We would have had to confront him sooner or later."

September grasped the Maengolauseren in her hand and thrust it out from its hiding place beneath the folds of the cloak. She cried out.

"What about this? Couldn't this magic stone have got rid of the evil in him?"

"I don't know lass. I don't know of any way of drawing evil out of a person once it's inside them but I don't know what powers that stone has."

September sank back into the boat, still shaking.

"Just remember, Cludydd, that despite what happened, Tudfwlch himself would rather have died than let you come to harm or allow the Maengolauseren to fall within the powers of the Adwyth. If anything you put what was left of him out of his misery."

September returned the knife to its scabbard on the belt at her waist. She realised the irritation in her side had stopped. The boat powered onwards, cutting through the calm waters smoothly and swiftly. The Sun, past its zenith, now pointed the way ahead, but still there was no sign of their destination. The waters of the lake surrounded them with no hint of land in any direction nor were there any other vessels in sight.

"Is the lake always this deserted?" September asked.

"Now, yes, but in the past no. When I was making frequent trips, Llyn Pysgod was a busy place. Many boats made the journey across it and there were boats moving from one community to another on its banks and the fishermen would cast their nets all across it. Now the people keep to the edges and the trading boats are few in number."

"All because of the Malevolence?"

"Yes. As we've seen already, the evil troubles everyone even if they have not been attacked by manifestations. The breakdown of trust sets each community apart."

"Do you think this evil can be beaten?"

"I don't know lass. The Malevolence has grown so strong and will become more powerful yet. I do not know if the people have the strength to withstand it."

"And what about me? When we set off you said you didn't know whether I would be of any help."

"I still don't know, girl," Cynddylig said gruffly, "I'm sorry, I wish I did. I have never been taught all the tales as Tudfwlch was and I've never been convinced that the goodness of the people was a strong enough defence against the evil. Not even the Cemegwr, if they exist, have opposed the evil. While the seasons went round, year after year, I couldn't accept that the growing power of the Malevolence could be defeated as it has been before by the appearance of the Cludydd o Maengolauseren," his voice softened, "but over the last couple of weeks I have learned that you do have power, that the stone can defeat the servants of the Adwyth. Whether it will be enough to drive the evil off the Earth and back above the sphere of stars, I don't know. But lass, you have brought hope and that is important in itself."

September had listened to this speech feeling wretched and disconsolate, but his final words cheered her somewhat.

"Thank you, Cynddylig. I hope that when we are with the Mordeyrn again, he will be able to show me what I have to do."

"Let us hope so, Cludydd."

They sailed on, as far as September could tell, in a straight line. The Sun sank below the horizon ahead of them and the sky quickly turned from blue, to violet then black. She lay back in the boat and looked up. Soon her eyes grew accustomed to the dark and she marvelled at what she could see. Camping each night beneath the trees had given little opportunity to look up at the night sky, but out here on the centre of the lake there was nothing between her and the universe. She felt that she was surrounded by a great dome of stars. She had never seen so many, had never been anywhere at night so free of light pollution. Astronomy had not interested her so she had never learnt the constellations, but she did recognise the Plough, up there on her right in the northern sky.

"It's wonderful," she sighed.

"Aye, it is lass."

"You can keep us on course by following the stars?"

"I hope so."

"You know the stars?"

"Well some. You don't need a guide to navigate the river, but from time to time I crossed Llyn Pysgod at night so I've learned how to maintain our direction. I keep the Seren Gogledd to our right."

"Seren Gogledd?"

"The star in the north that does not move."

"Oh, I think that's called the Pole Star."

Cynddylig pointed to it and explained how to find it using the pattern of stars that she knew as the Plough. September recalled something she heard at school.

"It's right over the North Pole so seems to keep still while the Earth turns."

"What do you mean the Earth turns?" Cynddylig said, "The Earth is motionless and the sphere of stars revolves around us."

September recalled something similar said by the Mordeyrn on her first visit.

"Oh yes, you think the Sun, Moon, planets and all the stars orbit around the Earth and that's all there is in the universe."

"Of course, how else can it be?"

"And what is beyond the stars?"

"The realm of the Malevolence, from which all evil comes."

"And where the unborn go, is that what someone told me?"

"So they say, I don't know."

September shook her head. The beliefs of the people in the Land were completely at odds with what her teachers had painstakingly drummed into her. It still confused her. At home the Earth was just an insignificant speck in a vast, unfeeling universe while here it was the centre of a small and threatened enclave of good. At home there were no monsters, nor magic stones and spells that could turn her into a mermaid when she needed it, but here there were. At home her twin sister had simply been stillborn; here she may still exist amongst the stars in some evil guise. A thought came into her head.

"What about those that have lived. What happens when they die?"

"Their goodness sinks into the Earth to be reborn in new life."

"And what about the evil things? What happens to them when they have been killed?"

"They are of the Adwyth."

"So are they dead?" September felt a sudden shiver, "Is Tudfwlch really dead?"

"Is evil ever truly destroyed? I don't know. As for Tudfwlch... well the boy you knew has gone, and what was left did the Malevolence's bidding; I don't know much more than that. Your blow with the knife was enough to kill a man. He sank into the depths and neither of us saw him again. He should be gone."

September was not convinced by Cynddylig's reasoning and neither, she thought, was Cynddylig himself. The air had grown cool now that night was upon them.

"Come next to me," Cynddylig called, "we can keep each other warm." September crawled over the bag to sit next to the old man with the tiller between them. He placed his right arm around her shoulders pulling her against him while placing his left hand on the tiller.

"Thank you, Cynddylig."

"What for lass?"

"For looking after me."

"I should be thanking you. You've saved my life enough times in the last weeks."

Later, they shared some fruit and nuts and water from their barrel. September took the copper horn from her pouch and placed it to her ear. She blew into it softly and very quickly the Mordeyrn's voice came to her. As she told him of Tudfwlch's attack her eyes filled with tears and once again she felt remorse and loss. She sobbed through her account of driving her knife into him and his fall into the lake. Aurddolen was sympathetic.

"I am sorry, Cludydd. My guidance has been wanting. I too should have recognised the signs in what you have told me about Tudfwlch's manner but even I, who should know so much, have been surprised by the rise in power of the Malevolence. I did not think that someone with Tudfwlch's training and desire could so quickly fall into evil. Now I wish I had waited in Amaethaderyn for your arrival so that we could journey together, but I am weakened and of course I did not know when you would reappear."

"I wish you were here too, but Cynddylig has supported me a lot."

"I thought he would prove to be a strong companion as well as an able guide, but tell me what happened after you fought off Tudfwlch's attack."

September recounted the loss of the Maengolauseren and her successful search for it aided by Eluned's mercury. The Mordeyrn was surprised and complimentary about September's resourcefulness.

"It was Eluned's spell," she said.

"Nevertheless, you have shown remarkable prowess in making use of it," he insisted. He wished her a quiet night on the calm waters of the lake and she put the horn away. She settled amongst the sacks with her warm sleeping bag draped loosely over her and the gentle rocking of the boat soon lulled her to sleep.

She awoke to find it still dark, the stars still shining overhead. She looked towards the stern. Cynddylig sat at the tiller impassive. Beyond him, away in the east, just above the horizon hung a crescent moon. Cynddylig saw her gazing.

"Ah, you are awake. Come and take the tiller, while I get some relief." September crawled to the back of the boat while Cynddylig moved carefully to the side and knelt on the gunwale. "Thank you, September. It won't be long before daylight now."

"Are we on course?"

"I hope so."

"I don't really know where we are going except we have to find the river on the other side of the lake."

"Ah, you will shortly see one of the wonders of Gwlad. The great wall of Clogwyn Llwyd Uchel"

"A wall? Clog...what?"

"The great grey cliffs. You'll see."

"But how will we be able to carry on if there are cliffs ahead?"

"The river has carved our passage – Hafn Afon Deheuol – a great cleft in the rocks."

It sounded like a sight worth travelling to see, but when the Sun crept into the sky behind them, they were still completely surrounded by water with only a distant haze on the horizon. They ate fruit and nuts again for breakfast and drank fresh water. September washed herself as best she could using the water from the lake.

"Will we get there in daylight?"

"We must; I daren't try to enter the gorge in the dark."

"Will we do it?"

"If we do not suffer any more bad weather or delays, then I think we should."

While the Sun passed over their heads, September lay in the middle of the boat, occasionally taking the tiller while Cynddylig stretched. She could tell he was getting tired but only he could steer the boat in a straight course across the featureless water. Around noon September realised that the grey line on the horizon ahead of them had grown a little. She watched in fascination as minute by minute, hour by hour, it grew from a line into a band and finally took on the form of a cliff. They were still hours away and September began to realise how the cliffs had got their name. She had once been on a ferry across the English Channel and had stared at the white cliffs in wonder. Those were nothing in comparison she now realised. Late in the afternoon when they were still kilometres away from land, the grey cliffs reared over them. They must be a thousand metres high, September thought, vertical cliffs rising directly out of the water and stretching for hundreds if not thousands of kilometres north and south. She realised that Cynddylig was peering anxiously in each direction along the immense grey wall.

"Can you see the gorge, September? My eyes are not what they once were." September joined in the search. The grey cliffs seemed almost featureless, almost as if they were an immense slab of concrete. But there, was that it? A vertical line, slightly darker than the rest of the cliff. She stood up, and pointed excitedly a few degrees to the left of their present course.

"There, is that it? Do you see it, Cynddylig?" He aimed the boat in the direction she pointed to. Minutes passed before he nodded. He looked up at the Sun, a few hand widths above the cliff.

"Well done lass. If the Sun had been just a little lower the shadow would have obscured it. We should be safely ashore for nightfall."

They drew closer and closer to the cliffs. So intimidating had their height become that they seemed to topple right over them. September knew it was an illusion but it gave her an uncomfortable feeling nevertheless. The thin crack opened up to become an alleyway, then a corridor into the cliffs. The boat was buffeted by the current of the river water pouring from the gorge. It wasn't a broad waterway, no more than ten of their boat lengths wide, but it carried a huge volume of water. The little boat shuddered as its magical motor struggled to make headway.

The great jaws of the gorge opened on either side of them as Cynddylig aimed for the centre of the gap. September leaned back and craned her neck to see the top of the cliffs but it was an impossible task. Now that the cliff face was close she could see that it wasn't completely smooth. There were small crevices and overhangs, places where a gull could land if not actually make a nest, and she could see birds wheeling in the air and diving into the water for fish.

Then they were inside the gorge and the jaws seemed to close behind them. The river filled the bottom of the gorge with the cliffs rising vertically from the water on either side.

"How are we going to land?" she called.

"Don't worry; it's not as forbidding as it looks."

The first few hundred metres of the gorge were straight as if cleaved by a gigantic axe. The river flowed swiftly past them. Then ahead, with the light fading as the Sun sank below the cliff top far above them, September saw a bend in the river. On the far side the waves broke against the cliff walls but on the near side there was a small promontory.

Cynddylig directed the boat into the side.

"Get the rope, girl. You'll have to jump ashore and hold the boat while I make her fast." September crept to the bow, the trailing hem of the cloak getting under her feet. She found the rope, hitched the cloak up around her waist and stood with one foot on the bow, waiting for the moment. The flow of water was less here, shielded by the bend, and Cynddylig manoeuvred the boat skilfully. September saw a small platform in the cliff, a metre above the water level.

"There you are, lass. Jump!" September leapt. She staggered and slid for a moment as her sandals found a grip on the small flat area of rock. With her feet steady she leaned back against the cliff wall and hauled on the rope. Cynddylig brought the stern in gently and hopped onto the landing with the stern rope.

"You'll find rings in the rock," he said. September looked behind her and, sure enough, there was a black, iron ring hanging from a spike driven into the rock. She tied the rope to it while Cynddylig did the same with a similar ring.

"There," he sighed, "we've made it. And just in time too." Almost like switching off a light, the shadow fell over them and it was dark. They unloaded what they needed from the boat to make their campsite on the small, flat area of rock. Now September realised why they had loaded firewood on to the boat at their last camp. There were no trees in the gorge. While collecting bags, September discovered Tudfwlch's short sword in its scabbard lying discarded in the bottom of the boat.

"What should we do with this?" she asked, holding it up for Cynddylig to see.

"Keep it for now, and perhaps return it to Cludydd Iorwerth if the occasion arises. You may have need of a larger blade than your knife."

They soon had a small fire lit and September was grateful for Cynddylig's cookery after two days without hot food. But after they had eaten, Cynddylig looked exhausted.

"You need to sleep, Cynddylig," she said, "I'll keep watch."

"Thank you, Cludydd. I am in need of rest but please wake me if anything troubles you." He settled into his sleeping bag and was soon snoring softly. September wrapped herself in her cloak and sleeping bag and sat with her back resting against the cliff. It wasn't particularly comfortable but she needed to stay awake. She looked up. Most of her view was of the rearing bulk of the cliff, but directly above was a slice of star-filled night sky.

A soft horn note had her fumbling for her leather pouch. She was grateful for the contact with Aurddolen – another means of keeping her awake. He was very thankful they had managed to have a successful day and were safely moored in the gorge.

"Despite the flow of the river, you should reach the twin towns in two or three days. I am wary of announcing your arrival, but I shall send guides to escort you from there into the hills."

"I am looking forward to that."

"I am worried that with the Malevolence growing so powerful, you may face further trials. Even with the cloak masking your presence, the occasions when the Maengolauseren has been exposed have been beacons of your progress. The evil may be drawn to your route but I have no power to protect you."

The Mordeyrn's words worried September. Even with the starstone to defend them the threat of attacks by monsters scared her.

"May you travel safely," the Mordeyrn said in farewell.

September put the horn away and sat gripping the locket under her cloak in one hand. She thought for a moment then took the scabbard of Tudfwlch's sword and fitted it onto her leather belt. Then she sat again against the cliff with the stone in one hand and Tudfwlch's sword in the other.

The night seemed to last forever although September was not certain she had been awake the whole time. It was still dark when Cynddylig stirred. He yawned and stretched.

"Ah, that's better," he said. He glanced up at the sliver of night sky, "There are still a couple of hours of night left. You get some sleep, lass."

September wondered whether she would drop off having struggled to remain awake, but in a few moments she was unaware of the hard rock beneath her.

Sounds of movement and the boat bumping against the rock awoke her. It still seemed dark under the cliff but as she opened her eyes she saw twinkles of sunlight reflecting off the ripples in the river and overhead the splinter of sky was a light blue. Cynddylig was loading the boat.

"Good morning, lass," he said cheerfully, "time to be moving."

September rubbed her tired eyes and got up. Quickly, she prepared herself for the day's journey and soon she was untying the rope, stepping into the bow and pushing off from the rock. Cynddylig pulled out into the stream and September looked back to the thin shaft of light that marked the entrance to the gorge and the Sun just above the distant horizon. Then they turned the bend and were back into dark shadow.

The gorge zigged and zagged like a crack in glass. Each 'zig' was several hundred metres long and almost the whole time they seemed to be in a shadow cast by the left or right wall of the gorge. At each bend the river crashed against the rocks as the water was forced to change direction, and the flow of water kept their speed below what September had become accustomed to. The sound of the water was a constant undertone to their travel. There was no other noise, but whenever one of them spoke their voice echoed off the walls of the gorge. They saw no other boats and there were no communities as there was no land. September found the day's journey in the depths of the gorge sinister. She felt trapped and worried that there was nowhere to escape from the river and the immense cliffs. There were however more of the small landing stages cut into the vertical bank at intervals along the gorge, and when the sunlight disappeared from the bottom of the gorge Cynddylig made for one such spot.

They camped and prepared their evening meal quietly. September almost felt afraid to disturb the intimidating atmosphere of the gorge with their reverberating voices. When the Mordeyrn called, he was relieved that they had experienced an uneventful day but he sympathised with her feeling of unease in the deep canyon.

"Hafn Afon Deheuol is a mysterious place," he agreed, "Few birds can find a secure perch on its smooth vertical walls and the river in flood scours the sides of the gorge of all vegetation. But you approach the end of your journey by water, and Dwytrefrhaedr has a very different atmosphere."

"I'm looking forward to seeing people again." As she spoke the words September saw again the crowd of evil-maddened people at Glanyrafon and Tudfwlch with the same red staring eyes. It was good, happy people she hoped to meet, not more of those invaded by the Malevolence.

19

The time had come for her to leave the dark and enter the universe of light. She swept through the slowly spinning sphere of glowing orbs and on towards the world at the centre. She avoided the planets swinging along on their orbits as they still had the gravity to pull her from her goal, and even at a distance she felt the goodness emanating from them and was disgusted. She commanded the lost souls to accompany her and they pressed on towards their destination.

Her plans were made. She knew what there was to be done. The one with whom she was connected bore a jewel of such power that it threatened her victory. It would be hers and the bearer destroyed. Then all the universe of light would be hers to control and she could wreak her vengeance with impunity. She longed for that moment when she could exercise her power.

She arrived above the blue-green world. Her quarry was invisible to her but the jewel left signs of its passage. She needed more information so that she could taunt and torment her victims. She commanded the souls to vent their hate and directed them to fashion the elements into her servants. At last Malice could begin her retribution.

20

Cynddylig woke her from a restless sleep. Over and over again the wild face of Tudfwlch had leaned over her grasping for the starstone. Time and time again she had shaken her head and denied him and each time she had been drenched by his blood. She opened her eyes to a dull day. It was still early, the unseen sun had just risen over the hidden horizon but the gorge was still dark, and the glimpse of sky overhead was overcast. September didn't like the look of the sky; bad things seemed to happen when the weather turned poor. Perhaps the Malevolence controls the weather, she thought, but decided not to mention it to Cynddylig. He seemed untroubled as he packed the boat.

"It's difficult to know precisely where you are in Hafn Afon Deheuol," he said, "but tomorrow we will arrive at Dwytrefrhaedr."

"The Mordeyrn says there will be a guide waiting for us," September said.

"That is good because I have never travelled amongst the hills of the stars. Now we must make a start."

Soon they were travelling along the river. The sky remained covered by thick cloud and the warmth and humidity of the air drained September of energy. She and Cynddylig took turns at steering the boat and Cynddylig talked of previous visits to the twin towns, happy times when there had been gatherings of friends and celebrations. September guessed that another of his women had been an inhabitant of the vibrant port. He still wouldn't explain why there were two towns together. He smiled,

"It would spoil it for you if I explained," he said.

A steady drizzle began late in the afternoon which soaked everything. When they stopped for the night the mooring place was slick with water and rock dust. September slipped when she jumped ashore and grazed her shin. When the boat was fast, Cynddylig looked at the injury.

"Use your arian, on it," he advised. September lifted the locket and chain from around her neck and contorted herself into a position so that she could rest the silver against her shin while still remaining covered by the cloak. She imagined her shin healed and was amazed to see the bleeding stop and fresh skin form over the graze. In moments there was no sign of the wound at all. She replaced the chain around her neck.

"It's magic," she said as she joined Cynddylig trying to light the fire with damp twigs.

"Just the power of the planets and the metals united by the good of the Earth," he replied, matter of factly.

They ate with the drizzle still falling on them and then September spoke to the Mordeyrn as usual.

"Your guide will be waiting at the harbour for your arrival tomorrow," he said, "and I look forward to your arrival here at the Arsyllfa a few days hence."

Once again September took the first watch. She sat with her back against the cliff holding Tudfwlch's sword in her hand. She slipped it in and out of its scabbard. While it reminded her of Tudfwlch and the terror of his transformation, the sword gave her some feeling of safety. It was miserable sitting in the wet but September was heartened by the thought that the river trip was nearly over.

The good news the following morning was that the rain had stopped but instead there was a thick fog. The top of the cliffs were completely lost in the damp, grey mist and Cynddylig had difficulty in maintaining a steady course along the winding gorge with the bends obscured until they were almost upon them. The rocky sides of the gorge passed by them slowly and hypnotically. September nodded off in her seat.

A screech overhead brought her to alertness. Her birthmark was itching furiously. What bird had such a loud, deep call? Yet it seemed familiar. She looked up into the mist behind them and screamed.

"What is it?" Cynddylig yelled.

"It's them. The adar.. whatever, the scary birds."

There were three of the Adarllwchgwin, the huge brown

birds with horned riders that had attacked her and the village the morning after she had arrived. The great eagle-like creatures swooped down towards them with huge boulders grasped in their talons. One after the other they soared over the boat dropping their load. The rocks fell to either side of the narrow boat sending up plumes of water that soaked them. As they swooped over them the riders fired flames from their three-pointed spears. Two gobbets of fire fell into the water extinguishing with a loud hiss. The third thudded into a bag in the bow of the boat. The bag erupted into flame. Smoke rose and the fire quickly spread to other bags and the wooden hull.

"Do something!" Cynddylig shouted as he steered the boat on an erratic course, "They'll be back."

The giant birds of prey had risen into the mist, but their calls rebounded off the walls of the gorge. September tried to work out where they had gone or where they would come from next but the echoes confused her. The sudden attack had shocked her, the flames in the boat scared her but now she had her wits about her. She stood up in the middle of the boat and flung her cloak over her shoulders. The silver pendant was in her left hand; she flicked the locket open and held up the Maengolauseren with her arm outstretched. She drew Tudfwlch's iron sword and held it in her right hand. She faced the bow then turned to the stern, just in time to see the Adarllwchgwin appear out of the mist, in line, their wings almost filling the width of the gorge. Their legs and talons were poised to strike and their riders held their flaming tridents in their hands ready to fire.

September felt the fear and the anger rise in her. Her hip hurt as if it was burning. She felt the twelve red eyes of the birds and their riders focussed on her. The birds' hooked beaks opened to let out a deafening squawk as they spread their talons to grasp their victim. She gripped the stone tightly, and raised the sword. Both arms were stretched towards the attackers. The first bird was nearly upon them. The rider flung its spear. Cynddylig thrust the tiller first this way and that, the boat yawed and rolled. September stumbled but regained her footing.

"Be gone!" September screamed out. A blinding blast of

blue light shot from the stone. It illuminated the gorge behind them and thunder echoed off the walls. The leading bird, hit by the force of the light was flung back, its wings crumpled and it fell into the river. September lost her balance and fell into the bottom of the hull but saw the second bird veer off its course, hit the cliff and tumble into the water, thrashing wildly as it sank. The third rose into the mist. A spear of flame gouged a charred furrow along the side of the hull.

Flames were spreading along the boat from the bow. One sack after another of clothes, bedding and kindling ignited.

"What can I do?" September cried scrambling onto her knees, stone and sword still gripped in her hands.

"Water, get water," Cynddylig called. September thrust the sword into its scabbard and dropped the starstone to hang between her breasts. Where was the cooking pot, a bucket, anything to scoop water into? She glanced up at the bow. Through the smoke and flames she saw the last Adarllwchgwin flying towards them. It was low, its talons almost in the water. Its great wings beat slowly but with great force. The rider was almost standing on its back, its fiery spear raised and aimed. The boat lurched to the right as Cynddylig wrenched the tiller and September fell again. The bird swooped past and turned tightly, its wingtip brushing the water. Now they were broadside on as it soared towards them again.

September was half kneeling half lying across the boat, but the stone was in her hand again.

"Be gone!" she cried, again and again blue light flashed from her hand. The beam hit the bird's head. With a roar of thunder and an explosion of light the bird disintegrated into smoke that fell around them. September blinked and covered her nose and mouth to avoid the sulphurous stink. They were about to hit the wall of the gorge when Cynddylig thrust on the tiller and steered the boat back on to its course. The cloud began to thin and September smelled the burning wood of the boat. She hoped that perhaps the attack was over but still her birthmark burned. There was something in the mist behind them. She squeezed her eyes to see more clearly.

"No," she whispered, "it can't be."

"What? What is it?" Cynddylig tried to turn to look behind

him.

Striding towards them over the water was the figure of a man. The trousers and tunic were familiar and so were the hair and the face.

"Tudfwlch?" September stared. Tudfwlch approached rapidly, taking huge strides that barely touched the surface of the river. It was Tudfwlch, she was sure, somehow still alive. Her heart reached out to him, she so wanted him to be living.

"It's not him, it's a Pwca," Cynddylig said, "get rid of it. Use the stone."

"Do I have to kill him again?"

September stared but slowly it dawned on her that the fog had affected her sense of perspective. As the figure got closer he loomed taller and taller, a giant Tudfwlch, with a red torrent pouring from the wound in his side.

"By the absent Cemegwr! It's not him, I say." Cynddylig appealed to her.

The figure opened its mouth and its deep voice resonated down the gorge towards them.

"September, September. Help me."

"Don't listen to it. It's not Tudfwlch."

"But how can it say my name? It must have Tudfwlch's memories."

"Perhaps, but they are not part of Tudfwlch anymore. It's the Adwyth."

"September, give me the Maengolauseren." The giant figure appealed reaching out its hand. It was only a few metres behind them now.

"Oh, stars above!" Cynddylig said.

"What now?" September turned away from the approaching facsimile of Tudfwlch to look forward. Smoke and flames obscured her view but emerging out of the fog were the galloping figures of three pale Ceffyl dwr; their turquoise manes and tails streaming out behind them and their pounding legs stirring the water up into a great wave that was rushing towards them.

"Give it to me."

September looked up to see the gigantic figure of Tudfwlch bending down over her, stinking mud dripping from its mouth. Its hand reached towards her. She raised the stone in her hand.

"No, you won't have it," she bellowed. The blue beam shot out and hit the Tudfwlch figure in its chest. It let out a huge sigh and began to topple forwards. The body hit the water, its head just short of the boat's stern and dissipated with a blast of hot air and a wave that lifted the boat and surged it forward. September fell again.

"Cludydd!" Cynddylig cried.

She rolled over to see the flames half way along the boat and beyond, the blue-green horses. The great wave was almost on them. The horses reared up, their huge hooves pawing the air, and the wave rose and rose above the boat. Lying in the bottom she struggled to raise the stone into the air. She screamed.

"Ymadaelwch!"

Intense, dazzling light filled the gorge and there was a great roaring noise of a tornado. The three horses blew apart in three fountains of water that reached up to the top of the cliffs as the wave hit the boat.

The bow of the boat rose, tipping Cynddylig off the stern with September slipping and sliding into the river after him. The wave broke and crashed down on top of them. September sank into the boiling, writhing, foaming water, pulled down by the weight of the sword and its scabbard attached to her belt. She tried to breathe, took a mouthful of water and clamped her lips closed. The swirling vortices flung her around and around until she was dizzy and her chest was aching. And then, calm. September fought her way back to the surface despite the weight tugging her down. At last she gasped air.

The Ceffyl dwr and the Pwca that was Tudfwlch were gone. The ripples on the river were dying away but there was no sign of their boat. September found the river current was pushing her along and she was sinking again. She kicked her legs and waved her arms but her head kept being pulled under water. Her hand struck rock. The side of the gorge was sheer and there were no hand holds but she was able to push her head to the surface. She peered through water-filled eyes and saw the gorge rising up over her. The current dragged her, bumping along the rock face as she tried to grasp something, anything. Through her bleary vision she caught sight of something ahead; a shadow in the wall. It was one of the landing stages, a part of the cliff gouged out to make a flat platform. It was above her head and she was going to be swept past it. Stretching an arm up, her fingers found the edge and although they scraped against the rock, gradually she slowed. Her other hand found the ledge and she strained to lift herself out of the clinging embrace of the water. For moments she hung half out of the water, half in. Her arms ached. The river was pulling her back down to sink forever. With all her remaining energy she willed her body to rise. She swung a leg to the side. A knee found the rim. She levered herself up and, with a final heave, rolled onto the ledge. Exhausted, she lay still, panting.

She stayed lying on the stone, her head almost over the edge, her eyes nearly closed, watching but not seeing the river flow by. Something floated into her view. At first she wasn't sure what it was, a log, a sack. Then she realised. It was a body. The head was almost submerged but with grey hair floating in the current. It was swept swiftly by.

"Cynddylig, oh, Cynddylig," September sobbed.

Still unmoving, unable to move for a time that she could not estimate, September just breathed, feeling fatigue in every limb. Eventually her senses told her that the fog had cleared and the Sun's rays were reaching down to the bottom of the gorge to warm her. She rolled over painfully, sat up and examined herself. She felt sore all over but apart from some grazing on her fingers she seemed to be uninjured and the pain had gone from her hip. Her search also told her that she still had her damp clothes and the cloak around her, the Maengolauseren and the phial of arianbyw were still around her neck and her knife, pouch and Tudfwlch's sword were still attached to the belt around her waist. She was whole but alone.

September opened up the damp leather pouch and took out the copper horn. It seemed undamaged. She raised it to her lips and blew. A weak cracked note sounded. The echo bounced back and forth across the gorge, a sad, forlorn sound, fading to silence.

"Cludydd? Is that you?" The Mordeyrn's distant,

concerned voice answered.

September sighed and sobbed.

"Yes, it's me, but Cynddylig is gone. The boat's gone."

"What happened? Where are you?"

Through her sobs, word by word, she recounted the attack.

"It all happened at once. The horses, Tudfwlch. I couldn't cope with them all together. The boat was overturned, we fell into the river and Cynddylig's gone."

"Are you sure?"

"I saw his body. It just floated by, he wasn't moving. His face was under the water."

"But you are safe? You have the Maengolauseren?"

"Yes, yes."

"I'll get someone to you. Stay where you are."

September looked around the small ledge, at the overhanging cliff and the river flowing by.

"I'm not going anywhere."

21

September sat on the rock ledge with her head resting on her knees and the cloak of tin and lead wrapped around her. She rocked forwards and backwards trying to dismiss the memory of the attack by the Malevolence and the loss of Cynddylig. Now she felt completely alone despite the Mordeyrn's assurance that help was on its way. Both the companions she had been with for nearly the whole of her time in Gwlad were gone. Why couldn't I save him, September muttered to herself, why did I delay? If I had got rid of the monster Tudfwlch I could have destroyed the water horses before they overturned the boat.

It was past noon now and while she was in shade the air was warmed by the sunlight that reached the bottom of the gorge. She watched the water moving smoothly by. There was no sign of the turmoil that had scattered all their stores and belongings and had drowned Cynddylig. September remembered how he had seemed gruff and negative when they had first met but she had grown to respect his knowledge of the river and his doubts about the fight against the evil that was growing in the Land.

September was hungry and thirsty but all she could do was sit and wait and rock and think.

"Hey there!"

September looked up. A boat was turning against the flow of the river and heading towards her. It was barely longer than the boat the three of them had travelled in but was broader and was being rowed by four bare-chested, muscular men sitting two abreast. What drew September's eye though was the figure standing in the bow. She was a tall young woman with long blonde hair that blew out behind her. She had a pale face and wore a long white gown that shimmered in the sunlight. A golden brooch was fastened between her breasts. She looked like a princess but September reminded herself that as far as she was aware, there were no princesses in Gwlad. September unfolded her legs and got to her feet. She straightened up, the folds of the silver grey cloak falling around her.

"Cludydd," the woman called, "I have come to take you to Dwytrefrhaedr."

"You are from the Mordeyrn?"

"I am Heulwen, daughter of the Mordeyrn Aurddolen." The distance between the boat and the shore became smaller. A thought entered September's head.

"How do I know you are who you say you are and not servants of the Malevolence?"

"My father will vouch for me."

September fumbled in her pouch for the horn and blew into it. Before the echo had faded, the voice of Aurddolen emerged from it.

"Cludydd, has my daughter found you?"

"She says she is your daughter, but how can I be sure that she is not some monster that has taken on her form?"

September was sure she heard the Mordeyrn chuckle.

"I am sure Heulwen would not appreciate being likened to a vile servant of the Malevolence but you are right to be wary after your experiences. She wears a brooch of aur. Look at it and tell me what you see."

The oarsmen fought the current and manoeuvred the bow of the boat close to the landing stage. Standing on the edge of the ledge September was just an arm's reach from the imposing young lady. She looked at the golden brooch shaped as a disc with flames around it like an image of the Sun. It began to glow brightly. The disc of light expanded and while still bright became clouded. An image appeared, of the Mordeyrn Aurddolen, his golden hair like flames around his head. He held his great gold plate in his hands. The image faded and the brooch returned to its former appearance.

"What did you see?" Heulwen asked.

"I saw the Mordeyrn holding his gold dish. But I thought that had been destroyed."

"Alas, that is true," The Mordeyn's voice whispered in September's ear, "the image is from an earlier time. Does it convince you that the brooch and its bearer are linked through the power of Haul to me?"

"Um, I suppose so."

"Then be assured that the bearer is my daughter, Heulwen, and she will escort you first to Dwytrefrhaedr and then to join me here at the Arsyllfa."

Heulwen reached out her hand. September grasped it and stepped onto the boat. She stood in front of the young woman. They were a similar height and they looked into each other's eyes, examining and wondering. There was a wooden chair behind Heulwen. She sat down.

"Please sit," she said. September looked for somewhere where she could settle comfortably. There was no other seat so she lowered herself into the bow of the boat and rested both arms on the gunwales. She watched as the oarsmen sculled the boat into the river and then with long strokes turned against the current. Soon they were moving smoothly upstream.

"So, you are the Cludydd o Maengolauseren," Heulwen said, her eyes scanning over September.

"So I'm told," September felt uncomfortable being examined.

"You are as my father described; the image of the Cludydd from the stories."

"You've got one on me there because he never mentioned you. He said he would send a guide."

"And that is what I shall be for you. I will guide you into the presence of the Mordeyrn and assist you in your task."

"But he never said the guide would be his daughter."

"He didn't intend it to be me. If you had arrived as expected at the twin towns another of his minions would have guided you into the hills, but this, ah, emergency changes things. I was in the town and thought it would be entertaining to come and find you."

"Entertaining?"

"Well, you seem to have had an exciting journey," Heulwen smiled sweetly. September felt anger and pain like a solid lump in her chest.

"That excitement cost me two friends, to say nothing of a whole village and the crew of a boat who have died because of the Malevolence."

"Ooh, you are upset. Surely the power of the Maengolauseren in the hands of the Cludydd could overcome the powers of the Adwyth."

September turned away and looked upstream. This woman, this girl, this 'princess', may have rescued her but September felt her temperature rising at her taunts. She turned back to glare at the girl sitting smugly on her little throne.

"Well, yes, perhaps I am to blame that Tudfwlch and Cynddylig are dead. Perhaps if I had a better idea about what this stone was supposed to do I could have saved them, and everyone else. But that was why I was on this journey – to learn from your father."

"My father certainly has a lot to teach you. I am sorry about your friends. I am sure you did everything you could." Heulwen smiled again, a condescending smile with her lips; her eyes remained gazing coldly and contemptuously at her. "Would you like a drink?" She reached down to pick up a leather water bottle and passed it to September. September took it and grunted an ungrateful thank you. She put it to her lips realising how thirsty she was after the hours sitting on the ledge.

"We'll be in Dwytrefrhaedr in a couple of hours. The men are strong."

September handed the bottle back and watched the oarsmen taking their long powerful strokes in rhythm. She turned again to look forward, searching the sky for Adarllwchgwin and the river for Ceffyl dwr but the sky above the cliff top was blue and the water was smooth and dark green. The Malevolence seemed to have given up its attack.

September didn't feel in the mood to engage in conversation with this daughter of the Mordeyrn who had suddenly appeared and treated her as if she was a weak girl who had to be rescued and protected. Her opinion of her may have been correct, September reflected – she was a silly girl with no talent to speak of – but Heulwen's manner was hardly designed to boost her confidence. Heulwen seemed content to journey in silence too.

After a time following the river's course through the gorge September began to notice something. It was a sound. At first it was faint, almost inaudible above the sound of the river and the oars dipping into the water, the sound of the sea heard in a seashell. She wasn't sure whether it was a real sound or if it was just the sound of her own blood rushing through her arteries, but it slowly became louder. It was the sound of a running tap, of water rushing down a pipe.

"What is that noise?" she asked turning to face Heulwen. This time the girl smiled with all her face.

"You will see soon enough. Nothing I could say will prepare you for it."

September recalled Cynddylig saying something similar and her eyes filled with tears.

The noise continued to build in volume and September noticed that the gorge was widening, the vertical walls receding little by little. Now the noise was a constant roar, filling her ears.

"Whatever it is it must be really close," she shouted to Heulwen who merely smiled back.

September stared ahead looking in vain for a source of the sound. She was convinced it was rushing water, but how could it make such a noise? Still it grew louder until it felt as if her head was being pummelled by a torrent of water, and then the boat turned a bend. The sight ahead made September stop breathing.

The gorge opened out into a semi-circular lake surrounded by the white cliffs. Ahead the passage was blocked by a black wall of rock over which poured a thousand metre high waterfall. The incessant pounding of the water as it fell into the lake was the source of the noise. September stared at the curtain of white water, the clouds that hung over it and the maelstrom at its bottom. She began to breathe again but was still speechless. She took her eyes off the deluge and looked around the lake. To the left on the south side there was a cluster of stone buildings huddled against the cliff. Having entered the lake the boat turned towards the town.

"That's Dwytrefrhaedr?" she shouted over the noise of the waterfall, pointing towards their destination.

"Yes, one part anyway. The other part is at the top of the cliff," Heulwen replied, also pointing, but to the top of the cliff beside where the water poured over the edge. September stared.

"Two towns?" she hollered.

"Two towns by the waterfall, Dwytrefrhaedr," Heulwen replied, although her words were almost lost in the noise of the waterfall.

"How do you get up there?" September asked, staring up at the impossibly sheer cliff face.

"By basket, look," again Heulwen pointed but this time to something halfway between the lake and the top of the waterfall. The boat was closer now to the dark cliff. Even though it was in the shadow of the afternoon sun, September could just make out two tiny objects moving almost imperceptibly, one rising, one falling. It's a sort of cable car, she thought.

The oars rattled in their rowlocks as the oarsmen ceased rowing. September dragged her attention away from the cliff just as the boat coasted into a jetty. It was the only one free. There were dozens of the pontoons jutting at right-angles from the shore. The others were filled with boats of all shapes and sizes including two of the large barges like the Gleisiad and Dyfrgi. There were people waiting to grab ropes handed over by the oarsmen and a crowd was assembling on the shoreline and along the other jetties. When the boat was tied fast Heulwen stood up and stepped onto the wooden landing. She held out a hand towards September. She took it grudgingly and hauled herself out of the boat. Heulwen guided her along until they reached the quayside and the crowd. September was suddenly aware that it had been many days since she had last been surrounded by people, not counting the crazed zombies of Glanyrafon. She had often felt uncomfortable in the company of a lot of people, thinking that they were looking at her and commenting on her fatness or how stupid she looked. It was silly she knew – people in a crowd had other things on their minds – but now being the centre of attention and after what had happened she felt vulnerable, even afraid. The mind-numbing noise of the waterfall and the pressing crowd made her dizzy. Heulwen seemed to sense her reluctance to walk through the throng and grabbed her hand.

"Make way for Heulwen and the Cludydd," someone called

and a passage opened up across the stone ground. They came to the door of one of the buildings that lined the harbour. The building appeared as if it was part of the cliff as it was built from the same rock. They stepped inside and Heulwen closed the heavy wooden door on the masses that pushed and shoved behind them. They stood in a cool, dimly lit room, the noise of the waterfall dulled by the thick walls and door. There were a few chairs and a table. September stared back at the door, still hearing the muffled sounds of the crowd beyond.

"How do they know who I am?" September said in a loud whisper in Heulwen's ear.

"The word was spread when we called for volunteers to row to your rescue."

"Why?"

"The boatmen were afraid. Your battle with the Malevolence could be seen and heard even here."

"Seen and heard?"

"Yes, the blue light of the starstone lit up the sky even through the morning mist and the thunder of its force echoed along the gorge."

"I didn't realise."

"Few of the people of Dwytrefrhaedr would dare face the evil but for the four brave men who rowed me to you." Heulwen glowed with pride.

"And you of course. You were brave."

Heulwen waved her hand.

"Oh, I had the power of aur, and the skills my father has taught me to protect myself."

"You are a cludydd?"

"I am... I will be," for a moment Heulwen seemed flustered, "I am my father's apprentice."

September was taken aback but Heulwen's manner began to fall into place. Her father was a powerful man, perhaps the most powerful in the Land, and if she had inherited even some of his skill with the gold then she had some reason to feel superior. September felt that it may explain her manner if not justify it.

"Please sit," Heulwen continued, "someone will bring food and drink and you can rest here until we journey to the

Arsyllfa."

September sat in an armchair grateful for the first comfortable seat on dry land in nearly three weeks. The chair was made of wood but padded with cloth-covered cushions. She felt safe, but was she?

"Are we, am I, safe here?" she drew her cloak around her.

"I am here to protect you," Heulwen said holding herself erect, her hand grasping her gold brooch, "and there will be others here to defend you."

"But?"

Heulwen sagged a little and looked away from September.

"The Malevolence grows stronger and could attack at anytime, anywhere," she recovered herself and faced September again, "but we will defeat it."

A door opened on the opposite side of the room from their entrance and a woman came in holding a tray of food. She was followed by a short man with greying hair and a developing paunch. He carried a short sword not unlike the one that rested beside September's thigh. The woman placed the tray on the table next to September, smiled and blushed then turned and left.

"Ah, good," Heulwen began, "this is Iddig, cludydd o haearn and leader of the guardians of Dwytrefrhaedr."

Iddig nodded to September who examined him with some surprise. He didn't look like a fierce warrior.

"It is an honour to welcome you to our towns, Cludydd," he said.

"Iddig will stay with you while you eat," Heulwen said, and immediately left the room. Iddig pulled a chair closer to September's and sat down.

"Where has she gone?" September asked, wondering how much she should trust this new acquaintance. She felt alone despite all the people around her.

Iddig surveyed the array of bread, cheese, meats, vegetables and fruit on the tray before taking a hunk of bread.

"Who knows? She looks after her own business does that one."

September realised that she was hungry too and selected a smaller slice of bread and some cheese and salad leaves.

"She's the Mordeyrn's daughter," she said.

"Aye, don't we all know it."

"Is she in charge here?"

"Thinks she is," Iddig rolled up a slice of meat and squeezed it into his mouth, "Heulwen likes to act as if she is the Mordeyrn's deputy not just his daughter, but as she said, I'm in charge of defence against evil."

"Have you been attacked?"

"A few times in the last year, Adarllwchgwin have raided us, but we're well protected here underneath the cliff with our stone houses. The Hafn Afon Deheuol is different. Many boats have been attacked while travelling through the gorge," he reached for a peach and bit into it, "and that is how the evil affects us all. Trade has almost stopped and we rely on trade for everything here. People are afraid and don't trust others anymore."

September nodded, it was the same story that Cynddylig had told. The Malevolence was seeping into the society of Gwlad making everyone fear everyone else. Thinking about Cynddylig and the evil that was everywhere suddenly filled her with dread. She shivered.

"What is the matter, Cludydd? Are you unwell?"

September could not stop herself sobbing.

"I'm sorry, it's just everything got to me. This whole Malevolence thing."

"But you have met and defeated the Malevolence. We saw the signs this morning." Iddig said.

September was sombre.

"Yes, we met the Malevolence. But I wouldn't say we defeated it. Cynddylig died."

"Old Cynddylig the boatman?"

"Yes. Did you know him?"

"Did I know him? Everyone in the twin towns knew that old rascal. Always a miserable bugger, but give him an ale and a willing woman and he was happy. The finest boatman on the Deheuol," Iddig subsided, "He's dead?"

"Yes," September said sadly, "He guided us nearly all the way here and then I failed him."

"What do you mean?"

"I didn't use the stone quickly enough. If I had I could have destroyed the Ceffyl dwr before the wave covered us and overturned our boat. Cynddylig drowned."

"He never did learn to swim. Said that he was boatman not a fish," Iddig laid his broad arms around September's shoulders, "tell me all about it, your journey, and this fine cloak you are wearing."

September looked down at the silver cloak wrapped around her.

"This was supposed to protect us."

"What is it? I don't recognise its manufacture."

"It was made by the two cludydd in Amaethaderyn. Aurddolen instructed them to use the two metals; I can't remember what you call them, tin and lead."

"Ah, alcam and plwm. I think I understand."

"Mixed together and made into this cloak the metals were supposed to shield me and the stone from the Malevolence."

"I can see the Mordeyrn's thinking behind it. Did it work?"

"I don't know. We ran into evil things along the river when I had to get the stone out and use it to defend us. Aurddolen thinks that sent a signal to the Malevolence and attracted the monsters to our route."

"Tell me about it."

September warmed to this genial guard and began to recount all the battles they had fought along the river, Tudfwlch's conversion to evil and the final attack by the Adarllwchgwin, the Pwca and the Ceffyl dwr. At the end she felt exhausted.

"I think you have shown you are a worthy bearer of the Maengolauseren. Not one of us could have fought off so many of the evil manifestations as you have done."

September smiled weakly.

"I've been lucky. I don't really know what I'm doing with this stone," she touched the pendant beneath her cloak, "and I worry what will happen next time."

"Next time?"

"The next time I'm attacked. There will be a next time, I know it." She decided not to mention the warning her birthmark gave her, late though it was.

"Yes, well of course, the Malevolence is growing in strength. Unless the Mordeyrn and the other Prif-cludydd, and you of course, can devise a plan to overcome it, we're all going to be attacked more often. But that is why we must get you safely to the Arsyllfa as soon as possible and why I must protect you."

"But that is just what I am afraid of. The people who help me get hurt, like Eluned, or killed like Tudfwlch and Cynddylig. I know I am the focus of these monsters' attacks. If the Malevolence, whatever it is, finds where I am no one around me is safe," she paused and sniffed, "Heulwen just thought it was exciting."

"That girl doesn't understand what you have been– um, are going through. Heulwen does not have a fraction of the power that you have, and I bet she knows it. She is envious of her father's position and seeks it for herself one day. Be wary that she does not lead you into danger through her lust for glory."

"But what if the Malevolence attacks?"

"I and my guardians are equipped to deal with them. As you have found, the attacks can occur at anytime, anywhere, regardless of whether you are a special target. We are prepared. If we are attacked then your power will be a welcome addition to our own, but you can't take responsibility for our lives. They are our own concerns. Now rest my girl."

September closed her eyes, grateful for Iddig's reassurance, and despite her unease was soon asleep.

September was awoken by sounds of the rustling of a long dress and Heulwen's petulant voice.

"Oh, you're asleep. There's no time for that."

September really wanted to ignore the girl and continue her doze, but she guessed that Heulwen probably wouldn't allow her to do that. She opened her eyes and saw the girl standing with her arms on her hips glaring impatiently.

"At last," she said. "We have to move."

"Where to?"

"We are going to the upper town, right now."

"To the top of the cliff? In that basket thing?"

"Yes."

"Why can't I stay here, just for a while?"

"Because my father's house is in the upper town. We need

to be there to prepare for our journey to the Arsyllfa. Father wants you there as soon as possible."

September groaned and got to her feet. She saw that Iddig had been sitting in another chair. He too rose.

"I'll escort you two ladies to the elevator," he said.

"Thank you, Iddig. I will enjoy your company," September said. Iddig opened the door onto the quay and Heulwen swept out. September hurried after her but paused as the noise of the waterfall hit her with its full might. At least her rest had revived her. She saw that the sun had sunk lower in the sky so she must have been asleep for an hour or two. Telling the time by the sun's position had become almost automatic during her journey.

There were four men equipped like Iddig with short swords standing by the house. They were presumably Iddig's guardians. They didn't look like a particularly well-trained military force but they came to attention when they saw Iddig and gathered around them. There were fewer people on the quay but those that were soon clustered around them. Heulwen ignored them and strode off in the direction of the waterfall. Iddig stood by September's side, fending off the growing crowd and instructing his men to keep close.

"We had better keep up with the lady," he shouted. September nodded and hurried along by his side.

They walked around the edge of the lake towards the basket lift she had seen from the boat. Now she had a chance to look around the lower of the two towns. It was really just a single row of stone buildings on a flat bed of rock no more than twenty metres wide. The buildings were built right against the cliff face. September wondered whether they were indeed dug into the cliff itself. There were not enough buildings to house all the people that thronged the quay and the jetties. She wondered where they all lived, not many of the boats tied up at the jetties were suitable for living aboard. Looking up at the cliff that towered over them she saw the answer. Between the stone buildings, ladders reached up to caves cut in the cliff with neat doorways and windows. There were three or four stories of the cliff dwellings linked by ladders and walkways that clung precariously to the rock face. September was rather glad that Heulwen had not taken her up the rickety looking ladders.

A few minutes brisk walk brought them to the lift. September was amused that Iddig had called it an elevator when all it looked like was a wicker basket with a rope attached. Just half a dozen people could fit in the lift and fewer if there was any luggage. September bent her head back following the line of the rope as it rose vertically to the top of the cliff. She couldn't see the rope after about halfway but she could just make out something sticking out from the top of the cliff.

An old man stood by the empty basket. Heulwen stepped up a flight of wooden steps and into the basket. She beckoned to September. It was no use trying to speak as the noise of the waterfall, the edge of which was a continuous pillar of water just tens of metres away, drowned all speech. September climbed into the basket. It hardly seemed strong enough to hoist them a thousand metres into the air, but Iddig and one of his guards joined them. The wicker was lined on the inside with a waxed cloth. The old man pulled on a thin cord which also ran up to the top of the cliff. A few moments later the basket lurched. September grabbed hold of the side of the basket as they were hoisted off the ground. In a few moments September had a view of the lower town of Dwytrefrhaedr, the narrow row of buildings tucked under the cliff, the equally narrow waterfront and the rows of boats moored at the jetties. There were lots of people, working on the boats, hurrying to and from the buildings and up and down the ladders to the cave dwellings. She looked out across the lake to the opening to the gorge, almost invisible through the spray from the waterfall that roared next to her. Conversation on the journey was impossible so she continued to look around. Her eyes roved across the sky looking for huge winged monsters but the only birds were small water birds that occasionally dived into the lake.

As the buildings and boats of the lower town shrank to the size of toys, September began to feel worried. She looked up at the rope to check for any sign of fraying, not that there was anything she could do about it. Her companions seemed untroubled and rested against the sides of the basket unconcerned by the immense height that they were rising to.

Looking up September saw an object descending on top of them. Her heart leapt for a moment before she realised that it was the other basket on its way down. It passed by very close and fast. There were no passengers, but as it dropped below them September could see water sloshing inside the basket acting as a counterbalance to their weight.

Now September could see where they were heading, a structure built out over the edge of the cliff and a wheel that the rope passed over. It was still small and silhouetted against the sky which would have been clear blue but for the spray from the waterfall that hung in the air above them. The water was settling on her and as they rose September became cool. She wrapped her cloak around herself to keep dry and warm.

The town below had become tiny and the people invisible while the structure above them grew. The basket slowed its rise for the last few metres until they drew level with a platform that jutted out from the cliff. Heulwen climbed the steps out of the basket and stepped onto the wooden platform. She gestured impatiently to September to follow. September felt very nervous about stepping across the gap between the basket and the platform. It may have been just a few centimetres wide but she could still look down to the bottom of the gorge a thousand metres below. A man took her hand and guided her from the basket. She was thankful that there was a fence on the side of the wooden platform and she was able to step quickly onto safe, solid rock. The wheel that held the weight of the two baskets and the rope was a couple of metres in diameter and connected by an axle, itself about a metre broad, to a much larger wheel, half of which disappeared into the ground. Two narrow channels carried water from the river to the sides of the wheel. A man stood by each channel.

Beyond the wheel there was another cluster of buildings beside the river. There were also trees and further away, fields and then the peaks. Heulwen was already past the wheel and heading into the upper town. Iddig came to September's side.

"Welcome to Upper Town. Come, we had better keep up with the lady." There was a little less noise from the waterfall here at the top so hearing each other speak was easier even though Iddig had to shout.

"She seems to be in a hurry," September replied. They set off in pursuit. In a few moments they were in the town. The buildings were a mix of stone and wood and looked more homely than the stark rock hewn dwellings of the lower town. Once again people stopped what they were doing to look at them. Heulwen approached the door of one of the larger stone houses. She paused on the doorstep, glanced to see that they were just behind, and entered.

September, Iddig and the guard reached the doorway and stepped inside. The sight that awaited September was quite unexpected. The other homes she had seen were rough and spartan in their furnishings. She had become used to thinking of the Land as primitive. This was different. There was a carpet on the floor, a window fitted with shutters with curtains hanging from a pole, and the walls, though plain, were decorated with paintings of landscapes. There was a comfortable sofa and chairs in the middle of the room and a simple but elegant desk on the far side.

"Welcome to my home, Cludydd," Heulwen said, spreading her arms and beaming with pride.

"Thank you, Heulwen. It looks very smart." September replied, still astonished at her surroundings.

"Aye, the Mordeyrn makes sure his daughter is comfortable here," Iddig said. Heulwen seemed to glower at him for a moment then smiled graciously to September.

"Come and sit and I'll call for refreshment."

September took a place on the sofa while Iddig lowered himself into an ample armchair. The guard remained standing looking out of the window. Heulwen went to the desk and rang a small copper bell. Almost immediately the door on the opposite side of the room opened and a woman entered. She was dressed in the rough everyday linen dresses of the women and was considerably older than Heulwen. She rubbed her hands and looked at the guests. When she saw September she rushed forward.

"Oh, Cludydd, we are so pleased to see you here fit and well."

"Meryl, could you get us something to eat and drink," Heulwen said.

Meryl turned to the young woman and September thought she saw an angry glare pass swiftly across her face.

"I shall Heulwen, once I have greeted our visitor," she turned back to September, smiling broadly, "You have come a long way and from what we have heard you have had a difficult journey."

"Thank you. Yes, it has been hard."

"Right, well we shall look after you then." Meryl turned and swept out of the room.

"Who is Meryl?" September asked. Heulwen seemed to treat her like a servant but she had spoken as an independent woman. There had been no mistress/servant relationships in Amaethaderyn; everyone there treated each other as equals.

"Meryl helps me look after the house," Heulwen said, waving her hand dismissively.

"Meryl is a fine cook and keeps this house for the Mordeyrn," Iddig said, getting another glare from Heulwen.

"Yes, well that's beside the point. Cludydd, we must prepare for our journey to the Arsyllfa. We will leave early tomorrow morning. I will show you to your room for tonight." Heulwen got up and led September from the room and up a flight of wooden stairs to a landing. There were four doors. Heulwen chose one and stopped by the open door to allow September to enter. September saw the most wonderful sight – a real bed. While the bedroom looked like it should be in a museum, the mattress on its wooden frame with sheets and blanket, a table with a washing bowl and jug of water, a wardrobe and a chest of drawers in a dark wood provided comforts that September had not seen since she was summoned from home. The sun, low in the sky, shone through the small window filling the room with yellow light that gave it a joyful atmosphere. She sat on the bed and felt a tiredness sweep over her. All she wanted was to lie down and enjoy the pleasure of a comfortable night's sleep.

"I'll just leave you to sort yourself out," Heulwen said, "Meryl will have supper prepared soon so come down when you are ready."

"I haven't got any baggage to unpack," September said.

"No, of course not. Ah, but I did put something here for you." She went to the wardrobe and opened it. A pale blue, silk dress hung on a hanger. "Perhaps you would like to wear it for supper." September felt her judging her dirty and scuffed tunic and trousers beneath her cloak. "Oh, the toilet is downstairs," Heulwen added as she left.

Well, this is a change, September thought. Perhaps the society of Gwlad is not quite as equal as I thought, and there are rewards for being the Mordeyrn or his daughter. She unbuckled the belt from her waist and laid it on the bed then persuaded herself not to lie down, sure that she would fall asleep immediately if she did. She wriggled out of her clothes while keeping the cloak around herself and washed in the bowl using a piece of hard soap that lay beside it and a towel to dry herself. Then she pulled the silk dress on under the cloak, finding the soft smooth feel of the cloth unusual against her skin after weeks of the rough linen. She tugged her fingers through her thick, white hair, gave the bed a look of longing then descended to the front parlour.

Meryl was as good as her word and provided a tasty and filling stew with fresh bread and fruit. She was eager to hear September's tale of her journey while they ate. Heulwen sniffed and looked bored while September told her story again. Meryl oohed and aahed but when September couldn't help a sob recounting the end of Tudfwlch and Cynddylig she sympathised and provided a clean cloth to dab her eyes. By the time they had finished eating, the sun had set and the room became dark. Meryl lit a few candles, but Heulwen suggested that it was time for an early night. September was sure that the real reason was that she didn't want to hear any more of her exploits demonstrating the power of the starstone, but she was grateful to get up to that wonderful bed. She removed the dress but kept the metal cloak around her and slipped between the sheets. She took the copper horn from its leather case and blew softly. Aurddolen replied almost immediately.

"You are safe in my house, Cludydd?"

"Yes, I'm snuggled up in this wonderful bed. I didn't think you had such things."

"Ah, they are not common but my daughter likes to do things a certain way."

"I've noticed."

"Don't be hard on her, September. People expect a lot of her as my only child. It's my fault that she is a little demanding and proud."

"She's old enough to be responsible for herself."

"Ah, that is true and wisely said. She is indeed of an age when young people reach for their own destinies, but Heulwen is hampered in that regard by being my daughter. People have expectations of her and her freedoms are limited. So she naturally thinks that she is a leader in my absence."

"I think I see."

"She will do everything she can to help you on your journey, but now I think you need rest. Have a peaceful night."

"Thank you Mordeyrn, and you."

She put the horn back in its case and lifted the belt and the sword onto the floor.

The mattress was hard and quite lumpy but it was blissful after many nights lying on the ground. Her eyes closed in moments.

22

She dreamt of monstrous birds swooping down on her and giant horses galloping through water towards her. There were noises and screams and shouts. She was alone so who was making all that noise? She looked from left to right but there was no source of the clamour. She opened her eyes. The shouting was real. Her birthmark itched. The door of her bedroom was flung open and Iddig appeared, wide eyed, flushed and sweating.

"Cludydd you must come!"

"Why, what's all the shouting for?"

"A Draig tân is coming. It is directed at Upper town."

September was already crawling from the bed cursing herself for having undressed. Or was she still dreaming? All her life had become a battle against the monsters of the Malevolence. She wrapped the cloak tightly around her.

"One of those fiery comet things?"

"Yes. Heulwen thinks she can stop it with her brooch, but she doesn't have her father's power."

"No, I know."

She recalled her first visit to the Land and her first use of the Maengolauseren to support Aurddolen and his golden plate. Could she destroy a Draig tân on her own? Well she was going to find out. She hurried after Iddig down the stairs, out of the house and into the street. They ran to the clearing near the lift. The moon was high in the eastern sky, over half full. The sky was dark and filled with stars, but lower in the sky was the latest manifestation of the Malevolence. The bright red disc was already twice the size of the moon and it trailed a tail of flickering fire that curled over the horizon. Flares burst off its surface and it grew noticeably as she watched. Some of the people of the town stood staring at the thing coming towards them while others ran hither and thither. Heulwen was there too, her brooch unpinned from her dress and held aloft. It glowed brightly but did nothing else. Meryl was by her side. September just caught her words above the noise of the waterfall.

"It's no use, Heulwen," Meryl tugged at her sleeve, "Even if you had your father's great plate of aur you would not be able to stop the Draig tân. Come with me and get out of its path."

"No, it's coming to me. It is my duty to destroy it," Heulwen replied.

"It's not just you," Iddig shouted, "It aims to destroy us all." He had drawn his sword and had raised its point towards the growing comet, to no great purpose that September could see. She reached inside her cloak for the pendant and drawing it out flicked the clasp. The stone glowed with the same blue whiteness as the moon and stars.

"Let us try to stop it together," September said, feeling calm and still as if in a dream. It seemed the right thing to say. Meryl looked at her and added her encouragement.

"That's it, Heulwen. Join with the Cludydd. Together you can destroy it."

Heulwen took her eyes off the approaching comet and glanced at September and the starstone.

"Yes," she said breathlessly, "we'll destroy it, the two of us."

The comet was approaching from the direction of the gorge. It hardly seemed to move, just to grow. Its tail lashed from side to side across the plateau, and gouts of fire dropped from it to the ground.

More people had joined them, standing silently in a crowd behind the four of them.

"Right then. Together," September shouted; she was confident she knew what to do. She thrust the stone out in front of her, "Ymadaelwch," she cried and Heulwen echoed her.

A violet aura radiated out from the starstone, Heulwen's brooch shone a brighter yellow and Iddig's sword glowed red hot, but nothing approached the Draig tân. Now it was a roaring, fiery sphere ten times the diameter of the moon. Fear gripped September, it felt real, this wasn't her dream. The Draig tân really was bearing down on them all. What if she didn't have the power to destroy a Draig tân without the Mordeyrn?

"Again," she shouted to Heulwen. Once again she thrust her arm with the stone aloft. "Ymadaelwch!" A violet beam shot from the stone but faded and died in moments. Still the comet approached. Now she could see that it was over the eastern cliffs surrounding the lake. Globules of fire rained down. It's going to hit us, she thought, all this journey is for nothing. Tudfwlch and Cynddylig have died to get me here and it's all going to be a complete waste.

"Try again," Iddig appealed. "It's closer now."

And these good people are going to die with me, she thought.

"You can do it Cludydd!" Meryl shouted, "For your companions who died!"

Yes, the Malevolence mustn't win; I've got to do something for Tudfwlch and Cynddylig. September held the stone above her head. She rubbed her side annoyed by the growing irritation. She took a deep breath. The Draig tân was almost on them. It filled half the sky and its roaring was so loud that even the waterfall was drowned out. Fire was falling from it into the lake and the lower town below.

"Ymadaelwch!" September screamed out loud and long. The violet glow started tentatively. She felt the muscles in her arm stiffen and the stone seemed to grow heavy. Now the power flowed through her body. She felt it welling up from the ground, up her calves and thighs, through her trunk and up her arm. The beam stretched out, became brighter, broader. It reached towards the Draig tân. The violet light and the bright red fire met, merged, mixed. The comet swelled and flares fell to the ground setting trees and grass alight, and then the comet's centre darkened and became a black hole with the violet shaft a spear in its centre. The blackness expanded rapidly swallowing the comet's fire. The ring of flames blew away, dissipating. A gale blew across the plateau fanning the fires but the Draig tân was gone from the sky.

Heulwen collapsed to the ground and September felt a great fatigue. She had triumphed again but how often would she be called on to stand against the Malevolence? What would happen if she failed to summon the power of the Maengolauseren? Her arm bent and she looked at the stone. It glowed dimly now the danger was past. She closed its case and slipped it back inside her cloak.

"You did it," Iddig shouted merrily, "You and the Maengolauseren; you destroyed the Draig tân and saved us all." He grabbed her shoulders and shook her, laughing and crying with relief. September gazed around her. Everywhere seemed to be burning, the wheel of the lift, the buildings at the end of the street, trees and even the grass at her feet. The people were running to and fro. Already some had collected buckets of water to the throw on the fires. September could only watch. She felt no sense of triumph now she saw people striving to save their homes. She felt so tired that she could barely stand let alone move. Iddig saw the fatigue in her eyes.

"Let's get you back to the Mordeyrn's house."

September looked at the prostrate body of Heulwen and Meryl crouched beside her. "What about Heulwen?"

"Meryl's looking after her. Come away from the fires."

September leaned against the plump warrior as they staggered back along the high street. The fires were restricted to the end buildings and the rest of the town looked quiet and peaceful. They reached the house and Iddig guided her in to the settee. Soon after Meryl arrived with Heulwen draped over her. She too was deposited into a chair. Iddig ran off.

"I'll find something to restore your energy," Meryl announced, leaving September alone with Heulwen. The young woman sagged in the chair but opened her eyes and stared at September. A smile spread across her face.

"We did it," she said proudly.

"Did what?" September asked.

"We destroyed the Draig tân. You and I, my aur and your Maengolauseren."

September was about to say that Heulwen had done nothing and that it was the starstone alone that had stopped the comet but she paused. She remembered Mother's instructions not to brag and to show kindness. She didn't feel particularly kind towards this proud and selfish young woman but she also didn't want to make things difficult with the Mordeyrn and she didn't feel like a hero. She took a deep breath.

"Yes, we did, we got rid of it."

Meryl returned with a tray of mugs and a jug. She poured out two cupfuls of the liquid and gave one each to Heulwen and September.

September sipped. It wasn't water but a sparkling, sharp, fruity drink. It seemed to flow into every part of her washing away the fatigue. She sat up straight.

"My, that's wonderful stuff," she said.

"That it is," Meryl agreed, "I'm sure Iddig and the others will need some when they have put all the fires out. Now you two should get to bed. You've still got a journey ahead of you tomorrow."

September didn't need any further persuading despite the revitalising drink. She climbed the stairs to her bedroom and soon was beneath the sheets. The muted roar of the waterfall came through the window and the shouts and noise of the people still struggling to put out the fires, but her eyes soon closed and she heard no more.

23

It felt as though her eyes had just closed when there was a tap on the door and Meryl looked in. September felt so comfortable wrapped in the sheets and lying on a soft bed she didn't want to move but Meryl urged her to get up as it was light and they needed to move. September dragged herself from the bed, washed, dressed in her worn old clothes and buckled her belt around her waist. She looked at the starstone inside its silver case. It was dull and lifeless. She felt her hip. The birthmark was not sore this morning. September was relieved. She hoped that both signs meant that there was no evil threatening her for the moment. She wrapped the cloak around herself again.

Downstairs she found Heulwen, Meryl and Iddig sitting at the table together. Heulwen looked pale and tired, Meryl was lively and busy and Iddig was covered in sweat and soot.

"How are the fires? Is there much damage?" September asked.

"Thanks to you, very little," Iddig replied cheerfully, "The rope of the elevator is burned and must be replaced, but that will only take a few hours. The other fires did little real harm. But you prevented the Draig tân from flattening the whole town."

"It was me too," Heulwen insisted.

"Of course, lady," Iddig said, "but now we must get you off and into the hands of the Mordeyrn as soon as possible. My men are ready and waiting to escort you into the Bryn am Seren."

"Thank you Iddig. How are we travelling?"

"On foot."

September groaned silently. Long walks were not her favourite pastime but perhaps it made a change from the boat.

"We cannot use the river?" she asked nevertheless.

"The river flows from the north. We must head westwards

to the peak on which the Arsyllfa stands."

Walking and climbing. She didn't like the sound of this trek.

"Don't worry my lady. We will provide you with suitable shoes for walking and clothes for the cool mountain air. And there will be animals to carry your baggage."

"Baggage?"

"Food, water, tents and bedding."

"Oh, I see. How long will this walk take?"

"Three or four days, if you make good time and are not delayed by the Malevolence."

Some hope, September thought. The evil seemed to be doing its utmost to disturb her journey.

"But now you must eat and drink before you set off," said Meryl laying down a tray piled high with food beside her.

After she had eaten, Iddig brought her pairs of stout leather walking shoes to try on. She found a pair that fitted snugly and provided suitable support. It felt strange enclosing her feet after so long in simple sandals. She was given a bag with a further change of clothes and a quilted jacket to wear in the mountains. Heulwen insisted that she pack the blue silk dress. Outside, half a dozen small ponies were lined up laden with bags and each escorted by a handler with a short sword at his side and a bow and quiver of arrows on his shoulders. Iddig stood with September in front of the lead pony and introduced its handler, a tall, strong young man.

"Sieffre will guide you to the Arsyllfa," Iddig said, "well, with our lady Heulwen's permission of course."

Sieffre took September's hand.

"We are all very grateful for your great work last night. To destroy a Draig tân is a feat of power that even the Mordeyrn has struggled to match."

September felt bashful.

"It is the stone that has the power. I'm not sure how it works at all."

"That may be true but only a great Cludydd can wield the Maengolauseren to such good effect."

"Well, thank you for guiding me for the rest of my journey."

"It is my pleasure and I speak for the others too." Sieffre gestured along the line of ponies and men, each watching her carefully.

The townspeople had stopped their work and come to line the street, waving and calling to September. Finally it seemed that everything was ready except that Heulwen was not with them. After a few minutes of muttering amongst the onlookers, Heulwen emerged from the house. She too had changed into trousers and tunic but her outfit was of bright yellow silk. She joined Iddig, Sieffre and September.

"Let us go," she said. She still looked pale and tired but her voice was strong. Meryl dashed up to give September a farewell kiss on her cheek, and Iddig clasped her shoulders. The party set off and the watchers cheered and wished them a safe journey.

They walked up the dusty main street. September noted the side roads had an assortment of buildings and realised that this was a sizeable town. Nevertheless the track soon led out between fields bounded by hedges with scattered trees and the river, flowing swiftly towards the waterfall, some metres away to their right. The hills were in front of them, round, forested hills first and further in the distance, higher, steeper, craggier peaks. Soon the river turned away to the north but their track continued westwards rising and falling gently over the undulating pastureland until they dropped into a narrow, thickly wooded valley and joined a shallow stream. The track became a narrow mud path and the hillsides and trees pressed close. They walked in single file and September found herself quite enjoying the fresh air and the changing scene but she was thankful when Sieffre called a rest break. She was relieved that the shoes felt comfortable but she knew that there was a lot of walking in front of them. Sieffre handed fresh bread and fruit to her and Heulwen.

"Does this stream take us to the Arsyllfa?" September asked.

"No, unfortunately. The valley turns north and we must take the path that climbs over the ridge and into the next valley, and then into the next, and the next before we climb to the peak." Sieffre said smiling as he saw September sag, "Don't worry, I won't push us along too fast. We must conserve our energy to climb the highest mountain in the Bryn am Seren."

While they sat and ate their bread and cheese, September kept glancing at the sky. Sieffre noticed.

"You are worried, Cludydd? You search the skies for danger?"

"Yes. I'm scared. I've been attacked by monsters too many times. Good people who helped me have died."

"I understand. We are all under attack from the Malevolence but you, or rather the stone, attract the attentions of the servants of evil."

"Aurddolen thought this cloak would keep the stone hidden but every time I have had to use it I give my position away."

"So the Malevolence may have felt your presence in Dwytrefrhaedr when you destroyed the Draig tân; but we are no longer there so you are hidden again."

"But surely it can guess I'm on my way to the Arsyllfa."

"You are treating the Adwyth like a thinking being. It is not. It is a mindless power that is driven to attack all that is good and the instruments of good. The manifestations may have a semblance of independent thought but they are driven by one desire – to destroy you, me, all of us."

"You seem to understand all this stuff, Sieffre."

"I am just a traveller and a part-time warrior but as I journey with my pony I see things and meet people. I have heard all the stories of the previous risings of the Malevolence and how it was defeated."

"You've heard the story of Breuddwyd, the last Cludydd?"

"I have."

"I think she was my mother."

"Ah, I have heard it said that those that come to us from the other world are of one family line. No doubt the Mordeyrn will tell you more. We must make a move." Sieffre started to get up. September grabbed his arm.

"Wait. You travel this way often?"

"Yes, it is my job to deliver supplies and guests to the Arsyllfa."

"But you said you are also a warrior. Have you met the Malevolence on your travels?"

"Yes, Cludydd. We have been attacked and the homes of

the people who live in the hills have been attacked."

"But you have fought them off?"

"Yes. It has been hard and people have been injured, killed and worse."

"Worse?"

"Turned to evil, such that they in turn attack the good."

"But you can defeat them?"

"So far, Cludydd, yes, but it becomes more difficult as the Malevolence grows stronger. Little by little we lose, villages are overrun or destroyed, people die or are turned to evil and there are that many less to fight the next time. We cannot defeat the evil alone. You are the hope of all who live in Gwlad, Cludydd."

"Please call me September. It's my name. Calling me Cludydd feels strange."

They got back into line with Heulwen in the lead and Sieffre with his pony behind. September followed with the other ponies and guides. They followed the path beside the stream through the trees. When the stream turned north the path left the waterside and now began to climb. September found her heart pounding and her breath coming in gasps. At home she would have collapsed in a flabby heap of weak flesh. Three weeks of sitting in a boat had not helped her fitness but the body she had here was more accustomed to effort. She was determined not to fall behind Heulwen. The girl was like a golden beacon leading the way. She seemed to have recovered her strength and was striding up the valley side.

Eventually the path levelled off. They had reached the ridge but surrounded by tall pine trees they were unable to see a view. Heulwen did not pause but strode on down into the next valley. The path zigged and zagged to the valley bottom. At last they broke out of the forest. September saw ahead of her a narrow strip of meadow beside a bubbling, tumbling stream that flowed from north to south. Across the other side was another wooded escarpment, higher than the ridge they had just crossed.

Sieffre looked up at the sky, cloudless as it had been all day. The Sun was dropping behind the ridge ahead of them.

"We still have a couple of hours of daylight," Heulwen

said, "We can press on."

"But night will have fallen before we reach the ridge," Sieffre pointed out, "The valley side offers no campsites. I suggest we make camp on the other side of the stream on the edge of the forest."

"It is wasting time," Heulwen protested.

"But safer for the ponies," Sieffre insisted. Heulwen shrugged and stalked ahead to the stream. The water level was quite low and a row of stepping stones was exposed. Heulwen skipped across and Sieffre guided his pony through the water. September paused to dip her hand in the stream. The water was much colder than the great river she had sailed on through the lowlands. She stepped across to the meadow on the other side and gazed around looking at the many coloured flowers amongst the emerald green grass. A sweet perfume filled the air.

"This looks as though it should have cows grazing on it," she called to Sieffre.

"You're right, it should. This land belongs to a small village a few hundred paces downstream," he replied. September sensed there was something more.

"Where are they then?"

"The village, its people and its livestock were devastated by the Malevolence a few months ago. It is deserted now."

"Devastated? How?"

"A pestilence," Heulwen said, anger showing on her face, "pestilence that killed every living thing in the village."

"A pestilence? You mean some kind of disease. What caused it?"

"It was a Cyhyraeth." Heulwen said.

"What does that mean?" September asked, frustrated at Heulwen's answer.

"A manifestation of air," Sieffre, explained, "it comes like a wind down from the peaks. It blows around and through every building even when the doors and windows are closed. It moans and whistles through any gap. Anyone or anything that feels its whispering caress becomes sick. Within minutes their limbs swell, their skin becomes covered in pustules and their breath comes in short, hot gasps. They cry out, echoing the moans of the Cyhyraeth and then they die."

"That's terrible," September shivered.

"If you hear the moaning wind you know death will surround you," Heulwen said.

"Can't you stop it?"

"A gold bearer can ward off the wraith and silver can heal the sick in the hands of a skilled cludydd, but small settlements have neither."

"What can they do?"

"People are scared. They are leaving their homes in the hills and moving to places like Dwytrefrhaedr where there may be protection. Whatever happens, the Malevolence wins."

The other ponies and men had joined them and now they set to work pulling tents and bedding from the packs. In a short time the camp was set and a cook pot was heating over a fire. Although the sky was still light, shadow spread across the valley. Under the trees it was dark and September was grateful that they weren't groping their way up the hillside.

The story that Heulwen and Sieffre had told of the Cyhyraeth made September depressed. It was yet another way that the Malevolence exerted its terrible influence over the people of Gwlad. The way that the people carried on working, chatting and laughing while knowing that the evil could approach at any time was admirable. She shook herself and decided she needed some distraction. Having tended their ponies, four of the guides were sitting around the fire while the fifth prepared their meal.

"I'm sorry I don't know your names," September said joining them and surprising herself with her manner. At home she was shy and silent with new people. Her ordeals seemed to be changing her. They all greeted her and invited her to sit with them.

"I'm Alawn," the young man on her left said, "and this is Elystan, Nisien, Gwrion, and Collen." He pointed around the circle at a fair-haired youth, a dark-skinned man with a lined and worn face, another fair but older man, and lastly the cook who was the oldest of the team with grey-flecked, black hair.

September repeated the names, trying to place them in her memory. She wasn't sure she had succeeded.

"I'm September," she said cheerfully.

"You are the Cludydd," Collen said sombrely. The others nodded.

"Do you travel this way often?"

"We used to," Gwrion said, "but there is less need of us now. There are fewer people living amongst the Bryn am Seren."

"Some of us have not journeyed for weeks," Elystan said.

"The only work has been to help Iddig," Nisien added.

"Doing what?" September asked.

"Guarding the twin towns. Checking people as they arrive and looking out for manifestations of the Adwyth," Gwrion explained.

Sieffre and Heulwen emerged from a tent.

"We have informed my father of our progress," Heulwen announced. September wondered if she had a copper horn like she possessed or whether their shared skills with gold connected them in some way.

"And there is news," Sieffre added.

"What?" September and the other men asked together. Sieffre's face was grave.

"The Arsyllfa is being attacked by the Malevolence," Heulwen said.

"Being attacked?" September asked not understanding.

"Yes, it started this morning with attacks by flights of Adarllwchgwin. This afternoon there was a Draig tân and then a Pwca in the form of a giant bear tried to beat down the door. Now there are more Adarllwchgwin."

"Can they defend themselves against so much?" September was horrified.

Heulwen stood up straight and proud.

"Of course. My father will hold the Arsyllfa secure," she said.

"The Arsyllfa was built to withstand the Malevolence," Sieffre explained calmly, "Its builders incorporated their skills with metals to give it power to withstand the forces of the Adwyth."

"That sounds impressive."

"It is, but never before has the Arsyllfa been attacked by such a concentration of evil or for such a length of time," Sieffre's look of confidence seemed to have cracked somewhat, "and the Mordeyrn is without his great shield of power."

"My father is still strong enough to withstand all that the Malevolence can summon," Heulwen said defiantly.

"But it means we may have to fight our way into the stronghold," Sieffre added, "and the fewer days and nights we are out in the open amongst the hills the better."

September guessed what was coming.

"We must rest and move at first light," Heulwen said, "and move at speed. We must join my father as soon as possible."

The mood was sombre while they ate the meal that Collen had prepared and then the party prepared to settle for the night with the guards organising a rota. September was pleased that she had a small tent to herself with a warm sleeping bag on a thin but soft bedroll. She snuggled down aware of how much cooler it was in the hills than down in the valley of the great river. She took her horn from its pouch and summoned the Mordeyrn.

"Ah, Cludydd, you have made good progress I understand."

"Yes, but your daughter says you are being attacked."

"We can withstand the powers of the Malevolence. The walls of the Arsyllfa are strengthened by girders of haearn interweaved with rods of alcam and plwm and bound together by threads of aur. Together they give our observatory strength and power to rebuff any attacks. My predecessors spent centuries preparing for this time."

"That's good to hear."

"Have no fear for us here, September. My only wish is for you to complete your journey in safety. While you have met opposition throughout your journey, the final stretch could be the most testing. But sleep now and we will talk again tomorrow when you are closer."

September put the horn away and snuggled herself into her sleeping bag. After the previous night's disturbance and a day of unaccustomed walking she felt a great tiredness.

Elystan woke her while it was still dark. September joined the others to wash in the cold stream and they all ate breakfast together. Then, when the sky above the ridge they had crossed the previous day was lightening, they set off. It was dark under the canopy of trees but the ponies found their footings easily enough and Heulwen and Sieffre strode ahead, familiar with their route. The path quickly climbed, weaving back and fore to lessen the incline. This ridge was considerably higher and the approach steeper than the first, so the morning was well on before they emerged from the trees onto a bare and rocky escarpment. It was the first opportunity that September had to see a view since they had left the twin towns and her breath was taken away. Behind were the rolling, tree-covered lines of hills but ahead rose the rocky peaks. In the foreground was another valley running from north to south but September could see that the valley floor was much higher than the valley they had left. They would not take long in their descent, but the next ridge rose steeper and higher still and beyond were the even higher peaks. The air here was clear and fresh, but the hilltops were surrounded by dark cloud and September saw flashes of red lightning.

"Is that where the Arsyllfa is?" September asked Sieffre, pointing to the hidden peaks.

"Yes, and the Malevolence is attacking with all its might."

"You mean the lightning?"

"Spears of fire tossed by the riders of the Adarllwchgwin."

"Are you sure they can hold out?"

"Of that I am certain, but fighting our way into the Arsyllfa, of that I am less sure. We must make haste."

Without further pause, Sieffre and Heulwen led them down into the valley and up the far side. The path was steep and rugged. The ponies found their way easily enough but even they tired as they climbed. September had no energy to watch how the others were coping. She had to concentrate on lifting one foot after another. Her thighs ached and tiredness spread through every bone and muscle. She plodded on, her eyes on the back legs of the pony in front that showed her where to plant her feet.

It came as a complete surprise when the next step was not upwards but level. September looked up and found sky in front of her. They had reached the top of the last ridge. Not even grass grew here. The rock was carved by wind into a knife edge. The wind blew now, a cold blast from the north. September shivered and wrapped her cloak around her. Behind her was an almost sheer drop and in front the ground fell away as abruptly. Sieffre offered her a hand and hauled her onto a platform of rock no more than a square metre in area. She had a moment of vertigo as she realised that there was nothing to hold on to except Sieffre, and that she was exposed on the narrowest of ledges. In front of her now the mountain rose from the next ridge that bounded a wide and shallow valley. It was shrouded in mist and cloud. High above came the crash of thunder and flashes of light of the continuing battle. Sieffre held her tight.

"You're doing well, Cludydd. Just the final climb left."

"Today?"

"No." He looked at the Sun disappearing behind the mountain, "We have an hour or so of light. We can make camp down in the valley and go up to the Arsyllfa tomorrow." He held her hand firmly as they stepped down and began the descent into the valley. A stream snaked across the almost flat plain but unlike the previous valleys they had crossed there were no trees here. The air was cold and clear.

The final light of the day was fading when Heulwen called a halt and they made camp in the shelter of an outcrop of rock a few metres from the stream. Overhead the sounds of the continuing siege of the unseen Arsyllfa echoed off the valley sides. The men made camp and once again Collen cooked a tasty meal but although Alawn and Elystan tried to raise a song, the sound of the thunder and the knowledge of what was happening above their heads made the others reluctant to join in. Before long Sieffre declared that again an early start was needed so they might as well get as much rest as they could. Nisien remained on guard and the others retreated to their tents. September was more than ready to settle into the comfort of her sleeping bag. She hadn't felt as cold in all her time in Gwlad and was thankful for the quilted jacket that she had been given. She was especially grateful for the down-filled sleeping bag and curled up inside it with the copper horn to her cheek.

"Mordeyrn, are you there?"

"Yes, my girl, I am here and longing for the moment when

we meet again. Now less than one day."

"You are still under attack. We can hear the thunder caused by the Adarllwchgwin."

"Yes. They strive endlessly to pierce our defences, but my predecessors built well. They foresaw that the Arsyllfa would become a focus of the evil. But I do worry about your approach. Sieffre will guide you well but you will be exposed to the power of the Malevolence. I fear that though your cloak may hide the Maengolauseren from the evil senses, you and your companions' very presence on the mountain will draw some of the attack."

"That's what I was afraid of. What do we do?"

"Sieffre knows all the paths up the mountain. He will keep you shielded as far as possible, but at some stage I am sure you will all have to defend yourselves and if you are forced to expose the stone you will draw the full power of the Malevolence upon you."

"I'll fight it," September said but shuddered with fright as she said it.

"My spirit will be with you, Cludydd. Now rest; your biggest challenge yet is in front of you."

The horn went silent and September packed it away. She was scared. She had won each battle she had faced so far, if losing Tudfwlch and Cynddylig and the injury to Eluned could be counted as winning, but the crashing peels of thunder that came to her even wrapped in her thick sleeping bag warned that tomorrow she would face greater power than she had seen so far. Oh, why can't I go home and just be silly little me, she thought, I want to meet my friends and have a laugh, even go to school and sit through some boring lessons, anything but face this terror. She wrapped her head in the cloak and opened the locket holding the starstone. It flickered with blue light but there was no clarity, no image of her bedroom. No, it wasn't going to let her go yet. She closed it up and let it drop between her breasts.

Something had woken her up. She shivered. Even wrapped in her sleeping bag and quilt jacket the cold of the night had penetrated. But it wasn't the cold that had awoken her. Her birthmark was itching and there was something else. It was still completely dark, surely no-one was moving yet. There it was again. A soft moan. September dismissed it; it's just the wind blowing amongst the rocks and the tent ropes. Again. A low, sustained groan. Then, pandemonium. Shouting, flapping of cloth as someone rushed from a tent, stamping of feet, the ponies whinnying with fright. A face thrust through the entrance of her tent, a frightened face lit by the dim light of an oil lamp. It took a moment for September to recognise Sieffre, his expression was so contorted.

"Cludydd! A Cyhyraeth is upon us. Help us before we all die."

September struggled to extricate herself from her bedding.

"What can I do? Where is it?"

"It's all around us, above us. Can't you hear it moaning? It will find us all and its touch means death."

September grasped her pendant beneath her cloak, not sure whether she should bring the stone out.

"But what do I do?"

"Protect us! You must, quickly or it will be all over for us." The face withdrew.

Protect. How could she do that? The stone had defended her in the past against attackers. It had driven them off but could it simply shield them? She drew the pendant out and unclipped the catch. A mist swirled inside the stone. Perhaps it was an image of the Cyhyraeth. What words should she use? She didn't know enough of the strange ancient language that controlled the powers of Gwlad. She muttered, "Protect us, protect us," over and over again and clasped the Maengolauseren to her chest. "Protect us, protect us."

A ball of blue light grew out of the stone enclosing her hands. It grew slowly at first but expanded faster and faster. It enveloped her, then filled the tent, then beyond. She knelt with the stone pressed against her breast surrounded by a bright blue mist. She rocked back and forth, still muttering, "Protect us, protect us".

She heard someone enter the tent. Sieffre's voice came through the glowing blue haze.

"That's it Cludydd. You have created a dome of light that is repelling the Cyhyraeth."

"How will I know when to stop?" September said still

thinking, protect us, protect us.

"I don't know. Perhaps the Maengolauseren itself will know when the danger is past."

She carried on repeating her mantra while the blue light swirled around her. Then a feeling of relief washed through September. She knew that she had been successful. She had repulsed the unseen wraith. The blue glow faded. Dim light from Sieffre's oil lamp was all that illuminated the tent now. He looked away from her, concentrating on listening. For many seconds he remained frozen, then he relaxed.

"Yes, it's gone. You have dispersed the Cyhyraeth. I must check on everyone." He left again. September crawled over her bed and out into the cold night air. There were other people milling around the faint embers of the camp fire. Heulwen was there wrapped in a white dressing gown, Sieffre himself and Elystan, Alawn, Nisien, Collen. No Gwrion.

"Where's Gwrion?" September asked.

"It was his watch." Sieffre said, then he ran from the camp towards the shelter of a rock where the ponies had been left overnight. There was silence for a few moments then a cry. The whole party followed Sieffre. In the dull yellow light of the lamps September saw lumps on the ground, like small hillocks. The ponies, she realised, were all lying down, not moving.

"The ponies? What's wrong with them?" September asked.

"Dead," Elystan said, "Every one of them."

Sieffre was kneeling beside a smaller lump.

"Gwrion?" September asked, knowing the answer.

"Yes. He's dead. He ran to the ponies when he heard them panic. The Cyhyraeth got him and them before your dome expanded to protect us."

September covered her mouth with a hand to stifle a sob and ran forward. Gwrion was lying rigid with his limbs contorted into unusual positions by the pain of the Cyhyraeth's touch. His face, dimly visible in the light of the lamp was an unrecognisable mass of pustules, some burst and bloody and his hands too showed the same swellings. September felt sick but she wanted to see more.

"No, keep back," Sieffre said, "The bodies are lethal. One

touch and the Cyhyraeth's pestilence will spread to you. There's nothing we can do."

"There is," Heulwen spoke coldly from behind September. "We must leave this place and ascend to the Arsyllfa. Now!"

"What about our baggage?" Nisien said, "Without the ponies we cannot carry everything."

"Leave it," Heulwen replied, "Leave it all. We must make haste to reach the safety of the Arsyllfa before we draw the other forces of the Malevolence upon us."

September realised that she was still holding the stone, exposed. It glowed faintly. Oh my god, she thought, I've been broadcasting my position all this time. She shut the locket and shoved it under the cloak. At least the irritation in her hip had eased.

"Heulwen's right," Sieffre said, "We have no need of our belongings except for our weapons. We must escort the Cludydd to the safety of the Arsyllfa, and quickly."

The five men ran back to the campsite. Heulwen grasped September's shoulders.

"Well done, Cludydd. The Maengolauseren protected us from the Cyhyraeth but we will need all our powers to reach my father."

"Did well did I? One man and six ponies dead. It's never quite good enough."

She twisted out off Heulwen's embrace and stormed to her tent. In the darkness she felt for her belt and buckled it around her waist feeling reassured by the heavy short sword resting against her thigh. She wrapped her jacket tightly around herself and the cloak over it. The others were already waiting by the fire when she emerged. The lamps had been put out. Starlight alone illuminated the group.

"Let's hurry. Perhaps we can still evade the Malevolence, if we move quickly and keep the stone hidden," Heulwen said. Sieffre led the party off at a trot. September stumbled over the rough, rocky path but the others were sure-footed in the dark.

It was cold, dark and quiet. September realised that since waking up with the moan of the Cyhyraeth she had heard no sound of the battle for the Arsyllfa. She looked up. The mountain was a black shadow against the stars. She stopped and stared in wonder. High up with the air thinner even more stars were visible than she had seen long ago on the hill above Amaethaderyn or crossing the Llyn Pysgod. There hardly seemed any darkness between the stars, they were so numerous. There was a thump on her back.

"Oh, sorry, Cludydd, I didn't see you had stopped. Are you alright," Elystan said, grabbing her arm to stop her falling. September recovered herself.

"No, it's my fault. I just happened to look up at the sky and saw all the stars. It's beautiful."

"I know, I love being up here in the hills. This is why they are called Bryn am Seren, the hills of stars. The sky is often clear like it is tonight. But we must keep up with the others."

September realised that Sieffre and Heulwen had gone on ahead. She hurried after them looking for her footing across the rough valley floor.

"Have you noticed," she said as she caught them up, "that the attack on the Arsyllfa has stopped?"

Sieffre paused and turned to her.

"For now, that is true, but I fear it will not be over for good. I think our camp presented an alternative target for the Malevolence which has given the Arsyllfa some respite. But we must hurry and get as close as we can while there is some calm." He turned away again and resumed his trot. September kept pace but was already beginning to puff and pant.

Very soon they slowed as the path, or whatever signs they were following, began to rise. It grew steeper and steeper and September had to search in the darkness for each footing. At least there were steps cut into the rock. They became more frequent and closer together until it felt as though she was climbing an endless staircase. She couldn't imagine laden ponies finding this at all easy.

"Is this the main route to the Arsyllfa?" she said to Sieffre just in front of her.

"No, Cludydd. We have avoided the main track which winds up the east slope of the mountain. The Mordeyrn recommended this route which takes us up to the ridge then up the western face of the peak, around the back if you like, of the Arsyllfa. But we will have to come back round to the east at the last to make our entrance."

"Why did the Mordeyrn suggest this way?"

"The focus of the attacks has been on the east side of the Arsyllfa, the side that has the great metal doors, but that is the only entrance. The Mordeyrn thinks we might be able to keep out of the Adwyth's attention by taking this route."

"Whichever way we go we have to climb I suppose."

"That's correct my lady, and soon dawn will come and we will see how far we have to go."

They resumed the climb. September could think of nothing more than lifting one foot after another and following the back of the man in front of her. Soon her legs ached and despite the morning cold she sweated under her quilted jacket and the cloak. After a countless number of steps she noticed that she could see more and not just the grey wool of Sieffre's coat. The darkness was lifting; dawn was coming. She looked up again and saw the stars fading, but not just because the rising sun was banishing them from the night sky. A cloud was forming around the peak so that just as she was beginning to see more around her the chance of seeing their destination was taken from her like a curtain across a stage.

"The attack resumes," Sieffre noted quietly, and hardly had he spoken than the first flash of lightning illuminated the thickening cloud and thunder rolled across the valley. At the same time September felt the faint irritation on her hip. The Malevolence was certainly active.

"Hurry, we must get to the western face as soon as we can," Sieffre urged.

September found herself carried along at a greater pace despite the ache in her thighs. Nevertheless it was daylight by the time they reached the ridge. Heulwen did not pause to look at the view but disappeared down the west side. A few steps more and September also topped the ridge and saw that the path dropped a few metres and then turned south. It was level for a short distance but there in front of them was the bulk of the mountain. Above them it was now shrouded in dark cloud from which emerged an irregular drumbeat of thunderous explosions and bursts of light. She hurried after Sieffre and Heulwen relishing for a moment the horizontal path.

Soon they were in the shadow of the mountain and the first tendrils of fog drifted around them. The climb resumed but the steps were narrow and steep so that despite the greater light September still had to take great care where she put her feet. At least the sounds of the battle were muffled by the mass of the mountain in between.

Each step upwards took them deeper into the fog. It was cold and dank and stank. It had a sulphurous odour, which irritated September's throat. She knew it wasn't just her because the others were coughing. Heulwen called a halt and the party stopped in line as there was no level ground on which to congregate. Elystan, who was still behind her, passed September a leather water bottle.

"Clear the foul stench of the Malevolence from your mouth, Cludydd," he said. September took a long swig, grateful for the cool, refreshing water. She was also thankful for the pause, awkward though it was clinging to the mountainside. The fatigue seemed to flow from her legs and her breathing settled. The break was short and Heulwen set off again, quickly disappearing into the fog. September hurried to keep Sieffre in sight.

Step, breathe, cough, step. Their progress slowed as the climb became steeper, and the fog thicker. September held her arm across her mouth trying to stop the noxious air entering her lungs. The noise of the one sided battle also grew with each metre that they climbed towards the summit and the closer they got to the battle the more her birthmark troubled her, first feeling like just an annoyance then a growing soreness. The fog glowed with every flash and crash of pure energy flung from their spears by the unseen riders of the Adarllwchgwin. September heaved one foot after another up the narrow steps, using her hands to grasp the rocks to keep her balance on the precarious cliff, each step now a supreme effort, her body aching.

She bumped against Sieffre's legs not realising that he had stopped. She saw that Heulwen too had paused and they were pressed against the mountainside. Sieffre looked down at her.

"Not far now Cludydd. We're nearly at the point where we circle around to the east side of the mountain. Then it is just a short way to the entrance," Sieffre coughed and cleared his throat, "but this is where we will be attacked. The Arsyllfa itself has shielded us from the Malevolence and your cloak has kept you hidden, but once we reach the east wall we will be exposed and we will have to fight."

A shiver of fear passed through September. The burning in her hip was a constant reminder of the evil that lay ahead. Why do I worry? she thought, the stone has protected me. I can blast all these monsters away; they cannot fight against the power of the Maengolauseren. Nevertheless, she felt scared, her understanding of her power was vague and her knowledge of what she faced was incomplete. So far she had survived while her companions had not. Would she always be the lucky one?

"Tell Elystan and Collen to climb past you. Alawn and Nisien will guard your rear," Sieffre went on. She passed the message on and the two men squeezed around her. Then the party resumed the climb, slowly, watchfully. An especially loud clap of thunder warned September that the Adarllwchgwin were close.

The path levelled off and in front of her Elystan and Collen stood up and took their bows from off their shoulders. They each pulled an arrow from their quivers and drew their bowstrings. Sieffre stood by their side, his sword drawn and raised. Heulwen stood behind the three men, her gold brooch in her hand.

September and her two guards approached them. She covered her mouth with her hand to try to stop the air entering but it was difficult when she wanted to speak. She coughed and said, "Shall I get the stone out? Perhaps I can drive off the monsters before they attack us."

"Wait, Cludydd," Sieffre said, "Keep it hidden as long as you can. You may be able to repel one wave of the evil but there will be more. Wait until we are detected before revealing your power." He stepped forward. The path was flat and wide enough for the two archers to walk side-by-side, arrows poised. September realised that the cliff rising up to their left was no longer the rough rock of the mountain but the smooth surface of the wall of the Arsyllfa. To their right the fog obscured a sheer drop. The cloud ahead flashed with lightning and thunder ripped through the air. September walked as close to the wall as possible, flinching at every new burst of noise. About a hundred paces brought them to a corner.

An Adarllwchgwin loomed out of the fog heading directly towards them. Its beak opened to let out a deafening screech and its red-skinned rider drew back its arm holding a spear. Elystan and Collen were ready and released their arrows. Both found their target and the giant bird lurched to the side as its rider threw fire from its spear. Its aim was faulty and the flame hit the mountain side beneath them with an explosion of light and sound. The Adarllwchgwin fell into the fog. September almost breathed again but instantly they were beset by three of the eagle-like monsters. They came from left and right and above them, seemingly alerted by their fellow. September heard the fizz and twang of bows being released behind her, as Elystan and Collen shot off arrow after arrow. Spears of fire exploded into the ground in front of them and the wall behind them, but the shower of arrows seemed to deflect the birds and the riders from their target.

"To the door!" Sieffre shouted, raising his sword and running alongside the wall of the Arsyllfa. Heulwen and the archers followed, loosing off another pair of arrows. September's mind was befuddled by the pain in her hip, the lights and noise and the flapping of wings. A strong hand grabbed her arm and dragged her along.

"Come on Cludydd, we must get to the entrance," Nisien said at her side. September made her legs work and then screamed with horror.

The sky was suddenly full of Adarllwchgwin. In every direction they were emerging from the fog and flying towards her. The archers let off their arrows but, even if every shaft flew true, there were too many of the fierce birds. One swooped over the four runners. Sieffre slashed with his sword, gouging the bird's flank as its talons ripped into Collen's chest. The archer fell to the ground and the bird, flapping its gigantic wings, turned to the left, disappearing in the fog.

"No!" September cried and drew the locket from her cloak.

She flicked the case open and raised the stone above her head. It glowed more brightly than she had ever seen. "Be gone!" she screamed aiming the stone at the nearest Adarlwchgwin. A broad violet beam shot from the stone blasting the bird to vapour. She turned to another and another and another. Each attacker was blown away, but still there were more. She stumbled forward until she was standing next to the fallen Collen. Heulwen knelt by him, her brooch raised up, glowing but apparently to no purpose. The three remaining archers let fly and Sieffre swung his sword while the light from the Maengolauseren destroyed the attackers. The ache in September's arms grew; how much longer could she hold the stone up? How many more of the ferocious birds were there? This can't go on, she thought. Picking them off one by one is not enough, there are always more. I need one great burst of energy, like at Glanyrafon. How do I do it?

A shaft of fire hit Alawn in the chest. His body burst into a ball of flame.

"Not again!" September screamed. In her head she saw an explosion of an atom bomb, blowing away everything in the huge circle around it. She squeezed the stone in her hand and felt it respond. The blue light expanded in an instant, growing into a hemisphere that raced away from them. With a great roar of rushing wind, the Adarllwchgwin to left, right, centre and above were swept away and blown into oblivion, and the fog too. September found herself standing on a bare mountain top with the wall of the Arsyllfa rising behind, and the valley far below in front of her.

"Now, while we have a chance," Sieffre said, hauling Heulwen onto her feet, dragging her away from Collen's body towards the great gatehouse that was now visible fifty metres away. Nisien grabbed September's elbow and urged her along as well. Just a few seconds and they would be at the entrance and safe.

She saw Sieffre, Heulwen and Elystan stagger to a halt before she saw the bear. It was between them and the gatehouse. September felt that it had just materialised out of the air. It was white like a polar bear but standing on its rear legs it towered over them, ten times the height of a natural animal. It roared. Elystan loosed off an arrow. He couldn't miss but the creature ignored the pinprick.

"The Pwca," Nisien said. September did not need any more explanation. She raised the stone again, directing it at the bear that lurched towards them.

"Be gone!" she yelled. A broad violet beam shot out striking the bear in its chest. It staggered and toppled with a thud that shook the ground. The body started to melt into a formless heap. In moments nothing remained that resembled the giant bear.

"Come on," Sieffre shouted taking Heulwen's hand. They took a few steps forward.

"Wait, what's happening to the Pwca?" Heulwen said. The shapeless mass was squirming and wriggling. It started to take form as September stared. From the remains of the bear arose a new monster, a huge white lion with a flaming red mane. It roared and took a bound towards them, and another. September lifted the stone again.

"Be gone, I said," she shouted. Again the violet light sprang from the stone, a broad cone of luminescence. It engulfed the lion in mid leap. Its roar died and it fell to the ground. Once again the Pwca formed a sloppy puddle on the ground.

Again the party started to advance towards the gatehouse, but the remains of the Pwca lay in their path. September limped, the fire in her side making her gasp with the pain. As they approached September saw that it was writhing and rippling. Elystan was closest when from the puddled mass arose the hooded head of a huge white cobra. It uncoiled and rose above the archer, then with a hiss sank down onto him, closing its jaws round his head.

September froze for a moment in shock. Why hadn't the monster died? For a third time she raised the stone.

"Die, why don't you die," she screamed. Her arm shook with fury, as again the violet ray shone out. This time there was no temporary flash of light, the incandescence remained focussed on the monstrous snake. "Die, die," September repeated. The snake collapsed in a heap which bubbled and boiled. Vapours rose and dispersed and still September held the blue fire on the Pwca. The jellied mass shrank and evaporated until it was all gone. Only then did September let out a sigh and drop her arm, the light from the stone extinguished.

Sieffre and Heulwen ran the remaining metres to the gatehouse with September and Nisien a short distance behind. September looked up at the wall of the Arsyllfa seeing it for the first time. Despite the days of siege, the stones that fitted tightly together to make the wall were unmarked. The arched gateway was blocked by dark grey, iron doors, ten metres high and five metres wide. Inlaid into them were threads of silver-grey metal and gold in curving complex patterns. September saw but hardly registered the intricate designs unharmed by the talons of the Adarllwchgwin, the flaming spears of their riders or the pounding fists of the Pwca. The doors were swinging open. Heulwen and Sieffre slipped inside. Nisien followed.

September was about to pass between the great doors when something made her stop and look behind her. A small dark cloud hung in the air a few metres away from where the mountain side dropped away. As September watched the cloud began to take shape. She raised the stone again. Not another shape-shifter, she thought, but instead of commanding the light from the stone she watched to see what shape would emerge. Legs, arms and a head. The body was clothed in a long black dress that sucked in all light. The head was crowned by flowing, wavy, white hair. September stared. She recognised the features from looking in a mirror. It was her own face.

"You think yourself so powerful don't you, Cludydd o Maengolauseren," the vision said. September was speechless. She gazed at the image of herself.

"You think that my servants can be destroyed by the stone you wield, but you do not know what you do," the girl continued, "For every one that you destroy a hundred more take their place. You think you have power but I know you, September Weekes, and your power is nothing compared to mine. I have the might of the Malevolence in my hands and I will punish you all for the wrongs that you have done to me, for I am Malice."

The figure pointed to her and the pain of her birthmark became intolerable. She could feel the crescent burning into her flesh. She fell to her knees, sobbing.

"Hide in your fortress," her twin – for surely it was her – went on "It will be your tomb."

September gasped because behind the young woman appeared a swarm of Adarllwchgwin, swooping towards the Arsyllfa. She struggled to her feet, staggered backwards and began to fall. Arms caught her and lifted her up and carried her through the doorway. The huge metal doors of the Arsyllfa crashed shut.

The story continues in

Volume 2 of Evil Above the Stars

The Power of Seven

Acknowledgement

Writing is largely a solo activity but being a writer requires support and assistance from a lot of people. I couldn't cope without my wife, partner, best friend and chief critic, Alison, who encourages me with all my writing projects.

The idea for *Evil Above the Stars* grew out of a short assignment for Ludlow Writers' Group and I must thank all the members, but particularly Sally, for encouraging me to go on to develop it. All the comments have been much appreciated.

Then there are the folk at Elsewhen Press. It is a joy to find a company as enthusiastic about their business as Peter and Alison are. Their mixture of astuteness, skill and excitement is both reassuring and invigorating. I was delighted when they took on *EAtS* and have been proud to become a part of their publishing family. Then there is Deirdre who had the unenviable job of finding all my typographic, punctuation and grammatical errors and make patient and sensible suggestions for improvements. Thank you Deirdre. Another thank you goes to Sofia for the proofreading. Any errors that remain are all mine.

Finally I would like to thank you the reader. Nothing gives me more pleasure than knowing people are reading my work (the royalties are useful but secondary). If you are reading this before launching into the novel, then I hope you enjoy it. If you have completed it then I hope it was a pleasurable experience and that you look forward to further tales of September Weekes.

Elsewhen Press

an independent publisher specialising in Speculative Fiction

Visit the Elsewhen Press website at elsewhen.co.uk for the latest information on all of our titles, authors and events; to read our blog; find out where to buy our books and ebooks; or to place an order.

Elsewhen Press

an independent publisher specialising in Speculative Fiction

Volume 2 of Evil Above the Stars

The Power of Seven

Peter R. Ellis

September Weekes found a smooth stone which took her to *Gwlad*, the Land, where the people hailed her as the *Cludydd o Maengolauseren*, the bearer of the starstone, with the power to defend them against the evil known as the Malevolence. Now, having reached Arsyllfa she is re-united with the *Mordeyrn Aurddolen* with whom, together with the other senior metal bearers that make up the Council of *Gwlad*, she must plan the defence of the Land.

The time of the next Conjunction will soon be at hand. The planets, the Sun and the Moon will all be together in the sky. At that point the protection of the heavenly bodies will be at its weakest and *Gwlad* will be more dependent than ever on September. But now it seems that she must defeat Malice, the guiding force behind the Malevolence, if she is to save the Land and all its people. Will she be strong enough; and, if not, to whom can she turn for help?

The Power of Seven is the second volume in the thrilling fantasy series, *Evil Above the Stars*, by Peter R. Ellis, that appeals to readers, of all ages, of fantasy or science fiction, especially fans of JRR Tolkien and Stephen Donaldson. If old theories are correct until a new idea comes along, does the universe change with our perception of it? Were the ideas embodied in alchemy ever right? What realities were the basis of Celtic mythology?

ISBN: 9781908168719 (epub, kindle)
ISBN: 9781908168610 (288pp paperback)

Visit bit.ly/EvilAbove

Elsewhen Press

an independent publisher specialising in Speculative Fiction

Jacey's Kingdom
Dave Weaver

Jacey's Kingdom is an enthralling tale that revolves around a startlingly desperate reality: Jacey Jackson, a talented student destined for Cambridge, collapses with a brain tumour while sitting her final history exam at school. In her mind she struggles through a quasi-historical sixth century dreamscape whilst the surgeons fight to save her life.

Jacey is helped by a stranger called George, who finds himself trapped in her nightmare after a terrible car accident. There are quests, battles, and a love story ahead of them, before we find out if Jacey will awake from her coma or perish on the operating table. And who, or what, is George? In this book, Dave Weaver questions our perception of reality and the redemptive power of dreams; are our experiences of fear, conflict, friendship and love any less real or meaningful when they take place in the mind rather than the 'real' physical world?

Dave Weaver has been writing for ten years, with short stories published in anthologies, magazines and online in the UK and USA. Jacey's Kingdom is his first published novel. He cleverly weaves a tale that takes the almost unimaginable drama of an eighteen year-old girl whose life is in the balance, relying on modern surgery to bring her back from the brink, and conceives the world that she has constructed in her mind to deal with the trauma happening to her body. Developing the friendship between Jacey and George in a natural and witty style, despite their unlikely situation and the difference in their ages, Dave has produced a story that is both exciting and thought-provoking. This book will be a must-read story for adults and young adults alike.

ISBN: 9781908168313 (epub, kindle)
ISBN: 9781908168214 (272pp paperback)

Visit bit.ly/JaceysKingdom

About the author

Peter R. Ellis would like to say he's been a writer all his life but it is only since retiring as a teacher in 2010 that he has been able to devote enough time to writing to call it a career. Brought up in Cardiff, he studied Chemical Physics at the University of Kent at Canterbury, then taught chemistry (and a bit of physics) in Norwich, the Isle of Wight and Thames Valley. His first experience of publishing was in writing educational materials, which he has continued to do since retiring. Of his fictional writing, *Seventh Child* is his first published speculative fiction novel.

Peter has been a fan of science fiction and fantasy since he was young, has an (almost) complete collection of classic SF by Asimov, Ballard, Clarke, Heinlein and Niven, among others, while also enjoying fantasy by Tolkien, Donaldson and Ursula Le Guin. Of more recent authors Iain M Banks, Alastair Reynolds and China Mieville have his greatest respect. His Welsh upbringing also engendered a love of the language (even though he can't speak it) and of Welsh mythology like the *Mabinogion*. All these strands come together in the *Evil Above the Stars* series. He lives in Herefordshire with his wife, Alison, who is a great supporter.